"Good God, woman!" Lord Wade exclaimed loudly, looking at Portia with a horrified expression on his face. "Do you imagine you and I are friends?"

"Of course we are! The best of friends indeed. You would have saved my life if I was in danger last month."

"That was last month." He loomed closer suddenly. Wade was narrowly built but quite a bit taller than Portia. When she looked up at him, she felt her knees start to tremble, which was an odd discovery to make now when he'd never intimated her before. "Miss Hayes, we are not friends. We never were."

She blinked at him in surprise. "But…"

His eyes narrowed, and he suddenly drew back. "I found watching your reckless antics amusing for a time—you were always one kiss away from scandal—but those days are long past."

HEATHER BOYD

BESTSELLING AUTHOR

LORD OF SIN

Distinguished Rogues

10

Chapter One

June, 1815
London

Murder and death had only kept the *ton's* attention a few days before they forgot the losses and the shock and returned to the gaiety and decadence of the London season. Julian, Lord Wade, was no different. He was glad the ugly business was well and truly behind them. The murderess had been caught and buried a week ago. Given everyone he spoke to had suddenly felt much safer, a flurry of invitations to parties and other amusements had begun to arrive in a steady stream. Julian hurried up the marble staircase of Lord Birch's home, eager not to miss a moment of the festivities to celebrate Lady Birch's birthday.

It was the third time Lady Birch claimed to have turned five and twenty, too.

Not that he was counting.

He passed the butler his invitation and sauntered inside. Because Lady Birch was a jolly sort, married and generous with her time—as harmless as one could be—no one dreamed of contradicting her story about her age. Accuracy in a married lady's stated age was hardly ever to be relied upon anyway. It was only widows and debutantes, and never-married old spinsters that were made to feel lesser for reaching another milestone in years.

In fact, where truthfulness was concerned, Julian believed marriage was undoubtedly a gamble not to be entered into lightly. Many men lost their hearts and sanity when they ended up with nothing to show for the sacrifices they'd made in taking a bride. Time and again, he discovered the initial euphoria of attraction and desire of newlyweds tended to give way to frustration and outright rage over their spouses' oftentimes-bewildering behavior.

Julian had not been so foolish as to wed what his heart desired most when he'd first found her. Betrayal was always one flirtatious smile or one stolen kiss away when trust was given too soon or absolutely. It was not only gentlemen who behaved roguishly. Even seemingly proper ladies delighted in the occasional indiscretion.

Julian had been biding his time, hoping that soon his love would realize he was her best choice for a happy future.

They were to meet tonight at this ball, and he would take another small step toward winning her over. Thankfully her parents had always been rather shoddy, inattentive chaperones, and there had been many occasions when she had slipped away from their sides.

Not with him, though. Never with him. A line of gentlemen had routinely formed around Portia Hayes' perimeter, almost from the first night she was out in society.

He was consoled by the fact that there would be plenty of opportunities to be alone with her in the future. His love had captured many a heart, but was not yet ready to keep any. She so far showed no sign of serious infatuation with any of her admirers. Because of that, he was content to wait while she enjoyed herself thoroughly.

Julian reached the ballroom and glanced around the large candlelit area, eager to catch a glimpse of the delicious woman.

All of society had come out tonight, masks firmly in place to conceal their identities and to bask under the influence of too much champagne and laughter. Despite the masks, Wade recognized many in attendance. The wealthiest members of the *ton* were always distinctive.

He easily spotted the Earl and Countess Rothwell dancing scandalously close. The earl and his bride of last year, Arabella, whispered to each other as they came together. Everyone was waiting for Rothwell to stray but so far, he seemed entirely faithful.

Not far from them were the newly married Windermeres. Lord Windermere and wife, Esme, were *the* couple of the season. All eyes were on the pair as they moved in society, waiting, hoping probably too, for someone to come between them. But there was no mistaking the intent behind the hot glances that pair exchanged. They only had eyes for each other.

Julian was happy for both men, acquaintances of his for years. Their brides were worthy of every effort the pair must have made to win their dearest loves' hands in marriage. Julian especially enjoyed the outrageous gossip that had circulated when the connections had become known. He'd not been surprised or shocked by either marriage.

For years, Julian had paid attention to the ladies of society, and particularly noticed their suitors were not always the first ones to gain their attention. He had accurately predicted a number of unions—not that he was going to shout about it to anyone. He was responsible for no one's happiness, even if he had secretly played devil's advocate a fair few times.

He had not bothered with much of a disguise tonight. He couldn't afford to. He wore an ordinary black suit, tall, black-polished riding boots, and a soft velvet mask over his eyes so he would blend in. He wasn't in the market to attract attention, but the one he sought always did.

He found Portia Hayes easily enough, dancing prettily with Lord Grindlewood.

Julian moved toward a pillar and stopped to admire her grace in the arms of another. Portia was delicately dressed and masked in pink silk and pearls, a costume he'd never seen on her before. One that must have cost her father a fortune. Portia's family, though common born, had deep pockets and grand ambitions. They spent extravagantly on their daughter, ensuring she fitted in.

It wasn't the first time Julian had been relegated to the sidelines but he was happy as always to watch her dance. He never paid much attention to her partners—not even Grindlewood, who was wealthy again, titled, and possessed of an exceedingly handsome countenance.

Portia always did attract the pretty gentlemen to her circle.

Julian didn't begrudge Portia a roving eye, though for a long time he'd lamented she'd never look upon him with any favor. He always made sure she noticed him, though.

The set ended and Portia was escorted back to her parents, laughing at something Grindlewood had whispered to her. Portia laughed a lot when her partners whispered. She was an exuberant, passionate woman. An original. Someone he cared about very much.

Her dance partner lingered at her side a few moments more, and when Grindlewood finally took his leave of Portia, Julian headed in her direction.

Portia had piled her thick dark hair high on her head tonight and allowed some of it to spill down in chaotic ringlets around her pale throat. She looked as if she belonged in the forest under the stars. As usual her green eyes sparked with life and merriment—and for the first time, they stayed that way when her eyes fell on him.

Portia held out her hand to him. "My lord."

"Enchantress," he said, as he grasped it and bowed. "You take my breath away," he whispered.

He turned to Portia's parents to greet them but the pair, as ever, were soon looking elsewhere in the room for someone more important. He turned back to Portia and put his hands behind his back. "You danced well."

She arched one delicate brow. "Just *well*, my lord?"

He leveled her with a pained stare. Portia liked to be complimented, the more flowery the endearments the better, he'd recently discovered. But it was not easy for Julian to speak in such glowing terms of anyone, least of all someone he liked as much as he did her. However it must be done if he had any chance to win her one day. "Better than well, but you've always known my admiration knows no bounds. Can I tempt you to visit a dark and private corner so I can prove it?"

"No, you may not." She grinned impishly, clearly pleased with his suggestion. "But a lady always wants to hear the most ardent of admiration spoken of."

"Haven't you heard enough insincere flattery from your flock of mutton chops for one night? They must be losing their touch if you find their compliments lacking enough to demand mine."

She shrugged. "I thought you would be here earlier?"

He glanced away to hide his discomfort. "My aunt changed her mind about coming at the last moment."

Portia's brow furrowed and she inched closer, until her skirts brushed his leg. "I'm sorry to hear that," she whispered. Portia glanced down at her card, her brow furrowing. "My dance card is full," she admitted, appearing pained by the fact.

Julian was so used to not dancing with Portia that he shrugged away the news. "Another time, perhaps."

She worried her lip and drew closer still. "You're not disappointed I could not save a spot for you again?"

He hid a smile at her worried tone. Things had definitely changed between them in recent days, it seemed. Thanks to the actions of a murderess, Portia now wanted Julian around. This was a very great improvement on their past meetings.

To test just how much things had changed, he moved his fingers slightly, until he encountered the delicate material she wore so well about her body. A further flex of his fingers and he brushed her thigh lightly.

A little gasp escaped her lips, and she looked at him sharply.

He pretended he'd done nothing out of the ordinary. "I will as ever enjoy watching you dance."

"Yes," she grumbled with a hint of frustration, but she did

not move away. "I used to find that so annoying."

Used to. Julian hid another smile and brushed a little harder against her leg with his fingertips. The room was thankfully so crowded that it should not be seen, and so he continued behaving improperly.

She turned slightly, and he did not withdraw his hand. If he was not mistaken, he was able to trace the curve toward her inner thigh and back, knowing full well that he was presuming a great deal about their relationship by teasing her like this. He watched her breathing quicken and a flush of color begin to darken her pale cheeks.

Portia was a good girl, but he believed she was not entirely pure of thought or unaware of preliminary intimacies between lovers. Her parents had no clue the number of times she'd nearly ruined her reputation, and he wasn't about to tell on her. A well-timed cough and a quiet word of warning to the worst of the scoundrels had managed to scare off those without marrying dispositions. Deliberately tempting Portia *himself* was something of a first for them.

For too long, Portia Hayes had run close to the mark, and Julian had tried to stay away. She had her would-be suitors eating out of the palm of her hand most nights. They rushed to do her bidding, champagne, kisses and more... But not Julian. He would not play games for a short-lived thrill of just one night.

"I was very aware of your dislike of being watched." He shrugged, and the act of doing so naturally separated his fingers from her limb. "Who do you dance with next?"

"Lord Sullivan," she said somewhat breathlessly, then wet her plump lips.

Julian reluctantly dragged his eyes from Portia to look around for his old school chum amid the throng of masked guests. Julian would like to think he'd be able to spot his old roommate in any crowd, even if he were masked. "Where was he?"

Portia eased closer. "We were introduced tonight over by the ferns, and he asked me to dance immediately. Do you know him?"

"Indeed I do," Julian promised, looking in the other direction without any success. "You'll be in good hands with Sullivan. Excellent partner. The ladies used to love dancing with him. His wife certainly does, too."

Portia's expression changed to acute disappointment. "He never mentioned he had a wife."

"He will. You even remind me a bit of Clare, too. Especially when you laugh. I doubt he will comment on the similarity, though. His wife is all he ever thinks about."

No sooner where the words out of his mouth when a firm hand clamped hard on his shoulder.

Julian spun about, and then grinned as he looked up at his friend. Andrew Finch, Lord Sullivan, was tall at just over six foot and three inches. The rest of him hadn't changed much either. Dark overlong hair, bright blue eyes, and a sharp, square chin completed the illusion of aristocratic splendor. "Sullivan!"

"Bye Jove, it's Wee Wade," Lord Sullivan exclaimed before taking his hand and shaking it firmly. "You look like an underfed black drake peering around like that. How long has it been, old man?"

"A few years," Julian told him, thinking how fast the time had flown by since they'd last been in the same room. A lot had changed, not all of it good for Wade, but then he noticed Sullivan had aged in the past years, too. Obviously marriage was harder than it had first appeared to be for some. There were fine lines at the corner of his eyes, and a deep cleft between his brows that Julian did not remember. Sullivan had lost the jolly countenance he'd possessed at school that had gotten him out of many a scrape. When they were older and moving about in society, Sullivan had used that smile to charm his way into the affections of the season's diamond and had made Clare his wife as soon as possible.

They shook hands vigorously. Julian had never envied Sullivan his handsome face, but he *had* envied Sullivan for his choice of wife for a brief time. "What are you doing back in London? I thought you were settled in Kent making babies with Clare. Where is she, by the way? I should like to pay my respects."

Sullivan's face paled. "She's gone."

"Gone?" Julian said in confusion, and then his heart skipped a beat as the only possible meaning became clearer just by looking at Sullivan's sad expression.

"She died," Sullivan told him.

"Oh, I am so sorry," he said quickly. He drew close to his old friend and lowered his voice. "I'd not heard. Clare was a truly remarkable woman."

Sullivan nodded slowly and his expression grew bleaker still. "It's been a year now."

Julian mourned Clare. The sharp stab of pain to his heart almost unbearable. She had been great fun to be around before her marriage. She'd had a wicked wit that had appealed to him greatly. But he'd not lain eyes on her since her marriage to Sullivan. The pair had taken themselves off to Kent to be alone and never returned to partake of society. "How did it happen? How did she die?"

"In childbirth."

Julian closed his eyes briefly, imagining the horror that had befallen the lovely lady. This was a tragedy. "And the child?"

Sullivan shook his head quickly. "He did not survive to even draw breath."

The earl had lost the wife he loved and the son he'd always longed for. Julian grabbed his old friend's hand again and held it more firmly. Sullivan had adored Clare. So had Julian, too. "Again, I am so sorry. I wish I had known."

"Time has lessened my sorrow somewhat." Sullivan shook off his grip and then glanced past Julian. He drew in a sharp breath and affected a smile that didn't reach his eyes. "Ah, Miss Hayes, I believe they are about to announce our dance."

"Yes, indeed, Lord Sullivan." She smiled, quickly stepping forward, her expression full of compassion as she met Julian's suddenly watery gaze. "Do excuse us, Lord Wade. Perhaps we might continue our discussion later."

"Of course," he murmured, as he staggered back.

He forced a smile as Portia brushed past him, heading for Sullivan's outstretched arm. She settled her hand on Sullivan's sleeve with a shy smile. "My lord."

"Miss Hayes," Sullivan murmured. "I have been looking forward to our dance."

"I have too. Very much," she admitted, looking up at Julian's old friend as if he were a god upon the earth.

Julian grimaced and looked away. Why *wouldn't* Portia flirt with Sullivan? She did it with everyone as easily as breathing. She had no reason to hesitate. Sullivan was a widower now. If anything, that made the earl even more desirable as a dance partner. Portia knew nothing of their great loss, the light of Sullivan's life gone from the world.

Julian listened to their brief conversation as they drifted away toward the dance floor, but experienced a feeling of growing discomfort as he considered their budding acquaintance. Sullivan would be an excellent catch, now he was widowed. He was a handsome earl, wealthy because of his marriage to Clare, and out of mourning now. Julian had nothing to say against Sullivan as a potential spouse for any woman.

Many would assume Sullivan was back in London to replace his late wife with this year's diamond, too.

As Sullivan positioned Portia on the dance floor, smiling down on her and charming her with small talk, Julian realized that he probably *was* back in London to take another wife. He would need a son and heir soon.

Poor Clare. So soon to be replaced by another.

Julian turned away suddenly as a bitter lump lodged in his throat. He couldn't stay near Portia when his heart was so heavy for another woman. He headed for home to mourn Clare in private, where no one could see the depths of his unhappiness.

Chapter Two

Portia Hayes scanned her bedchamber in exasperation. "Mary, do you know where my paisley shawl has gone?"

"It was right there on the bed, Miss," her maid promised. "I put it out earlier."

Portia tilted her head toward the bed. "It's not there now."

Mary Phillip, her maid of a few years now, rushed to the bed and looked all around it and under. She stood up slowly, frowning. "Miss, I am sure I put it right there for you, as you asked."

Portia drew close to the girl and sighed. "Lavinia probably has it."

"Oh, I'm sorry, Miss. I never saw your sister come in."

Lavinia was developing a number of bad habits that Portia did not appreciate lately. "Don't worry about it now. Could you fetch me my lemon one? Time is flying by so quickly this morning. I cannot be late."

The maid rushed across the room and finally found Portia a shawl to wear downstairs. She slipped it around her shoulders and considered her appearance. She was wearing a new gown, one made of white muslin like everyone else seemed to wear, but she was not at all sure it really suited her complexion. It was a bit pale where Portia preferred to wear brighter jeweled tones. The gown was modest in design too. She wasn't sure if it was the color or the style that gave her pause, or both. "The lemon doesn't look at all bad with it."

"No, Miss," Mary said as she glanced away to the door, and then rushed to it to listen. "Your mother is calling for you."

Mary had excellent hearing, a desirable trait to possess in a lady's maid. Discretion and loyalty were, too. Portia quickly hid the forbidden novel she'd been reading with Mary that morning under her mattress so her mother would not find it, should she come in. Mother firmly believed novels were not suitable for unmarried ladies' minds. She said they encouraged rebellion and disappointment. It didn't help that the late Lady Scott had been a great reader, and a murderess too. Anything that reminded mother of that horrible woman had been immediately denounced as unacceptable.

Ready to face any callers that may come, Portia rushed from her bedchamber and into her mother's dressing room. Mother was at her mirror, admiring her reflection. Her once lustrous dark hair had faded to gray with age but her green eyes were still shrewd. She looked Portia up and down and nodded.

Portia moved to the mirror and twisted this way and that. "You don't think it is too modest?"

"My dear, a little mystery will only increase your appeal," her mother murmured as they prepared for the day's callers together. This had become their new ritual each day of what was left of the season, since those horrible murders had taken away her friends.

Only occasionally did Portia long for the days when she had more freedom. "Even at this time of year?"

"Especially now." Mother swept a hand over her brow, and then reached for her scissors. She pruned a loose thread on Portia's sleeve and smiled. "You are the most beautiful woman in the world."

Portia smiled ruefully. "Second most beautiful, next to you."

She quickly pecked a kiss on her mother's soft cheek and went to her jewelry box. Portia selected a favorite necklace her mother owned and wore often—a large drop of bright amber strung on a long gold chain and placed it around her mother's neck.

"Thank you, my dear."

Portia turned back to the jewelry box and examined the contents idly. Mother's jewels were modest but there were plenty to choose from. Portia found the matching amber earbobs and handed them over. "What interesting tidbits did you hear last night?"

Mother moved to the mirror and threaded the golden hooks through her ears then flicked the amber beads so they swung. "Only of Lord Sullivan, and you were certainly envied for gaining an introduction so swiftly. My only regret was that you had already given away the supper dance to Lord Stephens."

"It was Lord Stephens' turn to take me in. Lord Sullivan seemed very nice," Portia said. "He certainly danced well."

"You made a very elegant pair." Mother turned back. "I suppose Lord Wade had something to say about him?"

Not enough, really, and she was very curious. She hoped to see Wade again soon, so she might quiz him discreetly about Lord Sullivan, and vice versa. "Nothing at all bad. They went to school together. I believe Wade knew the earl's late wife."

And last night, she'd seen signs that Lord Wade would mourn her, too. She was sure there had been tears in his eyes when she'd drawn close.

Tears were the last emotion she'd expect from such a cynic.

Mother nodded. "Ah, perhaps they were rivals for her affections before the marriage."

Portia considered Lord Wade's emotional reaction to the news that Lady Sullivan had died and wondered if mother might not be right. It would explain the estrangement, the long interval since they'd seen each other, and the fact that he'd not learned firsthand of the woman's death. Close friends wrote to each other all the time. "Wade did seem genuinely upset over Lady Sullivan's death. I had no chance to learn more, as he disappeared. I think he might actually have left the ball very early."

"That is unfortunate. Perhaps he will call today and be persuaded to tell all about the mysterious earl and how his wife died."

Portia shuddered. "I already know. She died in childbirth. Lord Sullivan would have had a son."

"Ah." Mother shuddered, too, and then hugged her quickly. "I think we are as prepared as we can be for callers."

Mother liked to be ready early, always. "I'll go and fetch Lavinia."

"Thank you, my dear."

Mother wandered off toward the stairs while Portia went to find her younger sister. At seventeen, Lavinia was turning into such a beauty that she was already attracting attention on the street. She had yet to be presented at court, though, so she often missed out on amusements unless they were conducted at home. Some of Portia's gentleman callers cast an appreciative eye over her younger sister when she occasionally joined them in the drawing room. Lavinia was not officially out, but she was never banished to the nursery as many younger sisters often were.

At her sister's doorway, she knocked once and entered, catching Lavinia unawares. Portia's paisley shawl was wrapped around her slender shoulders but she was still in bed, wriggling under the covers.

"What a lazy little slugabed you are!" Portia held out her hand. "And that is my shawl."

"I was cold."

Lavinia had her own on a nearby chair. Portia snatched it up and tossed it onto the bed. "Give. Mine. Back."

Lavinia grumbled but returned it. In doing so, Portia discovered she'd been reading in bed again, too. "You are going to be in so much trouble."

"Don't tell." She held the book to her flat chest. "I'll die if I don't finish this."

Portia rolled her eyes. "You'll die if Mother catches you reading a scandalous novel. You now how she feels about that sort of thing now."

"But it's *your* book!" Lavinia cried.

That was true. Portia did have a small collection of novels that Mother didn't know anything about, very well hidden, usually. She'd lose them all if Lavinia were caught and tattled on her. "Well, I am clever enough to never be caught reading one in my bed so late in the day." She flung the covers off her sister. "Put the book away under the mattress and get up. Mother expects you downstairs to greet our callers."

Lavinia grudgingly did. "This is so unfair."

"It's only a book."

"The best book." Lavinia twirled about and pulled the bell for a maid. "I cannot wait to fall in love."

Her enthusiasm was catching, so Portia wrapped her arms about the girl and squeezed. "One day you *will* fall in love," Portia promised before dropping a kiss on her pale hair. Love was not in Portia's future, however. The family had expectations for her that went beyond matters of the heart. "I swear you will. Don't take too long coming down."

Portia had the unenviable responsibility of marrying well and raising the family's consequence in society. Although she had wished it could be otherwise many times, she had accepted that she'd not the luxury of marrying for love. She had to marry to please her parents. She was still under one and twenty, and must have their permission and approval.

Father would only agree to an earl or better for Portia. Anything less was considered beneath them. It was not an opinion Portia shared, but she kept her feelings to herself these days out of fear that they'd marry her off to an older man. In their eyes, she'd had almost two unsuccessful seasons. Her parents were starting to worry she'd never be wanted as anyone's wife.

Portia made her way downstairs and went into the sunny drawing room where mother was waiting. Portia took her usual place, and then Lavinia rushed in a moment later to entertain them with her practice on the pianoforte.

At the sound of the knocker, Lavinia fell silent and swiftly moved to sit at Portia's side.

Their butler announced the caller, and Portia looked toward the door with excitement. A very distinguished gentleman appeared, and her smile grew.

"Lord Grindlewood. What a pleasure to have you call on us today, my lord," Mother exclaimed as the earl strode into their drawing room and bowed.

Of all her potential suitors, Portia was quite particularly drawn to the Earl of Grindlewood's good looks. She had admired him even before he had restored his fortunes. He was tall, broad in the chest and rather dashing. He made many ladies sigh as he passed, especially so since he was wealthy again.

Having money had its drawbacks, though. Portia never took anyone's overtures of friendship at face value until she had learned all she could about them. Lord Grindlewood was no different from any other suitor. Fortune or not, he had been thoroughly investigated and vetted as soon as they had met.

He wasn't much for small talk or smiling but she found him good company. He did not brag or make fun of his fellow gentlemen. Lord Grindlewood had been orphaned young, raised by near strangers, and had lurked about town—Lord Wade's description, not hers—for several years. His newly recovered fortune made him acceptable everywhere. Grindlewood was, in a sense, perfect husband material.

Portia was not in love with him, but she liked him very much.

She held out her hand to him and he bowed over it. "Miss Hayes, how lovely you look."

"Thank you." Portia dipped into a perfect curtsy. "It is very good to see you again, my lord."

From behind his back, Lord Grindlewood produced a bunch of pink hothouse tulips. "For you."

The tulips were perfect but sadly not Portia's favorite flower. However, she took her time enthusing over their color and showing her mother. When complimented enough, the flowers were handed to a maid to be placed in water on a nearby side table. "Please do sit down, my lord."

"Thank you." He smiled broadly. "Did you enjoy the ball last night?"

"Indeed we did. I do love to dance," she enthused. "Did I hear you attended Lady Porter's musicale earlier in the week?"

"I did indeed. Were you there? I did not see you if you were."

"No, unfortunately not. I'm not acquainted with the lady, but I long to be. I should like to attend one day. Everyone talks about the superior performances the next day. As you might be aware, my sister has a particular interest in music."

The earl glanced at Lavinia and smiled. "I heard you as I arrived, and you do play very well."

"Thank you, my lord," Lavinia's face slowly turned pink with embarrassment, which the earl must have noticed because he turned away from her and caught Portia's eye. "I should be happy to introduce you, should the occasion arise."

"That would be a wish come true," Portia enthused. Lady Porter's musicales were legendary—but so too were her political talks afterward. That aspect of the lady intrigued her more than the music, but women were not supposed to concern themselves with such matters, so she hid her interest for now.

There was a tap at the door and when invited to enter, the butler announced Lord Sullivan.

Another handsome earl in her mother's drawing room. Mother would be beside herself with glee. Portia smiled happily as he bowed to them.

They chatted together for a little while, and then Lord Grindlewood said his goodbyes, leaving Lord Sullivan to keep them company.

At that point, his lips seemed to fuse together. There was an awkward silence as he smiled nervously. The fellow did not flatter them about their appearance, as Lord Grindlewood had done, and Portia liked him more because of it.

Mother sent for tea and Lord Sullivan exhaled slowly.

Sensing he was more nervous than expected, Portia took control of the conversation. "Did I hear that you and Lord

Wade attended the same school?"

"Eton. For the last year, we roomed together. How do you know Wade?"

"He was my very first dance partner after I made my debut." She'd been in awe of Lord Wade that night, but later, when he'd revealed a few too many bold observations, she learned he wasn't always a gentleman. "What was he like then?"

"Shorter." Lord Sullivan laughed. "I don't think he's changed very much. Absolutely hates to talk about himself. But he's a good man, dependable."

Portia smiled at his praise of Lord Wade. Obviously the earl was more at ease talking about other people. "Which of you excelled at school, and in what subjects?"

"Wade excelled at sport, while I considered a future as a poet, of all things." He laughed to himself.

Wade had not struck her as much of a sporting fellow, but *this* handsome man might have a passion for words in the right circumstances. "Do you write often? I should dearly love to read one of your works."

"I gave all that up when I married my Clare. I used to send her little poems each morning, inspired by our meetings the prior night. I thought myself very gifted, but she was the only one brave enough to confess that I had no talent for it."

"So the poetry did not win you the lady?"

He shrugged. "It was something else altogether that won me her hand. Something I never expected."

Portia smiled. She quite liked Lord Sullivan, but he was so different from Lord Wade that she had trouble imagining the pair had much in common. Obviously, the late Lady Sullivan had chosen this man for good reason. "I was very sorry to learn of your wife's passing. Please accept our condolences."

"Thank you." He frowned, and then stood abruptly. His expression was apologetic, almost panicked. "I really must be going."

"Oh, so soon," Mother cried, appearing as alarmed as Portia.

Lord Sullivan nodded decisively. "I look forward to seeing you again, Mrs. Hayes, Miss Hayes." He bowed, very elegantly, and then strode for the door without looking back.

"Oh, I should not have mentioned his wife," Portia cried softly when the front door shut so soundly. "He was just starting to become comfortable."

Mother turned to her and nodded. "On the contrary, I think it was wise to bring up his loss early in the acquaintance. His father the duke is in Dorset but his Kent estate is said to be quite modest. He has two brothers and three sisters, but they hardly ever come to Town. He will be the Duke of Northport one day don't forget." She nodded. "His father is said to be poorly. Lord Sullivan would make an excellent husband for you."

"Mother!" Portia chided. "He just lost his wife, and now you're wishing for his father's death, too. Lord Northport is in fine health. Why, I saw him only last week in Bond Street. Lord Wade pointed him out to us himself. He seemed quite hale and hearty as he strode along to me."

Mother's face fell. "Then you'll be a duchess in waiting, but only if you bring Lord Sullivan up to scratch before someone else catches his eye. Think of what that will mean for your sister."

The idea of becoming titled—a duchess perhaps, if she were fortunate—was all that mattered to Portia's mother and father. She was meant to elevate the family into the aristocracy and ensure her younger sister made an exceptional match, too.

Portia, however, was looking for something more in a husband than the obvious. Strength of character and a modest fortune at a minimum were essential. Although she was an heiress herself, her father would not allow her to marry just anyone. Many a fortune hunter had sought out her company, some had even shamelessly pretended to fall in love with her at first sight in a bid to win her affections.

Another knock sounded, and Mother quickly had the attending maid remove the tea tray. When all was perfect again, she bid the butler enter.

Portia gasped at who followed him. The Duke of Montrose was in their drawing room.

They both bounced to their feet quickly and dipped deep curtsies. They had never received a duke at home before, but they had talked about what to do should it ever come to pass.

Portia stepped forward first. "Lord Montrose, what an unexpected pleasure. How gracious of you to call on our home."

The Duke of Montrose towered over her, seeming to take up all the air in the room. She was grateful when he sat, and she did her best to slow her frantic heart. They had danced together two weeks ago but she'd not seen him since. Portia could not imagine what might have brought him to their door today.

Mother offered him tea, which he declined immediately.

He glanced around the room. "I imagine you are wondering why I have come."

"Whatever the reason, we are very glad to have you in our home," Mother said very quickly.

A brief wince appeared on the duke's face, and then he turned the full force of his attention on Portia. "Might we speak alone? Just a few minutes will do."

Portia could not have been more shocked. She glanced at her mother for advice. "I…"

"Your mother and sister may wait outside the open door if you'd prefer," he announced.

Regardless of what she hoped showed on her face, her mind was racing every which way and that. She wet her lips. "Is that all right, Mother?"

"Yes, of course," Mother agreed slowly, her eyes full of excitement. "I will be right outside should you need me."

Mother curtsied and fluttered her way to the door, dragging Lavinia with her. She made such a show of leaving the door ajar that Portia wanted to laugh. She did not, of course. She would never seem to make fun of her mother in front of anyone. When Mother could no longer be seen, she turned her attention to the duke.

He smiled quickly. "I've come to ask for your hand."

Portia knew her lips had parted in shock but she was unable to close her mouth. A proposal was the last thing she'd expected the Duke of Montrose to offer her. She wet her lips quickly. "Could you repeat that?"

"I've come to marry you."

"Hmm," Portia murmured, and then swallowed. Yes she had heard him correctly the first time, but still… "You're asking for my hand in marriage. *Me.*"

"There's no one else at this address of suitable age," he said with a slight smile.

The duke had a sense of humor. "Surely you jest."

"I am not known for it. You will find I am quite a direct man. I've considered all the ladies in society, and I think you would be a most appropriate choice to be my duchess."

Portia exhaled slowly, but her mind continued to race. The Duke of Montrose really was asking for her hand in marriage. Just like that. No flowers, no flattery. No courtship at all. "But you don't know me."

He nodded. "I know your father and mother, and what I have seen of you with my own eyes confirms their praise."

Portia looked down at her hands. "Thank you."

"Your modesty today recommends you even more, but I am afraid I do require an immediate answer," he murmured. "We can become better acquainted after you agree."

Portia swallowed. If she accepted Lord Montrose, she would fulfill her mother's dearest dream and make her family so happy.

However, she experienced a momentary pang of regret that she would never have a more romantic proposal. As a young girl, Portia had dreamed of this moment and imagined it so much more romantic than this. She'd talked about it with her friends and with her mother and sister too. Portia had once expected her suitor would fall to his knees and declared no one else would do for them.

But that was the dream and this was her reality.

This was why her parents had brought her to London and

spent a fortune on her seasons. All so an aristocrat, wealthy and powerful, would ask for her hand in marriage. She was expected to say yes. She had promised her mother and father that she would marry as well as she could too. She had always known she must marry to better the family's standing in society. Doing so would ensure her sister could marry as she liked and hopefully marry for love when Portia could not.

She swiftly pushed the niggling disappointment aside for what might have been and forced a smile. She nodded slowly, regally. "I would be honored to be your duchess, your grace."

The Duke of Montrose nodded and got to his feet swiftly. "Thank you."

Portia thought he was about to lean over and perhaps claim a kiss, but he turned for the door instead and looked out, left and right.

Mother apparently had not lingered long in the hall.

When he returned and sat down again, he was frowning. "We will be married next week."

"What? No! That is not enough time for the banns to be called."

He smiled slightly. "Banns are not necessary when one has the means to marry almost immediately."

"But your grace, it is too soon." Portia wet her lips and sat forward. "We hardly know each other."

"You did agree to marry me."

"But I only agreed because you promised I would have the time to get to know you in the coming weeks."

He frowned, his jaw worked. "Very well. The banns will be called on Sunday."

"Thank you, your grace." There would be time to get to know him, time to plan a sumptuous wedding breakfast, and for Lord and Lady Sorenson to return to London. She so wanted her friend Anna to be there to witness her most important day.

Mother and Father suddenly appeared at the open doorway, and Portia beckoned them inside. "His grace has proposed, and I have accepted."

Mother shrieked and ran to embrace Portia. "I'm so proud of you, my darling," she whispered though her tears of joy.

Mother turned to the duke, smiling, but she only dipped him a curtsy. "You have made a wise choice, Lord Montrose."

"It was an easy decision," he told her before departing with Father to discuss terms.

Portia watched him go, waiting for the moment when she might feel as happy as her mother.

Chapter Three

"As you can see, I've taken excellent care of the piece," Julian murmured as he stood back with a smile, but he couldn't dispel the sadness that had been his constant companion since he'd arisen that morning.

Clare was gone.

Mr. Jones, a fellow sent to him by a mutual acquaintance, squinted and ran his hand over the billiard table's perfect felt top. Jones was new money, a merchant looking to furnish his new home in Orchard Square. Jones moved around the table slowly, looking for imperfections in the heavily carved oak from all angles. He would find none. Julian had realized long ago that imperfections cost money. "What do you say, Jones?"

The man patted his belly, and then started nodding. "I'll take it at the price you want. I won't haggle over fine-quality workmanship like this. It's a good deal, but I don't know why you would part with it."

"I don't play anymore." That wasn't quite true. He played at the club but only occasionally. He also preferred to call upon his friends in their homes if he could. The table was an unnecessary indulgence. It had been purchased by Julian's father—along with many fine things that were meant to convey affluence and riches they'd never had. Father had liked to show off before his friends and enemies. Unfortunately, the billiard table and many other similarly useless extravagances had placed a considerable drain on the family fortune until the day he died.

Since then, Julian had been attempting to rebuild, but mostly all he'd managed to do was survive, to delay the inevitable fall. Father had not invested wisely, and the losses since his death just kept coming.

"The table has only been gathering dust. I do hope you enjoy it more than I had time for."

They shook hands, and Julian was pleased beyond measure that Jones handed over the funds immediately.

He tucked the proceeds into his pocket, feeling immense relief. The funds from this sale would go toward paying his servants' next quarterly wages and settle an outstanding bill of his aunt's from her dressmaker. The little that remained after would be locked away for any unforeseen expenses in the coming month.

Julian had learned to be frugal, but the worry of keeping up appearances was starting to take a toll on his emotions. Some days were harder than others.

Jones gestured his men forward and they grunted and heaved to get the piece out of the room. "This would go faster with a few more men to help carry the load," Jones grumbled, casting the elderly butler at his side a hopeful glance.

"My servants are busy elsewhere right now," Julian said as dismissively as he could before the butler could do something foolish, like offer his assistance or send for the boot boy. The few servants Julian kept were working hard enough, carrying on the duties of twice their number to keep the house Julian couldn't get rid of in fair order.

He glanced out the front window to the bustling square and presented his back, falling back on familiar habits. He pretended the required indifference to their struggle as befitting a gentleman in possession of a title. He had been born to be a viscount, not a laborer—although he could end up one, he supposed. For now, he'd do everything he could to keep his place in society.

Unfortunately, selling off an item as big as this was sure to draw attention to the townhouse. There was no help for it. Only the front door was wide enough to emit the table, and Julian needed the money from this sale rather desperately.

He had to continue to spout the same story, that he was bored with the game, so few would question his real motive.

Jones had gotten a good bargain in their deal and thankfully said not another word about needing more men or help. Eventually they got the piece out to the street and loaded onto a cart to begin their short trip around Hanover Square, bound for Orchard Square.

Jones returned, rushing into the room. "I almost forgot the other things for the table," he exclaimed apologetically, rushing to collect the billiard balls and sticks.

Julian nodded but then remembered an oversight. He heaved another sigh and strode to the mantel and carefully pulled down an item from the wall. He returned to Jones, forcing a smile. "To help you keep score against your opponents, and your enemies, too. No charge."

"Thank you, my lord. Thank you very much. But I cannot take something for nothing. Here." Mr. Jones shoved a handful of notes into Julian's hand. "I believe a man should pay a fair price."

Jones clutched the counter board tight to his chest and juggled the lot on his way out the door. The butler followed to shut the front doors and the house was finally silent.

It was also painfully emptier.

Julian shoved the extra notes in his pocket as the butler returned. He'd gotten more than the counter was worth, but glanced around the nearly empty front room and bare wall with a pang of regret. The emptiness would be noticed immediately by the next person to call on him.

Luckily, Julian had already considered what to do about that.

He strode to the next room and picked up an armchair.

The butler spluttered.

"It's time to do a little redecorating around the house," he muttered, looking at the man apologetically. "Mosely, could you fetch the small round table and put it beside this chair?"

Julian could do most of the little changes himself, but he should not do everything.

He'd moved two comfortable armchairs and another oval table to sit before the front window before his aunt swept into the room.

"Where's my billiard table?" she cried.

"My table," Julian corrected her. "I sold it."

Aunt Hesper's face fell, and the newssheet in her hand crinkled as she crushed it. "But I was seduced on that table after I won my first game."

The butler choked and quickly fled the room.

Julian shook his head. "I'm glad you waited until after the deal was struck and Mr. Jones was gone before you mentioned that fact out loud. Poor Mosely, though. He may never look at you the same way again."

"Lenthall was quite proud of me that day."

Aunt Hesper and her late husband had enjoyed a passionate marriage. Unfortunately, she sometimes liked to share those reminiscences out loud more often than Julian preferred.

His aunt came forward and sighed as she looked about the room. "It's not fair."

Acid burned in his stomach. "It is what it is, I'm afraid. We needed the money," he explained before he leaned down to kiss her wrinkled cheek.

His aunt was silent a while. "My pearls. You could sell them, too."

"No, absolutely not." The pearls were a treasured possession of hers, a gift from her husband on her wedding day, but not worth very much. Better that she keep them for as long as possible. "We're fine for now."

"For how long?"

"Long enough." Julian glanced around. "I need to finish this in case someone comes to visit. Why don't you take a seat by the window while I find a servant to help me move my desk to this room."

"Very well, dearie," she agreed as she shuffled to the new seating arrangement. She tossed the crumpled newssheet onto one chair before claiming the other.

Wade found the fellow easily enough below stairs, pulling him away from helping Cook prepare luncheon. Together, they got Julian's favorite furniture arranged nicely in the larger space, and then he closed up the adjoining empty room. "One less room to heat and clean for the winter," he murmured, pleased with that.

"Yes, my lord," the man agreed. "Can I assist you with anything else?"

"No, that will be all," he promised. "Thank you."

The few servants he had remaining were kind enough to have held their tongues about the strict economies he'd been making this past year out of some misplaced affection for the family. Unfortunately, he would have to let another man go later today, and he wished he didn't have to take such a step. He'd no need for a stable hand, since he'd already sold his last horse. He'd been putting the matter off in the hope that things could be turned around. The stables were empty now, and the fellow without chores to earn his keep.

"My poor brother would be turning in his grave to know the troubles he'd brought down upon you," Auntie whispered as he rejoined her in the newly organized study.

Julian actually liked the change of scenery and having money in his pocket for once. He would have a view of Hanover Square now. He could read by the window, too, and see who came and went without ever bothering to get up.

Julian headed for the liquor cabinet and unlocked it. He poured two small measures of whiskey and handed one to his aunt. He dropped a kiss on her forehead. "Father never gave the future a second thought. He was having too much fun being scandalous."

"It was fun while the money lasted," she murmured. "But this is deplorable. We should do something."

Julian agreed. "I have tried numerous times to sell the lease on the townhouse, but you keep pretending it's haunted when

I bring anyone around."

"This is my home," she whispered. "And it *is* haunted, too."

"It is not. And home is where your heart is, and where your family resides. Wherever that may be, I will always look after the living. If I cannot sell the lease, I was thinking of subletting the place next season. We could spend spring and summer with friends."

Julian took a sip, aware that the melancholy of their situation was worse for his aunt. She remembered when things had been good, when they had entertained and traveled widely. She hated that the family fortunes were in decline.

"You will have to marry," she announced suddenly.

They'd had this discussion before. It was unnecessary. He knew what choices he had left. Just the one—but the timing had to be right. For now, he chose to make light of the situation and his fears. "Or turn to thievery," he countered.

She chuckled. "You walk too heavily upon the earth to be a good thief. Most likely you would feel guilty, too, and put everything back the next day. What about gambling?"

"You need money to do that, and I will not risk what we have."

She nodded slowly. "Then a wife it is. A rich one."

"Yes," he said morosely. Portia possessed a dowry to solve every problem for the rest of his life, but he was nervous about asking her to marry him. He was not sure her heart had softened toward him enough. He was well aware that he might only have one chance. If she refused, he could never ask again. He would be too humiliated to try.

Auntie clucked her tongue. "Being married isn't painful, not for the husband, anyway."

He rolled his eyes at her quip. "Being proven a fortune hunter is, though. Because I certainly am one, even before I begin courting."

Auntie leaned forward. "She does seem to favor you now."

Julian knew whom she was speaking of without Portia Hayes' name being mentioned. They had both been watching Portia since her debut—Auntie encouraging her out of her mother's shadow, while Julian kept the true scoundrels of society, fortune hunters particularly, from ruining her just to claim her ridiculously large dowry.

Unfortunately, he'd not done so well at recommending himself as a potential spouse until recent events had brought them together. The lack of funds meant he could not afford to bring her daffodils when he called or send love notes by messenger to prove she meant more to him than her dowry.

Seeking distraction, Julian picked up the paper next to him and smoothed the pages. He flipped to the spot he'd been reading at breakfast, hoping for good news.

"Lord Mallory married last week by special license," Auntie said suddenly. "He chose Elaine Whittaker for his bride."

"Devil take it!" Julian threw the paper away, disappointed by this turn of events. "I liked her but he's an ass."

"They say it is a love match," Auntie said in a soothing tone. "Best not to interfere with those things."

"Of course they say that. But he also happens to be rich into the bargain, so of course she fell in love with him."

Auntie clucked her tongue. "It won't do you any good feeling sorry for yourself, dearie."

Julian bowed his head. Frustrated by his life. If his father was alive, he'd wring his bloody neck. "This is hopeless. If not for this accursed house, we'd be far better off."

"All the best families have lived in this square."

"I hope that is some consolation for you when winter comes and the house is freezing."

"You worry too much."

He leaned toward her. "There'll be no money for coal, dearie."

A look of stubborn determination crossed her face. "We'll come about. We've waded through thick and thin together all these years."

She started chuckling to herself, and Julian groaned. "That sort of thing wasn't funny when I was a boy, and it certainly is not now."

That only made her laugh harder.

He raked a hand through his hair. Once rumors of the billiard table sale circulated, his situation would be looked at more closely by those who knew him. Marrying a daughter to an impoverished viscount was hardly the stuff of dreams for any ambitious family, but he had no time to dally. "If I can convince her, then I'll stop worrying," he promised.

"Remember, you're as deserving as the next man."

"I know that. But the inequality of money will be the true stumbling block. You know how much trouble Sullivan had with Clare's family getting in his way. I can't imagine I'll have better luck." He burst to his feet. "I'll begin courting her tonight."

"If she has any sense, she'll only care about your heart."

He moved to the front windows and peered outside, impatience making his toe tap. "She's invited to the Daventry Ball tonight, too. We should get there early. The best I can hope for is to beat the others to claim the supper dance."

"What if she has promised it to another?"

He spread his hands wide. "I'll take anything else left. If not, abduction seems a reasonable alternative to a proper courtship, doesn't it?"

He was joking of course. He would never disrespect Portia by sullying her reputation. Not when he'd done all he could to keep it pristine.

"That happened a lot in my day." Auntie sighed. "Only the most ardent of lovers risked the run for the Scottish border with the angry family in hot pursuit."

"That's a little more than I planned," he said, and then glanced at his aunt. "Shouldn't you be trying to stop me from ruining her?"

"I know your heart is in the right place." Auntie leaned back and closed her eyes. "Those other fellows see only her dowry and what they can do with it. You don't." She started to chuckle. "Although with a dowry that plump, there is a great many things that could be done around here."

"Not here. I quite like her uncle's house."

Auntie pulled a face. "At least that is something in your

favor. You both seem to prefer the place, though why, I cannot imagine. Would you really move so far from Mayfair?"

"I would." Julian glanced around, grimacing. "Try not to scare off the next gentleman who expresses interest in taking on our lease. No matter how large Portia's dowry may be, we cannot be wasteful and try to live in two places at once."

"Oh very well, but I do want to have a say one day again," she grumbled.

"Everything but the decoration of her uncle Oliver's house." Julian quickly kissed her cheek.

"If the boy was here, he'd be on my side about all this," she complained.

The boy was Nigel, Julian's younger brother. "Nigel has already assured me he is perfectly fine with anything I decide. I bought him the commission he wanted. He's happy, I think."

Auntie pouted. "It's too quiet without him."

"We will see him again, as soon as he has leave to visit us."

She squinted at him. "You need children."

"Don't get too far ahead of the present." Julian laughed. The things Auntie said sometimes were beyond the pale. "Excuse me."

"Where are you going?"

"To tell the groom to make himself useful in the kitchen rather than the stables. I might have enough to keep him in employment if I am accepted in the next two weeks." He turned back to his aunt. "Oh, don't forget, you're coming to the Daventry ball tonight, too. I'll need you there to keep her mother occupied, should I somehow manage to claim the supper dance. Wear something pretty with your pearls and stay out of the wine cellar. I'll see you at eight in the front hall."

"Julian," Auntie called. "She will say yes to you."

"We'll find out tonight," he replied before hurrying off. "My luck has to change for the better soon."

Chapter Four

"Welcome to our little party, Mr. Hayes. Mrs. Hayes," Lord Daventry said to Portia's parents as they reached the head of the receiving line. "I hear congratulations are in order, too. Montrose has stolen away one of our favorite ladies."

That was quick.

"I'm still here," Portia said as she poked her head around her father's shoulder.

She had not expected anyone coming to the Daventry Ball to know about the engagement yet. It had only been a few short hours. But she should have known that the *ton* loved nothing more than a good gossip. Was there anyone left who she could surprise with the news?

"So you are, but not for long, I imagine," Daventry said with a hearty laugh.

Father puffed out his chest, smiling proudly. "We cannot be more pleased with the connection. Lord Montrose has chosen very well."

The earl agreed and her parents moved along. "Miss Hayes, so good of you to come," Daventry murmured before urging his wife forward. "I don't believe you've met my wife yet."

"No, but I long to. How do you do, my lady," she said quickly as the countess approached.

"Very well. A pleasure to meet you," Lady Daventry

murmured with a fond smile for her husband. The earl stepped away to greet another couple, leaving them standing alone for a moment. The tiny woman was hardly ever seen in London, preferring a retiring life away from the crowds prevalent at London amusements. She was said to be quite nervous of strangers, too.

"Thank you for inviting us tonight."

"It would not be a proper ball without you," Lady Daventry replied in a soft and kind voice. "My husband mentioned you were much loved as a dance partner. I am afraid we only just learned of your engagement late this afternoon, or we would have invited the duke to join us, too."

"I do understand," Portia promised. "And I am sure Lord Montrose would have been very pleased to attend." Lady Daventry was so tiny that Portia shrank down a little so she was not towering over the woman.

"There would have been ample room for one more, I'm sure." Lady Daventry leaned forward suddenly. "I adore the color of your gown. Such a striking shade of green."

"I was about to say the same of your gown. I wish I could persuade my mother to permit me to wear crimson," Portia admitted with a heavy sigh of admiration for the daring creation. She stared at Lady Daventry's gown more closely but the countess started to fidget under her prolonged scrutiny. There was barely any bodice or sleeves, and the longer Portia admired the gown, the more she noticed it was almost indecently sheer.

She grinned slowly, and Lady Daventry returned it shyly. It was a bold choice and very daring indeed.

"My husband's choice," Lady Daventry laughed softly, and Portia did, too.

"Lord Daventry has excellent taste."

"I do indeed," Daventry said as he suddenly returned to his wife and slid his arm around her back before he pressed a brief kiss to her brow. "I've told you to wear anything you like, my dear. To hell with what people think of us."

Portia grinned. She couldn't wait to be married so she

might have a husband who doted on her like that. She bid her hosts a fond farewell and hurried to catch up to her parents, who were already far ahead.

This was the first large ball the Daventrys had hosted since they'd married, and Portia's first foray into the house at all. She was astounded by the richly decorated home and the guests she recognized. Absolutely everyone was here. The couple had invited a great number of people, and it seemed all the rooms on this level and the one above were filled with happy, chattering guests.

They passed through what she thought could have been an elegant drawing room, if it had any furniture left in it, to where people were gathered together sipping champagne.

Portia was allowed one glass, perhaps a second toward the end of the evening, if her mother was in a good mood. She accepted her first glass, completely sure she deserved a second later to celebrate her good fortune, though she sipped slowly. She followed closely behind her parents, who greeted friends of theirs. Her parents were not widely acquainted with the Daventrys' many friends, though, and soon they were standing alone. There were faces she did not recognize in the room but clearly they were important if they were here.

She glanced up, admiring the splendid crystal chandelier dangling high above their heads. Lord Daventry was said to be obscenely rich, so she was not overwhelmed by surprise at what she saw about her. One day she might live in such a grand house. She must remember to ask Lord Montrose to describe what his home looked like.

Portia felt eyes upon her and looked around for the source. The room was very full, but for a second she imagined Lord Wade was watching her yet again. She craned her neck, looking for him with a feeling of unease. He should have heard the news of her engagement from her own lips, and she was desperate to tell him the exact details of Lord Montrose's sudden proposal so he would know truth from fiction.

She was ashamed to say that in the rush of excitement at accepting the duke, mostly encouraged by her mother and sister, she had forgotten to send a note to Lord Wade and his aunt to tell them immediately. They were good friends.

She looked around again, eager to see him now. She had actually missed him very much today, because she could not get over his sudden disappearance from Lady Birch's party last night. She was worried about how he was feeling. She thought he might have been upset over the death of Lord Sullivan's wife, too.

She owed him her support in his hour of need. After all, the viscount had unselfishly watched over her safety in recent weeks. Yes, she might once have resented, even loathed, the very sight of Lord Wade hovering at the perimeter of her awareness. She had become used to his admiration, not that their little flirtations could have ever amounted too more than that. But he was her friend. The best kind she could ever hope to have.

Although she looked everywhere, she could not see him yet. But Lord Wade was sure to be here tonight. It was Lord Wade who had introduced her family to Lord Daventry during her very first season.

It was only after she had agreed to dance with several gentlemen that night that she saw Lord Wade's aunt in the crowd. Portia liked her very much. She talked with an open frankness usually only experienced with close family members. Mrs. Hesper Lenthall was talking, glass in hand, on the far side of the room. When the older lady finally noticed her, Portia waved quickly and smiled, hoping to share her excitement.

Mrs. Lenthall seemed to squint at her...but then immediately returned to her conversation without waving back.

Portia lowered her hand slowly, and then glanced around to see if anyone had noticed she might have been snubbed. Mrs. Lenthall would not have given her the cut direct, of course not, but it may seem like it to others.

Portia finally saw Lord Wade. He was standing by himself, watching her as usual from a distance, his expression unreadable.

Relieved to see his familiar face at last, Portia excused herself to her mother and turned toward Lord Wade—except Lord Wade was no longer anywhere to be found.

Undeterred by his disappearance, Portia moved to where she'd last seen him standing.

A little farther along the ballroom, a door was slowly falling closed. Portia followed, sure that Lord Wade had darted behind it, though for what reason she couldn't imagine.

She slipped from the room, plunging into the near total darkness of a narrow unlit hallway. When her eyes adjusted, Lord Wade was standing right in front of her. "There you are."

"Here I am," he said in a frosty tone that made her shiver.

"Why didn't you come over and say hello?"

"Why do you think?"

Was he so angry to hear about her engagement via the gossips that he would sulk? "I really must talk to you."

Wade folded his arms across his chest. "I cannot imagine what about."

"I wanted to tell you myself that I am engaged to marry the Duke of Montrose, but I fear you already have heard. Lord Daventry seemed to know of it the moment we arrived."

Wade's nod was clipped. "Montrose is a bore."

"He's a duke," she protested.

"You don't say," Lord Wade exclaimed, but his tone dripped with sarcasm. "I only heard about his blasted title from him every single day when I was at school with the man."

"I'm sorry he did that. Children can be cruel to each other without considering the hurt they cause others. My own sister sometimes drives me to distraction. However, I'm sure he has changed since then."

Lord Wade looked away. "I hardly care if he has or not."

"Please, Wade," she put her hand on his arm, "don't be cross with me for not telling you about it myself. I know I should have sent a note round rather than letting you hear it third hand. It all happened so quickly, just this afternoon."

"You don't say," he repeated, still obviously put out with her.

She shook his arm. "I want my friends to celebrate my marriage with me. The banns will be called on Sunday, then in four or maybe five weeks there will be the wedding, and later visits to the country or the London townhouse when we host parties. He is supposed to have a grand house to the south, but I've never been there. Imagine the adventure that trip will be for all of us."

His expression soured even more. "I'm sure Lady Sorenson will be delighted to visit you anywhere."

"I meant you and your aunt, too. We're friends!"

"Good God, woman!" Lord Wade exclaimed loudly, looking at her with a horrified expression on his face. "Do you imagine you and I are friends?"

"Of course we are! The best of friends indeed. You would have saved my life if I was in danger last month."

"That was last month." He loomed closer suddenly. Wade was narrowly built but quite a bit taller than Portia. When she looked up at him, she felt her knees start to tremble, which was an odd discovery to make now when he'd never intimated her before. "Miss Hayes, we are not friends. We never were."

She blinked at him in surprise. "But…"

His eyes narrowed, and he suddenly drew back. "I found watching your reckless antics amusing for a time—you were always one kiss away from scandal—but those days are long past."

Why was he lying to her? He had never been amused by her behavior or her fascination with other men. "That is not true. I cannot believe you could say that to me after all we've been through these past weeks. You protected me when no one else tried to. Not even my parents know how much you sacrificed to keep me safe."

"One less virgin wasted by a murderer," he said sourly. "The aristocracy needed you alive for your dowry, and look how quickly Montrose swept you up in his loving arms once he surveyed the very small field of choices. It took barely a week after his arrival in Town for him to sweep in and claim you before anyone else realized what he was up to."

Portia's face burned with anger. "That was a cruel thing to say. It wasn't like that at all."

He shrugged in an off-handed way that she instantly despised. "And yet it has a ring of truth to it. There are so few heiresses available for marriage this year. Pickings are slim. Lady Scott did you a great favor in killing off your competition."

Portia glared at him. "I can't believe you would say that. Those ladies were my friends."

"They were your rivals. Competition. It is the truth, no matter how unpalatable you claim to find it." He scowled. "Tell me, were you so desperate to be his duchess that you didn't care that Montrose did not even take the time to bother to court you?"

Portia had noticed and in the few hours since she had accepted she was already a little disappointed in herself. She could have taken more time to give the duke an answer. But with his impatience so obvious and her parents expecting her to say yes anyway, she had been persuaded to accept immediately.

"Tell me he courted you with sweet words and stolen kisses? Poetry? Anything to prove you had reason to give yourself to a man you barely know?"

They stared at each other, and a chill went through her. It pained her that Wade asked the same questions she asked herself, since Montrose had first called on her to propose. "Yes, I might have eagerly accepted Lord Montrose's proposal, but I insisted on having the banns read so we could know each other before the marriage takes place. I did not make a rash decision, but a considered one."

"I beg to differ, but what does it matter what I say? When did it ever?" Wade shook his head. "You do what you like anyway. Go back to the ball, Portia, and bask in the adulation of the masses. Go back where you can learn to be as dull and as ordinary as all the rest."

She punched her hands to her hips. Lord Wade simply could not be happy for her, no matter what she said. She shouldn't have to explain herself. Stubbornness, however, kept her there. She would not let him have the last word. "I will never be dull or ordinary."

"You will be." He shrugged. "Go back where it's safer."

"I am safe with you."

"Safe with me? You really have no sense, do you?" He snorted—but then he moved suddenly toward her. Her back hit the wall, and he stopped. His expression was grim as he caged her between his outstretched arms and lowered his head. "You have not the faintest idea about me, or what I hoped for you. Montrose will have the chore now of holding back the lecherous scoundrels nipping around your skirts like hungry dogs. You do little to stop them coming back for one more attempt to get you alone like this. I warn you, though; Montrose is as rigid as they come. He will not forget or forgive any indiscretions, should you be caught in another man's arms."

Portia gaped. "You're jealous. Jealous that he is a duke."

Wade drew back suddenly. "I'm not jealous of his title."

She didn't believe him. "He can't help that he was born to be a duke. My parents approved him, so surely my friends can, too."

He should his head. "I am not jealous of his title or his blasted money. Your parents have no idea what they've done to you. He will destroy everything I—" He winced. "Everything that makes you who you were always meant to be."

Portia shook her head. "You knew all along I could never marry just anyone or defy my family wishes. A duke is as high as I could hope for, and they couldn't be happier. I have to think of my family, my sister."

"You could have done better," Wade bit out. "You should have thought of yourself too."

He stormed off before she could call him back.

Chapter Five

Julian shook Sullivan's hand perfunctorily once his old friend had settled into the hack but looked away quickly again. He was not in a good mood, however Sullivan's note had lured him from his home where he'd been brooding over Portia's decision to marry so suddenly. He couldn't believe she'd chosen Montrose over all other gentlemen vying for her affections. "You wanted to see me."

"And a good morning to you, too." Sullivan frowned as he looked about the hack with obvious distaste and settled his hat on his lap rather than beside him on the stained seat. He was dressed very well today, much better than he used to, and naturally far above Julian's years-old attire. Julian feared it wouldn't take him very long to notice the differences between them were poles apart. "What happened to that ramshackle contraption you usually get about in?"

"It finally fell to pieces, so I've ordered a new one," he lied, smoothly he hoped. His old carriage was perfectly sound, it was just living elsewhere now. "In the meantime, I'll make do with what's easiest to hand."

"I never thought you would be without the old beast."

"Well, I am." He'd reclaimed twenty pounds for the carriage and another ten for the matched pair of horse that pulled it. He missed having a carriage of his own, even if it was ancient and the horses pulling it had been old and plodding. It was small comfort that at least the horses were probably better off where they were now.

"Clare told me she admired that rickety thing. She used to tease me about not having one of my own at first, too. Said she liked me better for not pretending I had a fancier one. For being honest about my circumstances. You were right about that…and so many things then. You were so good to us."

Julian's smile felt forced because he was still sad that Clare was gone. She had been an Original. Portia was an Original, too…or could have remained one if she were marrying anyone else. He pushed aside his bitter disappointment before it took hold again and tried to feel enthusiastic about the day. "So you're back in London."

"Yes, as you see, I've leased a house on Upper Brooke Street—for the season and next year, too, I think. You'll be seeing a lot more of me in the coming weeks."

So Sullivan was in London for a reason, most likely hunting a new bride. Julian wished him well. "I'm glad of that. Hardly anyone interesting comes to London anymore."

Sullivan laughed. "If I know you at all, you'll soon be pointing out the most outrageous ladies I should know."

"What few are left, that is," Julian lamented. "Sadly, our murderess, Lady Scott, culled the best of the flock."

"I read about that business in the papers. His grace was most concerned about the situation."

Julian had been, too. He'd been close enough to Lady Scott on that final night to hear just how deranged she'd become. It was no wonder her godson, Lord Carmichael, had fled London. The question on everyone's lips was how long he would stay away. Julian hoped not for long, because Carmichael was a man he had admired, though there'd been no reason to tell him at the time. "How *is* Northport these days?"

"The same." Sullivan pursed his lips a moment before he spoke again. "Concerned for the future of the duchy."

Sullivan was never an easy man to read. What he didn't say

often spoke volumes to Julian. If the duke hadn't changed—and Julian doubted he was capable of that—he was worried about the succession again. "Is he pressing you to take another wife already?"

"How did you guess?"

"Your face. It's been a year since Clare died, which isn't long enough to grieve for her. You're here, where you vowed never to be again." Sullivan began to nod. "It was a miracle you married the first time you know," Julian noted.

Sullivan was an oddity. Although he was handsome and titled, he had not always been sure of himself. He might seem confident and charming to acquaintances at a ball, but the closer a lady got to claiming his heart, the more nervous and evasive he tended to become. It had been absolutely necessary for Julian to meddle in Sullivan's courtship of Clare, too—even if doing so had forever put her out of his reach.

"Only thanks to you. I owe you a debt I can never fully repay," Sullivan assured him.

Julian turned a withering glance on Sullivan. Yes, he was adept at steering friends toward happiness, but powerless to secure his own joy. He expected nothing for his efforts on behalf of others and preferred they not know or mention any help, too. "I did nothing but tell the truth," he cautioned.

"You did more than that, and you know it." Sullivan glanced down. "I may need your assistance again, I'm afraid. It is difficult to imagine anyone could take Clare's place."

He brushed lint from his knee, hiding his irritation. "I doubt you should consider another woman as Clare's replacement, because there could never be another woman like her."

"You are right. I know you are." Sullivan rubbed a hand over his mouth. "I didn't mean it the way it must have sounded. The situation has my tongue tied in knots. I called on Miss Hayes yesterday, and at the first mention of Clare, I could scarce get another word out."

Julian grunted in sympathy. At least coming to London did not sound like it had been Sullivan's choice. No doubt the duke was pulling his strings once more.

The last time Julian and Sullivan had been in London together, they'd vied for the affections of the same woman. Clare Johnson had chosen with her heart, even if she became a countess by marrying the impoverished Lord Sullivan. Julian had been very envious at the time, but what was the point of holding a grudge now? They'd been in love.

Sullivan was watching him closely, so Julian shrugged away his unhappiness. "Did you have someone in mind already?"

"Not really. It is all so terribly uncomfortable. The wealthiest will always marry the most titled. It's hard not to know where I should focus my attention first, even if my heart rebels."

Julian let his gaze roam over Sullivan's attire. Judging by the fine quality of his garments, he'd found time to visit a tailor and boot maker already. He was very well turned out. The ladies in want of a title would be panting after him soon enough. He could take his pick of anyone. "I'm sure you'll find someone to suit your needs."

"I don't think I'm in any rush, but coming to London will appease his grace for a little while." Sullivan grinned. "And what about you?"

"What about me?" Julian glanced out the window, heart sinking though the floor of the carriage. Last night had not been a success, as far as claiming a wife was concerned. Quite the opposite. He had the worst luck of anyone when it came to women.

Sullivan tapped his fingers against this knee. "You know, I thought I saw a flare of interest in your eyes at the Birch Ball for a certain lady with dark hair."

His stomach knotted. "I don't know what you are talking about."

"Surely you remember how fetching Miss Hayes looked that night. You could barely take your eyes from her."

Julian glanced out the window. "She was a friend."

"Well, that is excellent news. You hardly like anyone."

"Indeed," Julian agreed, grimacing slightly.

He was still stunned about her sudden engagement, even though he should not be surprised. She had shown her true colors finally. Her family had always been clear that they wanted a title for Portia, the higher the better and he'd wrongly believed that Portia would have had the strength to defy them. That she would make a different choice. That she would marry for affection rather than social gain.

"She seemed quite lively. Clare would have enjoyed her company, I think."

Sullivan was grinning at him, unaware, of course, of Julian's disappointment. He hated that once again he'd gone home empty-handed, and lost to someone with a higher title.

"Yes, I liked her very much," Julian snapped, and then took a deep breath. "Better than anyone I've met since Clare."

Sullivan blinked at the ferocity of his tone. "I say, is there an understanding between you?"

"Of course not." Julian sighed as the carriage drew near their club. "She's just become engaged to marry Montrose. You remember that fine gentleman, don't you?"

"My God, is she a fool?"

He shook his head. Montrose was everything Portia should loathe in a husband. Controlling and cold. Montrose would sour her every waking moment. He would make Portia ordinary enough to conform to his exacting expectations while he did as he pleased. The snobbish dullard played by the rules, with no exceptions. "She will not enjoy being married to him," he murmured. "Shall we go in?"

"Wait." Sullivan put his hand up. "Don't say you asked her to marry you and were refused."

"No, and I am glad I did not take the trouble." Julian signaled the driver to stop before the club and alighted quickly. He'd no wish to discuss Portia with Sullivan. Certainly not on the street. Any right-minded woman would choose a duke over a mere viscount. But he was bitterly disappointed that Portia was not the daring woman he'd believed her to be all these years. He'd been blinded by his own hope—a foolish fantasy that she might finally care about him.

And if not him, then there were finer gentlemen in London than the Duke of Montrose.

Sullivan grabbed his arm before they could enter the club. "Wait. If you like her as much as I suspect, why did you not ask for her hand? I am certain I saw a sparkle in her eyes, too."

"There was definitely no sparkle in her eye for me. For you, perhaps, and any gentleman she considers handsome. Portia Hayes has known me long enough to make up her mind about my appeal, and she has never offered the slightest encouragement."

Well, perhaps once…but the next day, she'd accepted Montrose, so it didn't count.

"What have you done to win her?"

"Too much to name." He'd protected her, even from herself sometimes. He'd been willing to bleed for her if necessary, too. What a fool he'd been to think he had any chance. "I need a drink."

Sullivan did not release him. "What you need to do is what you recommended to *me*. Seduce her!"

Julian laughed bitterly. "It worked for you because Clare was already enamored and was being foolish about your lack of fortune at the time. She had no parents to please. Now, you'll not have to jump that fence for any lady ever again. Once society has discovered your pockets are still full to the brim, as I assume they must be, the ladies will be flocking to lie down and offer themselves on a platter. I, on the other hand, will not have the same luck."

"Are you saying you're truly hunting a bride?"

Julian shook his head angrily. "It's none of your damn business if I am or not."

"What about Miss Hayes?"

Julian calmed himself. *Portia.* There wasn't a thing he could do about her now but forget she existed. He'd done it with Clare; he could do so again, too. "Do you want to drink together or not?"

Sullivan's eyes narrowed on him. "We'll drink on my account. About time I put something on it."

"Good." Julian stalked forward into the club, unaccountably angry with Sullivan for no good reason. It was not Sullivan's fault that Clare had died and left him with all her money. It was not Sullivan's fault that ladies would prefer to marry a richer man than Julian could ever be.

At this hour of the day, a number of groups had formed around small tables in the club. They found a spot out of the way of the noisiest members and requested drinks for both of them. Julian did not care what he drank, but Sullivan requested the very best the establishment could offer.

Sullivan glanced around while they waited for the footman's return. "The place hasn't changed much since I was here last with you."

"The day you proposed to Clare." Julian nodded slowly, remembering the occasion. He accepted a drink from the footman and raised his glass. "To your late wife."

Sullivan lifted his, too. "To the love of my life. May she and our son be forever at peace."

Julian nodded, but his stomach twisted bitterly and his eyes stung anew. He drained his glass and signaled for refills to fight the emotion. He was of a mind to get drunk. The first time in a long while he'd felt that way.

"I say, is that Lord Sullivan I see," someone exclaimed suddenly, and Julian groaned as he recognized the voice as belonging to another old school friend—Lord Grigg. "By Jove, it is! What are you doing back in London, Lord Sullivan?"

Sullivan was drawn to stand and moved away a few steps. Lord Grigg was in line to be a duke one day, too. Much like Montrose, Lord Grigg thought himself a god among men of lesser rank. Julian kept his seat and sipped a second drink as Sullivan was drawn farther away by Grigg to meet mutual acquaintances across the room. Julian should have expected this to happen; he requested a paper and another round to pass the time.

He was sipping his forth drink when Sullivan came rushing back.

"Sorry," Sullivan mumbled, glancing at the table full of

glasses with obvious surprise. Julian's were empty; Sullivan's were lined up in a neat row. "Looks like I have some catching up to do."

"You were always a popular devil, and a slow drinker, too," Julian murmured without any real malice. The drink had mellowed him enough to put his losses in perspective. As long as he drew breath, there was still hope. But he would have to look elsewhere for a suitable wife and forget about love. "Future dukes are always much in demand. Grigg wasted no time pulling you away."

"People really don't change, do they," Sullivan said with a scowl for the far side of the room. He tossed back one drink and reached for another to sip.

Julian scowled. "I assume by that remark you will be the recipient of a dozen or more invitations to private engagements that will scandalize the *ton*, should they learn about them."

"Indeed, that was the suggestion," Sullivan confirmed as he sat back. "However, I'm only interested in being with my real friends."

Real friends who hadn't talked in years? Real friends who knew each other's business front to back? Julian missed those days, but he couldn't bear to share his troubles. "There could be pretty women there."

"Not the sort who interest me." Sullivan finished his glass and snatched up the next in line. "Besides, we can talk about women later. I have a feeling this afternoon will turn into a full day of spirited indulgence. You and I have a lot of catching up to do."

Julian took another sip of his drink, noticing the spirits had really improved his mood. He could feel a smile tugging at his lips. "I would like that very much."

Chapter Six

The banns had been called that morning so, officially, Portia was a duchess to be. The banns would be called for the next three weeks, and then the week after she would be married and a lavish celebration would be held in their honor. Portia was confident she had plenty of time to get to know her betrothed before they became man and wife.

She flittered about her room in a happy daze, picking up things and putting them down again. She did not have that many possessions really, mostly gowns and evening slippers. Before she'd made her debut, she'd spent most of her time wearing sturdy boots and sensible gowns. At times, she missed not having to be so particular about her wardrobe and how she looked in case someone important, besides her closest friends, saw her that way.

She had to admit, the most fun she'd had this year was the days she'd spent combing through Uncle Oliver's cluttered townhouse in an old gown she'd hidden there. Uncle's old house was dirty and dusty and quite ruinous for anything new. So whenever she went there, she changed into the old gown almost immediately, and then changed back before going home again.

Lord Wade's claim that her uncle had been odd, even for a known eccentric, had been right on the mark. Uncle Oliver had lived on his own—collecting many odd curios as he went through his life. He'd never married but had traveled extensively. He'd had affairs and been a character people wrote about too. The only part of his life she did not celebrate was that he'd died alone. He should have had a family around him.

Portia sighed. Regrets were unpleasant, and she had her own now too that she'd rather do without. It was imperative that she speak to Lord Wade again tonight and clear the air between them.

Upon reflection, she had not behaved well toward him. For as long as she'd known him, he'd spoken honestly, a frequent failing of his, and expressed his opinion far too candidly for her comfort. She had overreacted completely when it became clear he wasn't happy with her news. It was understandable but hard to hear. He didn't like the man that would be her husband. He was entitled to express an opinion contrary to her own. So were all her friends.

Lord Wade had known Lord Montrose longer and from a far different perspective than she ever could. But she would make him understand what had happened in the past would not influence her opinion about him, or Lord Montrose, either. They would remain friends no matter what.

She slipped down the main stairs, hearing the murmur of low voices drifting from the direction of her father's study. He was probably meeting with his man of business again. They usually did so at this time of day, so she did not risk disturbing them.

It was her mother that Portia needed to see immediately. Portia tapped on the morning room door where her mother usually was at this hour. She found her perusing the Ladies Monthly magazine and the fashion plates inside. "I've found the most perfect gown for your sister. Come and see," mother said without looking up.

Portia drew closer, gazing down on a lovely design. It was so lovely that Portia imagined herself in it. "It's a little daring, isn't it?"

"Oh no. Do you think so?"

"You wouldn't have let me wear a dress like that when I made my debut two years ago. You would have claimed it was too revealing and refused to have it made for me."

Mother lifted the magazine higher for a different view of the gown. "You might be right. I'll keep looking."

Portia sat down, glancing at the papers surrounding her mother. "What are you doing?"

"Planning a party."

"You don't have to go to too much trouble for me, Mother."

Mother's gaze lifted momentarily. "It is for your sister. Your father and I have decided to bring her out this year instead of waiting until next."

"But she's only seventeen."

"Seventeen and ten months. Your wedding day is an opportunity to show her off we cannot afford to miss. There is bound to be a lot of important members of society attending St. George's for the Duke of Montrose's wedding."

Portia was stunned by the remark. "It's my wedding too."

"Yes, my dear. I know that." But she made another notation. "I wonder if Lord Wade could be persuaded to be your sister's escort to the King dinner? We're not lucky enough to be invited yet, but it will be held right after she's made her court presentation."

"You can't ask him to do that," Portia warned. It was not a good time to ask Wade for anything, really.

Mother put her hand on her sleeve and patted her arm. "I can't wait till you're a duchess so it will be easier to show off your sister. For now, though, I'll discreetly gauge Lord Wade's interest in helping Lavinia next time he calls. He helped us tremendously in your first season."

"He did?"

Mother nodded. "Quite invaluable a connection really, even if he's only a viscount."

Portia had not realized that he'd done anything much out of the ordinary, but if he had, she did not like the way Mother spoke of using Lord Wade again. She'd have to warn him what she was up to. "What time should I be ready for tonight's ball?"

"Yes, about that. I don't think you should attend with us."

"But why?"

"Lord Montrose will not be there, and he is quite particular about appearances. He is not acquainted with our hosts, but your father and I will go and talk about Lavinia's upcoming presentation. Now that we mean to bring her out early, there's a chance one of your discarded suitors would favor her."

Portia blinked and she stared at her mother in horror. They were not "discarded suitors" but her male friends. It had taken time and perseverance to deserve the large acquaintance of male and female members of the *ton*, and she would not have those friendships cheapened this way. Marriage would change nothing in her circle of acquaintance except to increase it. Lavinia would make her own friends and attract her own suitors if given the chance. "I want to go. I told Lady Young that I was looking forward to being there. She expects me."

Mother stared at her. "We could say you have a headache."

"I never suffer them, and everyone knows I do not. She will think I snubbed her because Montrose was not invited." Portia licked her lips. "I promised her, and a Hayes always keeps their word."

Mother pulled a face. "Yes, I suppose you must go if you've said you would, but perhaps you should be less agreeable in the future. You should be seen with his grace more often than not."

"I will of course spend time with Montrose before we marry," she promised. Lord Wade's remark last night about the lack of courtship had niggled at her peace since the moment they'd parted. Lord Montrose really had never done anything remotely romantic, and he really should have a chance to do so. "How else can I get to know him?"

Mother looked up suddenly. "That reminds me. He wants to see you."

Portia grinned and checked the time. Had he sent a note to take her out in his carriage that afternoon, or perhaps a high-perch phaeton? She had been looking forward to sitting at his side as they rode through Hyde Park. "When?"

Mother glanced at the mantel where a little clock across the room sat and squinted. "At two o'clock in the drawing room."

That was too early. "Are you sure you didn't mean at four or perhaps five o'clock?"

"There is nothing wrong with my hearing, young lady. Montrose is in the library with your father now, going over the marriage contract. I expect he'll return later in the day to take you driving in the park so everyone can see you together if he has the time."

Portia hadn't realized her betrothed was in the house but she was excited to see him. "I hope he does suggest it. I will wear my new carriage dress with the gold buttons."

"Perfect," her mother agreed.

Portia jumped to her feet and rushed to a mirror. If she was to see her betrothed now, she had better make sure she looked her best.

"You look lovely," mother murmured without looking up. Mother returned to her paperwork and plotting Lavinia's sudden debut. Portia smoothed a few loose strands of her hair and smiled. Seeing that she still had a few minutes to spare, Portia slipped out into the hall. Mother never called her back. She was too focused on her work.

She moved toward the closed library door where her father and Lord Montrose were meeting, hoping her presence might look innocent if anyone saw her lingering in the hall. She was dying to know what they were talking about now. She had been assured that the marriage contracts and settlements had been drawn up already—very favorably in Portia's favor. There was nothing Father and Lord Montrose should be talking about that couldn't include her anymore.

She eased closer to the door and her eyes slowly widened at what she heard.

Father was talking about launching Lavinia, and Montrose was trying to talk him out of it.

"Surely another year will make no difference," Lord Montrose complained.

"My wife insists there couldn't be a better time to bring her out than now, especially with the wedding to come," Father explained to the duke. "You'll learn for the sake of peace that wives require considerable latitude in arranging such amusements. I'm sure you cannot object. It must be done right now to ensure she might marry just as well."

There was a very long silence before Lord Montrose spoke again. "Very well, if only to please your lady. I can wait for the banns to be completed. Ask her to not take too long to make her final preparation for the wedding. I would like to see Portia now."

"Yes, of course. I am sorry I could not accommodate you about the other matter. It is completely out of my hands. The will was very specific."

Portia frowned. *What will were they talking about?*

The chairs inside scraped across the floor, and Portia was rooted to the spot as Lord Montrose spoke again. "I suppose I must make the best of the delay. I will complete my business ahead of the wedding, instead of after."

When boot steps headed her way, Portia scrambled for the morning room as silently as she could. Mother was still poring over plans for Lavinia's debut.

Mother looked up though, and examined Portia from head to toe. "Oh, you are back. Right on time. Lord Montrose did stress punctuality above all things the other day."

The day Portia had accepted the Duke of Montrose as her husband had not included mention of punctuality. He hadn't said very much at all, so Portia could recall every single word. "When did he say that?"

"Oh, when he was here. Last Monday."

Portia drew close to her. "Mother, you are mistaken. Lord Montrose proposed on Friday."

"But he came to speak with your father and I several days before that. He was very keen."

Lord Montrose had arrived in London a week ago, on a Sunday. He must have come to see her parents the very next day. Lord Wade had been right about his haste, it seems. "You should have told me that he came. What else did you talk about?"

"Oh, a great many things. I swear I said nothing that could cause you any difficulty. I insisted you were ready to be married, prepared for the duties of a wife and very capable of managing a large household. I did not want to spoil the surprise of his proposal for you. He's been planning to marry for some time."

At the time of his proposal, Portia had not questioned what had brought Lord Montrose to the point. Her parents *had* been quick to encourage her agreement that day. They'd already made up their minds to accept Lord Montrose into the family. It had not been a shock for them, as it had been for Portia.

Portia followed her mother into the drawing room and stood where told, beside her mother just as the clock struck the hour.

There was a knock immediately after the clock chimes died away, and the butler escorted Lord Montrose in alone. "Good morning, Mrs. Hayes. Miss Hayes."

Lord Montrose produced a bunch of roses from behind his back and handed them, not to Portia, but to her blushing mother, instead. "Oh these are lovely," Mother exclaimed as she buried her nose to inhale the sickly sweet scent from the buds. "You needn't have gone to so much trouble on my behalf, your grace, but I do thank you."

"It is my pleasure." Montrose nodded and turned to Portia. "You look lovely today."

There were no flowers for Portia, so she curtsied and claimed a seat on the chaise next to her mother.

Lord Montrose took the opposite chair, sitting forward with his hands clasped together. "I trust you are in good health."

"Oh, yes, we are both in excellent health as always, your grace," Mother told him quickly.

A small smile crossed his lips as he turned more fully toward Portia. "And your sister, Miss Hayes?"

"She is well, too," Portia promised, viewing him with curiosity. Why had Montrose singled her out of all other ladies to marry? Was it just because there were so few heiresses to choose from as Lord Wade claimed? She didn't want that to be true. "Did you pass a pleasant evening last night?"

"Indeed. I went to my club as usual and met with friends there."

"You're a member of the Boodles Club, are you not?"

"Of course."

Portia waited for more but Lord Montrose buttoned his lips together. She couldn't ask outright whom he met there, gentlemen's clubs were terribly secretive, but she was very curious about what went on in them. Portia quickly glanced at her mother for help with the conversation.

Mother smoothly sailed into the breech. "We missed you at last night's ball. The Daventrys' event was very lively."

"I'm pleased to hear you enjoyed yourself." He glanced at Portia quickly. "Did you dance?"

"I did indeed." She smiled. "I do enjoy the amusements of the season."

"Even with Lord Daventry, which was quite a surprise," Mother remarked with a wide smile.

"And you allowed it?" Lord Montrose seemed appalled. "Where was his wife?"

"She was there," Portia promised, but she stared at the Duke of Montrose in consternation. "Lady Daventry cannot dance easily, so she watches her husband dance from the sidelines. He reports every word of his conversations back to her later for her amusement."

Lord Montrose drew back, looking anything but pleased. "Even if she is wise to be a little suspicious of the scoundrel she married, I do not agree that he must repeat his conversations. Indeed, I do not."

"Lord Daventry was a perfect gentleman," Portia protested in the earl's defense. "It is, I suspect, a great amusement between them. He is obviously devoted to his lady. She seemed perfectly content with their bargain."

"Bargain?"

"Lord Daventry enjoys dancing, and enjoyed several that night. The look in his eyes for his wife and the passion of their reunion between sets was utterly without guile. He truly loves her."

Lord Montrose drew back with a gasp. "You should not speak of such things."

Portia frowned. "Why ever not? Neither one hides their feelings from society."

"Well, I for one would not like anyone to discuss our union in such an unguarded way in the future." Lord Montrose's eyes narrowed slightly on her. "Whom else did you dance with?"

Portia narrowed her eyes on him, too. She would not account for her every action when he was not around, unless he shared more details about his. Besides, she'd done nothing out of the ordinary that night but argue with Lord Wade. "Friends."

His expression firmed, and then he glanced at his pocket watch. "We will discuss this matter another time. I am afraid I must be going."

Did he think he could just show up, demand answers to a few questions and rush off? He would not endear himself to her in this way. She liked people. She liked dancing and laughing and enjoying the amusements of London. "Please don't leave yet."

He frowned at her. "I am a busy man, Miss Hayes. I will call again tomorrow."

Portia gained her feet as he stood up, heart sinking. Lord Montrose wasn't a romantic. "Thank you for calling, your grace."

"A pleasure, Miss Hayes," he murmured. "Mrs. Hayes."

When he was gone, Portia requested tea and sank down into the nearest chair. She desperately wanted to wash the sourness of that encounter from her mouth and be rid of the uncertainty churning in her stomach. Would that be what married life would be like with him? She hoped not.

"You will make a fine pair," Mother promised, nodding in approval.

She glanced at her mother, annoyed that she could see nothing wrong with that brief meeting. Where was her courtship, flowers and an invitation to go driving with him that afternoon?

Abandonment was not at all what she'd expected. Not so soon, anyway. Many couples lived a life largely separate from their spouses later on in a marriage. It was the way of the aristocracy for lords and ladies to pursue their own interests eventually. But only after a wife had produced an heir and a spare for the continuation of the family.

She cast a suspicious glance at her mother, noting her serene smile. Her parents spent no time together anymore. Father was much too concerned with toadying up to anyone who might increase his influence. Mother was much involved with making friends in all the right places for the sake of her daughters' marriage prospects.

It was the way of the world, unfortunately.

Portia suddenly didn't want the world to be like that for *her*. She certainly hoped that she might fall in love with her husband, and he for her, too.

She nodded to herself, deciding instantly what she must do.

She would worm her way into his affections by being the most gracious, knowledgeable, kind lady ever to become a duchess. She would make him crave her company and conversation. Things would go far differently the next time they met.

She poured her father a cup of tea when he suddenly joined them.

Father took a sip with a sigh and sat back. "Well, that settles it."

"Settles what?"

Father nodded. "He doesn't want Oliver's home after all, so I'm going to go ahead and lease it."

"What!' Mother and Portia cried at once.

Father cringed. "He'd rather I sell it, but it is part of her dowry and willed to her unborn son. However, Montrose agrees that we can turn a profit from the lease for a few weeks, and then his man of business will take over the income and the managing of the place."

Portia took in her father's smug expression and fumed silently. Uncle's home and estate income was a gift, the reason the family had money to spare for an extended stay in London. "You cannot lease my home."

"It will be your son's home, not yours," he reminded her quickly. "Lord Montrose has been made aware of the unbreakable nature of your uncle's will. It was foolish of Oliver to be so exacting. Nobody has ever wanted to live in his house but him."

"I have always wanted to live there!" Portia cried. "It was meant to be mine. I should have a say what's to be done with it."

Father winced, and then looked at Portia's mother. "About the wedding. He is very keen to bring the wedding date forward. Is there any way it can be done without difficulty?"

"We cannot be married before the reading of the banns are complete," Portia argued.

"Oh no," Mother cried.

"He hinted he might be able to secure a special license."

"What about my plans for Lavinia? There's no time to do all that I want if the wedding happens too soon."

Portia sat back. A sudden proposal, and now a rushed wedding date? Did Montrose want society to think there was a nasty reason he was marrying her? "Why would he suggest such a thing now?"

Father looked away. "He's a busy man and insists he must return to his estate soon."

Portia and mother exchanged a glance, and it was mother who looked away first. By that look of guilt forming on Mother's face, Portia realized she had known Lord Montrose's wishes opposed Portia's for a proper wedding celebration. "Is anyone in this house willing to celebrate my marriage, or do you just wish to be rid of me as soon as possible so that Lavinia can be the center of attention?"

"Daughter, calm yourself," Mother snapped. "Let me think."

"You've always been special to us," Father promised, looking to his wife for answers.

"Is that so? First you try to keep me at home, away from friends, and now you want to rush me to the alter."

"He is most insistent, too." Father shrugged. "You *have* been out for two seasons."

"That is not at all long!" she cried as she burst to her feet. "Rushing to the alter now after telling everyone we will wait for the banns to be read will look suspicious. After all that mother has said about arrangements for the wedding breakfast, people will wonder if there is a reason I must be married in such a hurry. There certainly is not."

"Your best friend married in a hurry. Everyone accepted that, and he was only an earl."

"Anna married because she feared her life might have been in danger. Surely you both realize now how close to danger Anna was? Lady Scott was her mentor, her confidant, and utterly unhinged. I was in danger, too, don't you know?"

Father rose now, his hands beseeching her to calm down. "He just doesn't want a fuss made," Father began. "That does not mean we agree with him. The wedding will occur as planned and promised. Just as you want."

"It had better," she warned. "I will not have either of you making any more decisions about my future without at least warning me. I'm not a child, and this is my life you're deciding."

Father held out a hand to her. "Now don't fly into the high bows over this little incident and become difficult. We will hold firm. Your mother has already begun making arrangements for your sister, too, that cannot be changed without affecting her chances of making a good match."

Portia stared at her father with suspicion. "Tell me you haven't already begun negotiations with a gentleman interested in Lavinia."

"No. No," Father assured her. "But there is considerable interest already, I think."

"From whom?"

"I will not embarrass anyone by mentioning names here today, but I will say they have called upon us on several occasions. I think it a splendid match if it can be done."

Portia considered the gentlemen who had called on them this season. None would suit for her sister, certainly none who had pursued Portia for her dowry. She would be vigilant and make sure Lavinia was not forced into a marriage she did not want.

Chapter Seven

------◆------

Julian took breakfast at White's Club in the morning room once a week as usual. He'd been a member all his life, but he could not afford the indulgence more often, unfortunately, given the shortfall of his income. He sipped his coffee, ate ham and eggs, and studied the news in the morning paper alone in his favorite corner of the room, content that the bill would come later.

He'd had a quiet few days by himself, avoiding society—Sullivan and Portia, particularly. He had declined two events at the last minute that he'd already promised to attend, simply because he couldn't bear to face them again. He'd kept to his house, to his Spartan new study, and compiled a list of the unmarried women he knew who possessed a sufficient dowry for his modest needs. It had turned out to be quite a long list, actually, but almost all the women he'd found fault with for one reason or another.

A fortune hunter couldn't be particular, but he found that he had a conscience. He knew of men who'd seduced heiresses, and then hardly ever spoke to them again. He could do that, too, he supposed, but he might not like himself very much if he did. So he'd removed the names of the women who looked down their noses at the less fortunate, the one who already made his teeth ache, and the ladies he suspected were already being courted by other men—even if they were not aware.

The list had whittled down to two names. After supper the previous evening—a brief affair of watery soup, and bread and cheese—his aunt had mentioned in passing scandals he'd not heard about. One of his choices had run off suddenly to Gretna Green with a footman in her father's employ, and the other had been found in a compromising position in an older lady's bed.

Julian had returned to his chambers and, before bed, had scraped the page clean of all markings and returned it to his writing desk drawer. He obviously needed to meet someone new to have any hope of getting married.

After an hour of sitting in his corner alone, the members began to file in, ready to discuss the events of the past evening's amusements and to plan for the next. A pair of good friends came in, arguing heatedly.

"There, satisfied," Lord Stephens said as he dropped a handful of coins into another member's outstretched hand with an audible clink. "You win this round."

"Indeed," Lord James crowed as he put a line through something in the club's betting book. "When will you learn I've more sense than you?"

Lord Stephens grumbled and asked for ale.

"Ah, there you are at last, Wade. And I see another wager in the betting book has been completed," Sullivan murmured as he dropped into the chair beside Julian. "What was that one about?"

"I've no idea," Julian told him, not the least bit interested. Without money to spare, gambling had lost its appeal.

"I didn't know you would be here at this hour. I've been trying to meet with you for days. I called at your home first, but your aunt said you were already long gone. Thank heavens you always come here for breakfast on Tuesdays."

Julian hid a grimace. He'd been hoping Sullivan would have no reason to call at his home. Breakfast was only served to his aunt at home, and most days Julian did without. "I'm just catching a bite to eat before doing the rounds of social obligation."

Sullivan's eyes roved over him from head to toe, a frown appearing slowly. "I noticed you made some changes at home."

He nodded carefully, wondering what Sullivan would say or have concluded about the changes he'd made, but otherwise made no response.

"I think I will do that, too—move my study to the front of the house. I can see the benefits of viewing the passing parade from my favorite armchair." Sullivan squinted across the room. "So, is it still there?"

"Is what where?"

He jerked his head across the room. "That old wager in the betting book?"

Julian let out a soft sigh, thankful the topic of his reorganization had been mistaken for something else. He glanced over his shoulder to the betting book Sullivan was staring at now.

The first occasion Sullivan had come to the club, he'd read every wager in the betting book. One in particular had been of interest to him. "Oh, I've no idea about it. I stopped paying attention when you left London."

He'd stopped doing a lot of things when Sullivan married Clare. Most of them cost money.

"But you loved reading the wagers with me! Let's look today," Sullivan decided. Sullivan bounded to his feet and hurried to the betting book before Julian could talk him out of wasting his time. Wagers were frequent in the club, and it had been quite a while. It might be impossible to find the wager he was talking about now.

Julian lingered over his second plate of food another few moments, gobbling up the last of the ham and downing the shockingly bitter coffee quickly before he grudgingly followed.

Sullivan grinned. "I found Lord Stephens' latest wager. *Lord J bet Lord S that Lord M would warn Lord S away from Miss H.*"

He stared at the inscription and sighed deeply as he

understood it. It had begun. "Lord James must have bet Lord Stephens that Lord Montrose would warn him away from," Julian he swallowed the lump in his throat, "from Portia Hayes. He is nothing if not predictable."

"He was always a selfish, jealous bastard."

"True." Portia usually enjoyed dancing with Lord Stephens, too. He wondered briefly if Portia knew what Montrose had done yet.

"I've never met a more unhappy bastard in all my years. He could always drain the joy out of any day." Sullivan began flicking pages of the current betting book to get to the beginning.

"You'll probably want an older book," Julian warned as he pulled older editions down from the shelf until he found the right one. "There. It is still outstanding."

"*Lord W wagers Mr. Q fifty pounds that Lord M's prized possession will reappear during supper.* I cannot believe it is still outstanding after all this time."

Julian chuckled. "That supper is definitely over, so I'm sure that wager should be crossed off by now."

"Wagers never expire. And I still want to know what the bet was about, and by whom," Sullivan declared, turning to scan the room, his expression hopeful.

"We may never know." Without thinking too much about it, Julian lifted up the newer book so they could look through the most recent wagers placed in the club together. Julian let his gaze drift over the most recent pair of entries, noticing the reckless betting habits of his peers had not changed one bit. Large sums of money betting on how often another gentleman might sneeze during dinner was insane.

His attention snagged on one recent wager, a month old, and then he glanced at the older book. He'd left it still open to the page they'd been looking at before. His heartbeat quickened as he studied both. "Does this handwriting seem similar to you?"

Julian laid the pair of ledgers side by side as he and Sullivan compared them. "By Jove, I think it may be the same penmanship! Who wrote this newer one?"

"Lord W bet Lord B ten pounds that Lady W will sneak away with a younger man.

Julian's grin slowly grew wider the longer he considered the wager. A month ago, he might have appeared to sneak away with a married woman, not to seduce her, but to stop a seduction in progress. How fortunate the wager had been focused on the wrong party that night. It was crossed out, and further on, another wager in the same handwriting had been made just yesterday involving Lady W again.

Most of the *ton* remained abed at this hour, recovering from the previous night's amusements. He laughed at the realization he could play a part in the bet. "I really should read these wagers more often before I go out."

"Who is Lady W?"

"Lady Windermere," Julian explained. "Esme."

"Oh, right. Of course. So much for her fidelity." Sullivan shook his head in obvious disapproval. "So Windermere might have been the one who had a wager with Mr. Q years ago. I wonder why they never finished it."

Julian scratched his head. "I don't recall any mutual acquaintances starting with Q."

"Well, we have to find out what the item was. Let's ask," Sullivan declared, tugging on Julian's arm.

Intrigued, Julian allowed himself to be shoved into Sullivan's carriage. He experienced a pang of envy at the comfortable surroundings he found himself in. Hacks were convenient and cheap but the ride was damned uncomfortable at times. Sullivan's carriage smelled fresh and clean, and the cushions were deeply comfortable.

"Where does Lord Windermere live?" he asked.

"Portman Square," Julian called to the driver. "You do realize Windermere may not remember so old a wager?"

"He has to remember. We'll remind him. I have an excellent memory."

Sullivan's enthusiasm could be infectious, and it was not long before they were standing in Lord Windermere's front hall, waiting to be seen.

"Lord Windermere will see you now."

They entered a large room that reeked of money and bookish tendencies. Julian was impressed. He rarely envied his acquaintances, but he did today. Windermere set his book aside and gestured them to take a chair. "What an unexpected surprise?"

"We were just at the club, looking through the betting books, and then saw one of yours," Julian told him.

Windermere winced when their eyes met. "You're angry about last month, aren't you? Essie assured me you wouldn't mind."

"Of course I'm not upset. Your wife is very lovely."

"Do not get any ideas," Windermere warned, switching suddenly to a possessive husband in the blink of an eye.

Julian laughed outright at Windermere's hostile expression. "She wouldn't have me, and I wouldn't dream of asking."

"Good." Windermere's feathers settled and he gestured to the chairs. "What can I do for you gentlemen this morning?"

"We were hoping you could help us solve a mystery. For years, we noticed a wager in the betting book at White's remains incomplete. One we think you started."

Sullivan rattled off the entry accurately until Windermere began to grin.

Julian sat forward. "You do remember it?"

"Indeed I do. I wrote it with great pleasure."

Sullivan rubbed his hands together, sitting forward eagerly. "The wager remains incomplete. Can you tell us why?"

Windermere sighed. "The item in question was lost."

"Lost! No!"

Julian sat forward, too. "What was the item, if you don't mind telling us? Sullivan here never quits talking about it, and I desperately need some peace."

An expression of amusement crossed Windermere's face. "A phallus."

"A what?"

"A young acquaintance of mine posed to have his erect

member immortalized in carved wood. Boasted about it one night when we were all drinking together. He claimed that he used it on his lovers, and they were vastly satisfied to have him in two places at once. Or two in one. None of us believed any of his wild claims. Young men often exaggerate about their lovers and prowess in bed. So it was *acquired* in the interest of shutting him up. He was a boastful, vain young man and quite full of himself. The plan was to have it served up to his esteemed dinner guests the very next night. We never got to savor his reaction."

"How was it lost?"

"My co-conspirator passed away suddenly in his sleep. I never discovered what happened to the item, so I could not win or complete the wager. I could hardly explain to my late friend's family what I was searching for, given what it was, could I?"

"That would have been awkward indeed. Who was Q?" Sullivan asked, completely wrapped up in the tale.

"Oliver Quigley."

The hair on the back of Julian's neck rose. Portia's uncle, Mr. Oliver Quigley, had died suddenly in his sleep, and he might have been a chum of Lord Windermere's at one time, too, now he considered the matter. "Oh my."

"Do you remember him, Wade? He was quite keen on your aunt for a time, I think."

Oliver Quigley had been an enthusiast of women and scandals, according to his correspondence. Auntie had said much the same. Julian had read more about the fellow's antics than he should ever repeat to anyone. "Describe the phallus?"

Windermere blinked. "I beg your pardon."

"What was it made from?"

"Walnut. I've always found my lovers prefer the touch of marble, personally."

"Walnut…"

A month ago, Julian had been in Oliver Quigley's house. During the period that a murderess had been prowling London's ballrooms, Portia had run away from the protection of her parents. A ridiculous decision given they'd no idea who the murderer had been. He'd followed her there early one morning and stayed with her there a few days, even though she had protested his protection was unnecessary. Aunt Lenthall, and his brother, had been there too and had acted as chaperone so there had been no impropriety at all.

It had almost seemed like a holiday to him.

Julian had had ample time to explore the property from top to bottom, and poke about a bit too in some of the rooms. Especially the one he'd slept in. There had been a walnut phallus in Portia's uncle's bedchamber, if he remembered correctly. He'd had to quickly hide it from Portia when she'd suddenly come into the room to make certain he would be comfortable for the nights sleep. He'd meant to dispose of it later, when he was unobserved, and save her or her mother the embarrassment of viewing it. He'd forgotten about it until now, though. It could still be there, too, stashed under a pile of old love letters in a box. Ready to be burned…unless the house had been cleared.

But if he could fetch it back, he might just help Windermere win the wager.

He looked up at the earl and considered whether to say something.

Lord Windermere was watching him closely. "What are you thinking, Wade?"

"What if it could be found, my lord? If I help you locate the object, would you be willing to help me, too?"

"Yes, I suppose I could offer a reward, but only if it is the genuine article. I have seen it, unfortunately for me, so no counterfeit copy will suffice." Lord Windermere smiled slowly. "Lord Wilmot is hosting a dinner soon, and the owner of the object has returned to Town. He will be there, surely. If you discover it and bring it to me, I'll give you the wagered amount there and then."

Julian had been thinking more along the lines of obtaining Windermere's help to sell the lease on the Townhouse but the money was a definite attraction to see the wager through too.

Unfortunately, he'd have to use the hidden spare key to sneak into Portia's uncle's home to get his hands on it. There was no way he could ask permission. Perhaps before her engagement, but not now. Not when there was a chance she might run to Montrose and tell him what he wanted from the house, and what would be done with it, too. He did not know how close they'd become, but Montrose had absolutely no sense of humor. "I'll see what I can do."

"Double."

"What?"

Judging by the way Windermere nodded, he knew full well that Julian could get ahold of it if he tried. "I'll give you double the wager just to see the smug prig's face drain of color."

Julian bit his lip. Considering the matter carefully.

He knew how to get into Oliver's house undetected. He'd had to, once upon a time. Portia may not have given the key to her future husband yet or emptied the place, destroying what he sought. Perhaps it wouldn't hurt to at least pass by the Soho Square property and determine if it were already empty before he made any sort of commitment. If he found the house still cluttered, then he could either consider asking or go round the back and look for the key.

He would be stealing. Sort of.

And he'd be paid to do so.

His cheeks warmed, and he shook his head. No, he could not take anything that did not belong to him, especially since he was not speaking to Portia anymore.

"We should be going." Julian stood and held out his hand to Windermere, ready to depart without committing himself. Windermere might end up disappointed in him, but it was not as if the earl had ever imagined having his hands on the item again.

As soon as their hands connected, Julian felt the press of paper cut into his palm.

Windermere winked. "For that wager. Your share. It's only fair; you played your part better than we dreamed."

"Thank you," he muttered quietly, disturbed at being paid

to look out for his friends. This was money he did not deserve. But even as he considered giving it back, he realized this small amount would be a boon to his finances right now.

Sullivan was sure to want to enjoy London's amusements, and Julian would prefer to pay his own way when he could. "Give my best to your wife," he murmured. "Tell her I am always at her service."

On the stairs, Sullivan turned to him. "You've some cheek, leading him on like that. Where did you imagine you might find a walnut phallus? No one can carve that fast, and remember it must match Lord Windermere's memory. Did you notice he never said who it belonged to? I wonder what makes it so memorable?"

Julian shivered and shoved his hands in his pocket, hiding the money he'd been given. It would be best if Sullivan knew nothing of Julian's brush with temptation. "I have no idea."

Chapter Eight

Portia had been at the Sandersons' soiree for an hour before she finally saw Lord Wade leaning against the mantel on the far side of the drawing room. She couldn't be happier to see him. It had been a few days since their awful conversation, and she'd missed him. Unfortunately, he seemed to have declined a few invitations unexpectedly this week. It wasn't like him to be so hard to find.

If she'd not seen him tonight, Portia had been ready to call upon him at home, a scandalous thing for any unmarried lady to do, just to find out if he were ill or not. But he seemed more or less the same as he always did—his black hair too long for her taste, his skin perpetually pale across his lean cheeks.

She took a step in his direction, but a tall figure suddenly stepped directly into her path—blocking her way completely.

Portia glanced up in annoyance, and her eyes clashed with Lord Montrose's steely gaze.

She blinked in shock at seeing him here, and then hastily dipped a curtsy. "Your grace," she murmured in astonishment.

"Miss Hayes. Mrs. Hayes," he murmured after a bow with a quick nod to where her mother lingered as chaperone. "I am glad to have finally found you in this godawful crush."

She frowned. How had her betrothed somehow wrangled a

last-minute invitation to this ball? She'd been sure he'd been engaged elsewhere this evening. She studied him, and noticed how he glanced at those nearby with a perpetual frown. It occurred to her that he didn't want to be here, even though he was now.

"I'm surprised to see you here."

A muscle in his jaw ticked. "It seemed prudent."

"Surely you mean pleasurable. Do you like to dance, your grace?"

"Not particularly, but I will if required."

There were plenty of dances to be had tonight, though Portia's dance card was not yet full. She looked at the short list of gentlemen on her card discreetly. Now Montrose had come, she would have one less empty space. She had discovered during her time in London that, by this hour of the evening, gentlemen seldom forsook cards for a dance with an engaged lady.

It was not the first night since her engagement that Portia's dance card had lacked completeness by this hour, either.

Across the room, Lord Stephens was talking with Lord Hector Stockwick. Lord Stephens was a fine dancer, but had not yet asked her to dance, which was a curious oversight on his part. He was usually one of the first, but they hadn't even done more than acknowledge each other so far.

She'd heard all about the newly titled Viscount Stockwick, but they'd not been introduced as yet. From what she'd learned of him so far, it was probably unwise to rush to an introduction with the man. Stockwick had quickly gained a reputation for a fair degree of recklessness—both in his spending and in his romantic entanglements.

Her attention shifted back to Lord Wade, and she sighed because he was so far away still. Outwardly he seemed unchanged, but she thought the way he remained by the hearth was unusual for him. Usually he prowled these events, speaking to their mutual acquaintances. Perhaps he had been unwell and still felt fatigued.

She would have to seek him out as soon as she had the

opportunity.

"Let me see your dance card," Montrose demanded suddenly.

Portia showed him, surprised when he only claimed one dance, and at the very end of the night, before handing it back. That left her with two times that night she'd remain on the sidelines.

The sound of a throat clearing caught her attention, and she turned.

"Ah, Miss Hayes, is that you?" Sir John Singleton said as he drew closer to peer at her face.

Lord Montrose immediately moved slightly between them until Sir John moved back a step. She was surprised by his protective behavior, because Sir John was a very gentle man.

"Yes, indeed it is me, Sir John." Portia stepped around Lord Montrose quickly and extended her hand to the newcomer.

Sir John was not wearing his glasses again tonight, which was a great pity, really. Portia thought he looked quite dashing wearing them, but Sir John foolishly resented needing them because he felt they made him appear old to the ladies. Without them on, he tended to stand too close to everyone when he talked.

Sir John was slightly older than most of the gentlemen Portia regularly danced with, but quite a favorite of hers. He looked her up and down, squinting a little at her gown. "How lovely you look tonight," he murmured.

"Thank you, Sir John," she said, smiling. "And how happy I am to see you here. Tell me, is your mother feeling any better than the last time we spoke?"

"Oh, indeed she is, and it is most gracious of you to inquire." Sir John squinted at Portia's silent betrothed, and then moved a little closer to Portia. His eyes sought hers, and he didn't look away from her face as he spoke quietly for her ears alone. "She will be so pleased to learn you would remember her, especially now."

"Of course I could not forget her," Portia agreed, glancing

toward her betrothed quickly and then away. She was still not sure which members of the *ton* Montrose was acquainted with, but he did not seem interested in Sir John. "Do give her my best wishes for continued good health."

"She is here tonight and would be delighted to speak with you in person." His brow arched. "Perhaps you would permit me to escort you to her for a brief conversation after our dance, if you happen to have one still free?"

Portia nodded and held out her card to be signed. "Shall it be a quadrille or the Danse Espagnole?"

They were practically the same dance, but Sir John was still having trouble remembering the difference.

"The latter." Sir John blushed crimson. "I have been practicing since our last encounter. I am determined to master this once and for all."

"I'm sure you will, too," she whispered. If he wore glasses more often, Portia believed he would never have a problem on the dance floor. "Until later tonight, Sir John."

Sir John bowed, cast one last puzzled glance at Lord Montrose, and then backed away.

Montrose moved to claim her arm immediately. "Pity has its place, but you need not please old acquaintances if you want to keep the connection once we are married."

She looked up at his face but noticed Montrose's gaze locked on a distant view. "Do you know Sir John?"

"I do not."

She stared at Montrose until he looked down to acknowledge her. She smiled tightly. "Sir John is a dear friend, but quite shortsighted. Quite adept at a waltz, but terrible at recognizing anyone not immediately in front of him."

"I see."

So did Portia, unfortunately. Montrose had not liked the familiarity with which her friend had approached her, nor hers for Sir John. But Sir John was harmless. "Perhaps you will allow me to introduce you later? He is a good friend of mine, and I will dance with him whenever he asks, if my dance card has room for his name," she insisted.

"An introduction will not be necessary." Montrose nodded, and then he turned to her mother. "Madam, would you permit me to introduce your daughter to Lord Forbes? I see he has just arrived.

"Anything you say, your grace," she quickly agreed.

Montrose led Portia down the room and presented her to an elderly man and his equally aged wife. Lord Forbes and his wife had to be sixty years each, and neither one smiled at Portia at first. She learned that they lived near Lord Montrose's estate, and knew Montrose and his family very well indeed. They spoke of farming, sheep and wool, and the latest bill before parliament. Not once did the pair congratulate them on their upcoming marriage, though, which she felt was very disappointing.

When Portia realized she was in jeopardy of missing the first set, she had no choice but to interrupt their lengthy conversation. "Your grace, you must excuse me now."

Lord Montrose glanced down at her, frowning.

"I have promised to dance with Lord Phillip for the next set. He is very likely waiting with my mother for my return."

"Very well," he said slowly, and then apologized to Lord and Lady Forbes for the inconvenience of leaving them. "I will escort you, Miss Hayes. Later, we must talk."

Portia bid his friends goodbye quickly and started back up the large room with her betrothed at her side. As she drew level with the fireplace, she cast a sideways glance at Lord Wade.

He was watching her, glass in hand.

She smiled quickly and hurried down the room to Lord Phillips. Lord Phillips was a great tall fellow, and he accepted her apologies for her tardy return with an easy smile. "Given the news of your swift engagement, I would have understood if you had forgotten me," he murmured as they left Lord Montrose behind.

"I made a promise to dance with you," she chided. "And so we shall."

They found a place in the set and Portia curtsied to her partner. When she rose, her betrothed was standing directly in her line of sight, staring at her.

She cast him a quick smile but concentrated on dancing her best with Lord Phillips.

As her partner took her hand and drew her closer, he whispered. "Are you all right?"

She blinked at him. "Of course. Why do you ask?"

"You seem unusually flustered. Normally you have something clever to say to me."

"I'm sorry."

They turned, and her gaze fell on Lord Wade. He was not watching her now—and *that* she found even more unsettling than her betrothed's stare. "How is your sister?"

"Upset she had to stay at home tonight."

"Why was that?"

"The babe is coming."

"What? Now? Oh my!" Portia faltered but managed to contain her excitement. "But what are you doing here? Surely you should be at home waiting for news with the rest of your family."

"I might have stayed but they kicked her husband out. I went with him to keep an eye on him."

"Where is Lord Charles now?"

"Drinking over there with lords Wade and Sullivan. I cannot thank Wade enough for the distraction. For a while there, I feared Charles would bolt for home to meddle with the birthing."

She glanced over. "Lord Charles hardly seems at all anxious. How exactly does Lord Wade distract your brother-in-law?"

Even as she asked, she saw Wade lure another gentleman into the conversation, and then another departed. Gentlemen seemed to come and go from the group in a steady stream. Drinks were plentiful all round, too.

"The soon-to-be father is in too much demand for him to even think of his wife's struggle at home. With luck, he'll be quite drunk soon."

"It does seem a very lively group around the expectant

father," she noted before executing a turn that placed her far from Wade. However, she faced her betrothed again.

He stood with a lady now, a woman she'd never been introduced to but knew by reputation. The lady was not someone Portia *wanted* to meet. She had a reputation that put her on the outs with many of the highest sticklers. Montrose did not smile at the woman, and when he moved off without her, Portia was very pleased.

Portia yelped as Lord Phillips suddenly stomped on her toes. She hopped on one foot for a moment, wishing the pain would recede quickly so they could continue their dance.

"I am so sorry!" he exclaimed in horror.

"It is quite all right, my lord." But it wasn't. She found it hard to place any weight on her toes at all when she put her foot down. She held out her hand to him. "Could you help me from the dance floor?"

"I am so sorry, Miss Hayes. How terribly clumsy of me. Are you very hurt?"

She found a vacant chair in front of her suddenly, and she sat to clasp her stinging toes. She could move them but they really did hurt a lot. "I'll be fine in a moment."

Suddenly, Lord Wade was hunched down beside her. "You weren't paying attention."

"No," she agreed. She really had not been giving the dance her full attention. She'd had two gentlemen on her mind—one of whom had been ignoring her until this moment. "How did you get to me so quickly? Last time I looked, you were on the other side of the room."

Wade scowled at Lord Phillips. "You should be more careful with her."

"It was an accident," Portia promised, throwing a reassuring smile in Lord Phillips' direction.

Wade made a grumbling sound that disagreed with her statement, and then moved to kneel in front of her. "May I?"

"Why?" She looked around her quickly, noticing they were oddly protected from view behind a wall of people that she was sure hadn't been standing there a moment before. It was impossible to see the dance floor now, and no one could see them, either.

"I should like to determine if Phillips broke any of your toes before I consider whether to break his nose."

Reluctantly, Portia moved her foot toward Lord Wade's outstretched hand. "Quickly."

Lord Wade gently grasped her ankle and eased her foot from her slipper.

When she saw red on her stocking, she quickly grasped Lord Wade's shoulder. "Steady."

"It is only my own blood that affects me," he murmured. Wade carefully moved a few of her toes, those away from the blood first. He paused with his fingers beside the bloodspot. "Don't scream."

Then he took her bloody toe between his fingers and applied pressure.

Although it was dreadfully painful, all she did was hiss at the sting.

He looked up at her. "Well?"

"I do not think it broken."

"Thank goodness," he murmured. Lord Wade slid his palm back and forth along the underside of her foot. The gentleness of his touch caused her breath to catch, and the pain seemed to suddenly recede.

"He's looking for her," someone warned suddenly.

Lord Wade rushed to shove her poor foot back into her slipper. "You'll be fine."

Portia reached for Lord Wade's shoulder again, intending to thank him, but his upper body slipped through her fingers. Her fingertips could only drag down his coat, coming to rest scandalously upon the top of his silk-clad thigh. He was quite warm there, too, and all lean muscle.

"Gracious!" Portia snatched her hand back and looked up to find Lord Wade staring at her with a feverish light in his eyes. She blushed. "Forgive me."

"You could have touched me like that at any time before," he said with a wry smile. He shook his head, and his eyes lost that new spark. For a moment, she saw pain in his eyes, too, but then he quickly glanced around them. "You might have trouble dancing for a while. Take care of yourself, Portia."

He turned away suddenly, weaving through the throng until she couldn't see him anymore. Portia desperately wished she could call him back.

"Hello, dearie."

Portia spun around in her chair at the sound of Mrs. Lenthall's voice, blushing furiously to find the woman sitting next to her. She would have seen her touching her nephew.

"Hello," Portia choked out.

Mrs. Lenthall nodded to Portia's foot. "Took some damage on the battlefield, did you?"

"It is not broken."

Mrs. Lenthall's expression soured. "Not like a dozen or so hearts around us."

Portia glanced around them. The numbers standing about her had thinned but they were indeed her friends—male friends, once considered possible suitors. "You exaggerate."

"Perhaps I do. There is really only one truly disappointed heart of note."

Portia caught sight of her betrothed across the room between a pair of gentleman's legs. Montrose appeared to be looking for someone—probably her, she realized. She raised her hand to signal him for help, however, the gentlemen milling between her and the dance floor moved closer together, forming a wall of privacy in front of her and Mrs. Lenthall.

She looked at their backs in astonishment. "Why are they doing that?"

"Why do you think?" the older lady huffed. "Still so blind to the truth."

"Please," Portia whispered. "Let's not quarrel. I want to speak with your nephew tonight if I can find him again, to clear the air."

"Indeed you should." Mrs. Lenthall patted her hand suddenly. "Such a shame about you, after all the trouble we went to on your account. I do what I can for those I love, too." Mrs. Lenthall stood herself up using a cane for assistance. "Chin up and smile, dearie. It won't be too bad being married to a stuffed shirt. I liked the fire you had once, girl. Try to remember who you really are before it's too late."

The lady shuffled off…and Portia suddenly felt like crying. People had been acting very strangely toward her since the betrothal was announced when there was no reason. Even though she'd become a duchess on her marriage, she was still the same woman. She laughed, danced and enjoyed the company of other people. But somehow, she had obviously fallen far in Mrs. Lenthalls esteem because of her decision to marry Montrose.

Another pair of long well-muscled legs stopped in front of her. When she glanced up slowly, she found the Duke of Montrose towering above her. His eyes were cold, and she saw no concern in them, only suspicion. "Miss Hayes, should you not be with your mother by now?"

"I am on my way there," she promised quickly. Standing gingerly, she limped a few steps to see if she could manage on her own. Her toes were quite tender. She hoped there would be dancing in her future tonight, because she had promises to keep.

"Why are you limping,' he asked suddenly.

"An accident."

Her arm was suddenly grasped tightly, and she was pulled into Montrose's side. "I'll have your mother take you home to rest."

"I just need a few moments and then I will be right as rain."

"I must insist," he said in a firm tone that demanded immediate compliance with his wishes.

Portia resented that Montrose acted as if he already had the right to tell her what to do. No one but her parents could do that yet. "I cannot leave. My dance card is full."

It wasn't, but she knew who should ask her to dance. She managed to escape his grip easily enough and returned to her mother unaided.

Chapter Nine

Despite his best efforts, Julian somehow found himself within arm's length of Portia Hayes later again that night. He was also much closer to Montrose than he ever wanted to be. The overbearing snob couldn't help but scowl at anyone who tried to approach Portia.

Julian turned his back on Portia firmly, although it felt wrong to do so. She'd made her choice, and she had to live with the consequences now. Montrose would drive away all but the most determined of gentlemen.

He strolled away. He had other friends to talk to. Word had come that Lady Charles had birthed a son, and the new father had run off into the night like a man possessed. Lord Phillips had laughed and then given chase.

One of his newer acquaintances, Lord Hector Stockwick, strolled in his direction at the side of his friend Lord Clement. Stockwick had been a regular face about London for a few years, but his elevation to viscount after his father's death had brought him new distinction and funds to spare.

The Earl of Clement was, to some, the perfect man. Perfectly unavailable most of the year, as he spent most of his time in the country. His appearance here was sure to be fleeting.

They shook hands. "Was that a new phaeton I saw you driving in today, Stockwick?" Julian asked, doing his best to keep his envy in check. The phaeton had been very fine.

"Indeed yes. Collected it just yesterday. What do you think of it?"

"Quite elegant indeed," Julian promised. "I noticed many admiring it as you drove through the park this afternoon."

Stockwick offered a smug smile. "Any ladies among them?"

"Several, and not all of them with possessive husbands," Julian noted with a laugh.

Hector grinned wolfishly. "I have my hands full already, or I would certainly have asked for their directions."

Many newly titled gentlemen came to London with money to burn and left again with pockets to let. Lord Stockwick was undoubtedly the poorer for his elevation. His appetite for scandalous women seemed to be matching his spending. Julian smiled anyway. It wasn't his business to curtail anyone's pleasure. "Mustn't exhaust yourself."

"Isn't it a shame," Stockwick chuckled.

Lord Clement cleared his throat. "How have you been, Wade?"

Surviving. "Quite well. And you?"

"Much the same. Though I'm one sister short now. Ruth married last month."

Julian remembered Ruth less than fondly than he probably should admit. She'd been an utter cow to one and all. "Do give her my best, won't you?"

Clement nodded.

Stockwick moved closer. "I say, who is that beauty behind you? My word, what a woman!"

Julian did not really want to turn around, but cast a glance over his shoulder. Portia was again not far away, and obviously the only woman Stockwick could mean. "Someone out of your league, I'm afraid."

"What's her name?" Julian started shaking his head but Stockwick grinned. "I'll find out one way or another from someone else if need be. Perhaps she's lonely."

"That is the Duke of Montrose's betrothed," he announced, though the words hurt him to say aloud. "Miss Portia Hayes."

Hector's face fell. "Pity. Who's the other one?"

Julian looked again and saw Lavinia, Portia's younger sister, at her side. "Miss Lavinia Hayes."

A hungry light appeared in Hector's eyes. "I've always been intrigued by sisters. Care to introduce me?"

Julian stepped closer to the viscount and lowered his voice. "Look at either one of them in that manner again and you'll wish we'd never met."

Stockwick cast him a sharp look of surprise. "Steady on, man. They're not yours, are they?"

"They are friends of mine, and I protect my friends from each other, too. "

Stockwick scoffed but after Clement had a word in his ear, he looked away with a disgruntled expression. "Not worth my time then."

"No. It's not."

Stockwick pursed his lips. "I'm for the card room. Are you keen to try your luck against me?"

"No. But enjoy yourself. Both of you."

Julian watched them leave, temper slowly fading away. He should not have done that. Threatening a peer when he had no right to would make people wonder about him, and Portia or Lavinia.

Julian turned around to view the room slowly, feeling a sudden sensation that he wasn't alone anymore.

Portia Hayes was watching him from not far away, her eyes full of questions and unexpected appreciation.

Confused, he looked away and studied those dancing before he imagined anything else so ludicrous. The party was winding down but there were still a few dances left to be enjoyed. He could not recall seeing her dance with Lord Montrose yet. That was something of a surprise to him. She dearly loved to dance all night, every dance if she could manage it.

Her eyes met his again for a moment, and then she tilted her head toward an exit to the room.

Julian glanced around quickly to see whom she planned to meet with now. However, there seemed not to be anyone paying her the least attention.

What was she up to?

Portia suddenly leaned close to her mother and whispered in her ear before she moved away alone. She was leaving the room, without her betrothed or her mother by her side. A rendezvous was definitely underway.

Her gaze returned to him again—and he realized finally that *he* was being asked to follow her into the hallway beyond the ballroom. Although the direction she traveled led to the retiring room, he was almost certain she was not going there for the conveniences.

Julian debated following her for about three of her tiny strides before he turned around to exit the room via another door. To others, he'd appear to be headed for the card room, but of course he'd never bother.

There was a little hall between the ballroom and the ladies' retiring room, and she lingered there, glancing out of the shadowed doorway nearest to him.

He approached slowly, rather alarmed that she was smiling at him.

Portia darted out and grabbed him by the sleeve before he could get away and tugged him into the deep doorway. "We need to talk, my lord."

"Can't imagine what's left to discuss," he insisted, glancing over his shoulder to check for anyone coming. "A future duchess hardly has need of a poor viscount's conversation."

She made a small growl. Something akin to a cornered cat, and he almost laughed. "Are you going to hold that against me forever?"

"Probably." He drew back as far as he could and looked her up and down. She was quite literally the most stunning woman here tonight. Her mane of dark hair was dressed in ribbons that struggled to contain it. He lowered his eyes to her pert breasts, barely contained in another water-damped white silk gown, and grinned. "That's a pretty dress. I'd like to see you step out of it."

"Lord Wade!"

"As if you didn't wear such intoxicating creations to torture all gentlemen." He looked away in disgust. "I suppose your betrothed has feasted already."

Portia gasped, blushing a little. "He has not."

Wade shook his head. "Poor Portia. Engaged and not yet ravished. Proposed to but not even courted. What is the world coming to?"

She punched her hands on her hips and glared. "We are not going to talk about Lord Montrose. We are going to talk about us, and that is why you are here."

"The tilt of your head seemed to suggest you were again up to something that would likely put you out of favor. I do love a first look at a scandal before the twitters start," he said with an insincere smile. "But since it appears nothing is going on right now, I will take my leave and return to the ballroom, where there are ladies to admire."

He did not truly mean that, but Portia did tend to bring out the worst of his spite right now. He knew he had to leave her to Montrose and his lackluster passions. Julian just couldn't seem to stop running into her wherever he went. It was his own fault, really, for introducing her to everyone he knew. It was an exhaustive list of people, and he didn't want to avoid them, too.

Portia grabbed his arm and dragged him into the adjoining room. The chamber was dimly lit by only a few lamps, but blessedly empty except for a few armchairs and a thick Persian rug spread out before a cold hearth.

"What a cozy chamber for a bit of give and take between lovers," he remarked. "Care to sit on my lap and find out if the chair is sturdy enough for a hard ride?"

Portia whacked his arm. Hard. "This has to stop."

Julian snaked his arm around Portia's waist and pulled her close against him.

It was time to give her the shock she so richly deserved. He'd protected her from scoundrels for a long time. Now it was time to point out her greatest mistake was in underestimating his nature. "Montrose would not like this little rendezvous you've arranged with me. He would be quite put out if he ever learned how often we've met privately in the past, too. He has no idea who you are. Wouldn't you rather a lover who will take the time to please you?"

She seemed to sag against him. "Stop talking like that."

"Why? I'm just being myself. You know me better than anyone. I say what's on my mind and always will." He dusted light kisses around her temple. "You should have brought your betrothed to this room instead of me. He'd have had you on your back and been done in about the count of three. Quite unsatisfactory for you, I should think. I always imagined you'd be a handful in bed. Care to prove me right?"

"Nothing has ever happened between us." She wriggled but not enough to dislodge him. "Stop trying to distract me."

"In what way am I distracting you?" Julian murmured as he lowered his head. He brushed his lips across the shell of her ear briefly before he spoke. "What do you want from me?"

"For us to be the way we were," she cried, although her fingers had curled into his waistcoat. "Friends. Confidants."

"It's too late to turn back the clock." He nuzzled her neck just below her ear, drinking in the scent of her for what might be the very last time he had a chance to. "You cannot prevent the end of our acquaintance, Portia. Montrose dislikes me as much as I do him. It is a long-standing dislike, nothing to do with him marrying you. We can never know more about each other than we do now. When you are his wife, his duchess, he will certainly have a say about who you can flirt with in the future."

"Flirt with? Talking is not flirting."

Julian spread his fingers across her back and drew her more firmly into his body. "Silly Portia. I'm not talking to you; I'm seducing you right now, and you're allowing me to," he whispered softly against her skin. "I have wanted you like this for so long."

"What?!"

"We're not friends."

Portia pushed at his chest feebly. "Don't you dare say that again."

"Why shouldn't I, when what I want from you is more than a humble viscount deserves?" He let his lips rest against her throat and softly kissed her there. "You don't know him like I do. He does not share anything he feels belongs to him."

"I don't belong to him," she promised. "I will not change, either."

Julian ignored her promise and smiled sadly. "One of your most admirable qualities is your ability to do the unexpected. Montrose hasn't an impulsive bone in his body and will do his best to snuff out your extraordinary sparkle."

He caressed her back, holding Portia in his arms as he'd never done before. She fit perfectly against him, so warm, so lovely…and so far out of his reach still.

"Wade," she whispered, leaning into him despite the impropriety.

He released her abruptly and scowled. "Within a year of marriage, you'll be as dull and submissive as anyone who moves in his circle. And bored. You'll take lovers just to get the attention you crave, but he'll never try to win you back. He's not capable of loving anyone but himself. Everything I've admired about you will be gone by the time you realize I was right all along. Enjoy your time in London, Portia, while you still have a little freedom left to be yourself. If you ever find yourself a widow, we'll talk again then. If I'm still available."

Portia followed him. "He won't change me. He won't change my life."

"He already has," Julian murmured. She was fooling herself that it hadn't already started. The spark of mischief in her eyes had already dimmed whenever Montrose was near her. Gentlemen had been warned off already. It was surprising that Montrose didn't consider him any real threat, but he might if Portia kept chasing him. "Marriage changes everyone but the degree depends on the spouse. Excuse me. I have no wish to face your betrothed at dawn over a misunderstanding."

Portia grabbed his arm and held him back. "He wouldn't dare."

"Some would say he's within his rights even now. Look, there's still that sturdy-looking chair over there, big enough for two if you really want us to compete for the pleasure of your company. I could easily sit you down on my lap and," he leaned closer, allowing the heat of his breath to tease her ear lobe, "we could talk about why you really want me to stay with you. I don't think it's my outstanding conversational skills that interest you anymore."

He removed her hand from his coat and pressed a lingering kiss to the back of her fingers, and then turned her hand over to kiss her slender wrist.

Portia gasped aloud at his touch, and a rush of unwanted desire rushed through his entire body as she trembled. But he was trying to provoke her, not torture himself. He straightened slowly and looked into her familiar eyes, but tonight they were dazed by an unexpected emotion—lust. An expression she'd always reserved for other men before.

"Wade?"

He brushed his fingertips across her cheek. He had to go. "You are perfect as you are. Don't marry Montrose unless his touch excites you at least this much."

He stepped back from her just as the door burst open.

Two figures entered the room and then closed the door again. Lord and Lady Windermere smiled, and Julian cursed under his breath.

"Darling Wade, there you are at last!" Lady Windermere cried.

"Windermere. Lady Windermere." Julian's voice was rough as he answered, and he cleared his throat. "Good evening to you."

At his side, Portia dipped into a curtsy for the earl and his wife.

Julian stepped in front of her slightly. "Do you want the room?"

"No. No." Lord Windermere and his wife came closer,

neither one glancing at Portia. "But I wanted to ask if you wouldn't mind doing me a favor. Well my wife, really."

"How can I help?"

"Would you at all mind escorting my wife home tonight?"

"Of course I can escort your lady all the way home," Wade promised quickly. "It would be my pleasure."

"Thank you," Windermere said, and then turned to his wife. They kissed goodbye, and Julian heard Windermere whisper a warning to his wife. "Keep our friend out of trouble. He's not thinking clearly."

Lady Windermere laughed. "Trust me, darling. I know which scandal must be spread about tonight."

She turned to study Portia, her expression amused, as her husband rushed from the room. Julian prayed she'd not cause trouble.

"Do excuse the interruption of your fascinating discussion, but time really is of the essence." She glanced between them, a smile growing on her face. "Now, quickly, what shall we say we talked about tonight when asked about this meeting tomorrow?"

Portia frowned at Lady Windermere. "I don't understand."

"My dear girl, you know full well that we must create a story to explain why you left the ballroom to rendezvous here. Lord Wade cannot be connected with you, too. Not tonight."

Julian moved toward Lady Windermere and held out his arm for the countess to take. "She would never do anything that scandalous with me."

Lady Windermere laughed wickedly. "It looks like a tryst to me, and it will to others, too. How is my husband to win a wager if people have doubts?"

"We were disagreeing," Portia explained unnecessarily.

"Yes, I heard all about it. Your voices carried out into the hall. Have you not heard of lowering your voices or discretion? Anyone else walking past would have assumed it was a lovers' tiff and reported every word back to Montrose. I thought better of you, Wade, to be the *cause* of scandal rather than preventing them."

Portia stepped closer to Julian and rested her hand lightly on his back. "Meeting here was entirely my doing. He didn't want to stay beyond a moment."

Lady Windermere laughed heartily at that lie. "He would have kept you in that chair or on that rug by the hearth all night if he'd had his wicked way."

"That is not true," Julian protested as he looked at Portia again more closely. Yes, her feet had seemed to be welded to the floor the moment he'd drawn her into his arms. She usually reveled in the attention of scoundrels, and from him now, too, apparently. He had not expected that reaction at all, really. He'd thought his behavior would have driven her away but she really was defending him. "Our paths crossed quite by chance."

"A pretty pair of liars you both are, but no matter. I reserve the right to be as indelicate as I want since I discovered you here alone together. This is not well done of either of you. What about your betrothed, Miss Hayes? Shouldn't you be luring *him* off to dark corners instead of our dear friend Lord Wade?"

Julian shrugged. As far as he knew, Portia hadn't lured Montrose anywhere yet. But he had stopped watching Portia these past few days. The duke seemed entirely too wrapped up in his own consequence and rendezvous were hardly needed, now Portia was promised to him.

"Please don't tell Montrose," Portia begged, and then winced, no doubt imagining the trouble she'd be in if Montrose did find out.

Julian almost wanted that to happen. Almost but not quite. Montrose had a formidable temper. "It will not happen again," he promised, turning away from them both.

Lady Windermere clucked her tongue. "Perhaps it will. If it does, I expect you to do the right thing."

"Nothing happened, and don't you dare infer it will," Julian warned, turning back. "It's done. She's marrying Montrose."

"You're counting? Good." Lady Windermere nodded slowly, a smirk on her face. "Oh, I suppose you were right to back away now, but I was so looking forward to Christmas."

Portia's eyes lit up. "Oh?"

"We are all headed to the Duke of Exeter's country estate. Daventry and his wife were going to be there early, Wade and his aunt. Sorenson, too, since he married my husband's cousin, Anna. Our whole set haven't gathered together for a very long time. It should be great fun, and I so hoped you could be there with us."

Portia looked at him accusingly. "I didn't know you were going away."

Julian nodded. "My aunt and I thought we might leave London soon. There's not much to hold us here, now that my brother has joined the army. The Duke of Exeter's Christmas Party cannot be missed but its later in the year, we might travel before and that will hopefully distract my aunt from melancholy."

"It will not be Christmas without you," Portia protested.

"Unfortunately, the Duke of Montrose would never be invited to the Duke of Exeter's estate." Lady Windermere sighed deeply. "I am sorry you will have to miss it, my dear."

"So am I, my lady. Perhaps you'll come to us at Sherringford another year?"

"We'll see," Lady Windermere murmured, though she didn't sound enthusiastic.

Portia's face grew pale.

"I tried to warn you," Julian murmured softly. He held out his arm to Lady Windermere again and drew her toward the door. "Shall I escort you home now, my dear lady? I doubt there's anything left to be said."

"A dance first, if you don't mind." The countess smiled. "There are also a few young ladies new to Town we should talk about. You need a wife soon, too."

"Matchmaking?"

"It passes the time," Lady Windermere confirmed. "Besides, I am determined to see you as happily wed as I am."

Julian cast a quick glance at Portia to see if she cared. Aside from wearing a puzzled expression, he sensed no distress in her face. He turned back to the countess. "I was hoping you'd forgotten all about my bachelor status."

"Never. You must have a bride before Christmas. I can think of nothing better for you."

"But he's always acted as if marriage was the last thing on his mind," Portia said suddenly.

"There was a good reason to delay," he said with a shrug, without looking at her. "That reason no longer exists."

"I don't understand."

"No, it's clear that you never did," Julian agreed. Portia Hayes must have never known the depths of his adoration.

"Miss Hayes, would you care to walk with us?" Lady Windermere asked her suddenly.

Portia seemed troubled and shook her head. "No, thank you." Her voice was small, and Julian felt torn to leave her behind.

Lady Windermere, however, smiled widely. "Very well. Please allow us to leave the room first. Wade will cough if the hall is clear."

Julian agreed. "We wouldn't want Lord Montrose to misunderstand where you've been all this time."

"No," Portia said firmly before Julian swept the countess from the room. But he hated leaving her there. Who knew what trouble she would get into next.

Chapter Ten

Portia spun around as a floorboard behind her creaked unexpectedly. Seeing no one creeping up on her, she returned to poring over a boxful of sheet music she'd just discovered under Uncle Oliver's guest bedchamber bed. The house usually made all sorts of odd noises and Portia usually ignored them. Today she was jumping at every sound.

She'd been here since dawn, after enduring a restless night where she'd been trapped in a room with Lord Wade while Lord Montrose pounded on the door. She'd woken in a sweat and twisted sheets. What disturbed her the most was not her fear, but the fact she'd not felt any. Lord Wade's arm had been around her and his lips had caressed her throat in a way that made her pulse race even now.

It was a disturbing dream to have so close to being married.

Resolved to put the troubling dream firmly behind her, she'd gathered up her maid and come here to sort through more of her uncle's possessions. She was squeezed tight between two sea chests she couldn't find keys to open. Portia did not even find the cramped confines of Uncle Oliver's old dwelling at all restricting or embarrassing. Her uncle had taken a lifetime to accumulate it all, and it might just take all of hers to see it all, too.

She blew back a lock of fallen hair, frustrated she could not seem to keep it contained by her ribbons and pins today. Her hair was getting in her way of having a good time.

And then Portia froze as a door suddenly shut somewhere in the house—beneath her.

She cocked her head, listening to heavy footfalls on the stairs, moving up from the bowels of the house. She considered calling out but then remembered no one at home knew to find her here except her maid, and it was far too soon for her to return from the errand she'd been sent off on.

Nervously, with one eye on her door, Portia reached blindly for the nearest heavy object, ready to hurl it at the intruder and defend herself with it if necessary. Her fingers curled around an old pistol, but she knew it was not loaded or truly that dangerous. Regardless, she raised it aloft, held it by the barrel, and inched toward the door as gently as she could so the floorboards didn't creak beneath her feet. The handle was made of ivory and should make enough of a dent in whoever-it-was' head to give them a reason to run away from her.

Portia placed her hand on the door handle when she heard footsteps stop just outside the room she was in. Definitely not her maid, who would have called out long before now.

Portia gripped the pistol tighter and jerked open the door—only to be very surprised.

"Wade!"

"Portia!" Wade clutched at his chest, his brow scrunching as he pointed at her raised hand. "What the devil were you going to do with that thing?"

Portia lowered the pistol immediately. "You surprised me. What are you doing here?"

Wade licked his lips, a sure sign of nervousness. "I have a good reason."

"You had better." She tossed the weapon back onto the dresser and stepped out into the hall with him. In truth, she was very glad to see Wade here again, because she'd started to feel very lonely in this big empty house. Wade had been just as intrigued by her uncle's collection as she was, and she hoped he might stay awhile. They had much to talk about.

First of all, she wanted to know when he'd decided that marriage might not be as bad as he'd always claimed. That was quite a big step for him, and one that troubled her. He shouldn't rush into anything. But then, as she looked at him closely, and longed to fetch a comb for his shaggy hair, she thought a wife might be good for him. He also needed a better valet and a decent haircut. "I do hope you intend to be a gentleman today."

The corner of his mouth lifted in a smile. "I might give it a try."

"Try very hard, my lord, or there's always that pistol." She didn't want to hurt him. "You used the spare key."

"Yes," he said as he leaned closer. "You're not angry that I did, are you?"

"Why would I be angry? It's not the first time you've arrived unannounced." She looked him over from head to toe. He needed a better suit, one that fit him. His current attire seemed unnecessarily unfitted. "At least this time I don't have an injury to tend."

The first time Lord Wade had called at this house, he'd broken a window and cut his hand. "No." Wade flexed his fingers on the railing he gripped.

She stared at his gloved hand and thought of the skin beneath. "I've been meaning to ask about your hand. Did the wound heal? Is there a scar?"

"Yes and yes."

"Show me," she asked impulsively.

Although his brow rose at her request, he tugged off a glove and presented his hand for her to inspect. "See, all better."

"It was the other one, Lord Wade."

He huffed slightly and showed her the other, too.

There was a faint red line, but it had healed very nicely. She ran the tip of her finger across the scar, feeling only the slightest hint of unevenness. "I'm glad it wasn't deeper."

"Are you always this familiar with your friends?"

Portia grinned. He'd called himself her friend, and that

made her happy. "I might be."

He laughed softly as he tugged his gloves back on. "I'm fine, Portia. Another month or so and there will be nothing left to see."

"But I'll remember."

"No doubt you will be too busy to mention it again," he said, and then looked away. "I suppose I should explain why I am here without asking permission to come first."

"You are always welcome to call on me anywhere, but tell me what has brought you back here today?"

"Your uncle was an eccentric collector of a great many things."

She nodded. "Indeed. I'm always surprised."

He gnawed on his lip a moment. "I was hoping you might let me take a look at one item of his, if it is still here. If it's not too much to ask."

Portia couldn't be more surprised. "Do you want something belonging to my uncle?"

"It was not his in the first place." He gestured to the stairs. "Perhaps we might sit if you don't mind the dust on the stairs while I explain."

"The stairs are probably the cleanest part of the house. The whole house really is in need of a thorough airing." She moved to sit and Wade perched at her side. "Tell me what it is that you want?"

"I cannot say what it is."

She leaned close to him. "Then how can I agree when you won't tell me?"

"You mistake me. I know exactly what I'm searching for and where it might be, but I cannot tell you what it is because it is rather risqué. You'd undoubtedly be shocked."

Well, that was a fair reason not to tell her. "Are you certain it's in this house?"

"I *think* I saw the item last in Oliver's bedchamber when you were in hiding here last month, but I wanted to check to be sure first. Do you remember how shocked you were by the correspondence you read in Uncle Oliver's study?"

"Oh, well, you may certainly take his letters."

"The item was put under another lot of letters I discovered up here in his room."

Portia frowned. "Ah, well if you cannot tell me what it is, then surely you can say why you need it."

"I'd be happy to." He twisted around, to face Portia. "There's an old wager in the White's betting book I want to help settle. My friend Sullivan has always been intrigued by the foolishness written there, and as we were flicking through the pages recently, we uncovered a clue about one of the oldest wagers. Suffice to say, I found out your uncle was intimately involved in the matter before his death—the day before, actually—and I believe he has the item wagered upon still hidden in this house."

"Then go and fetch it!" Portia cried, immediately caught up in the hunt for treasure. "I'll come along and help you if you like."

He shook his head violently. "I do not want to offend your delicate sensibilities."

"This is my house. Come on, I've read enough sheet music here to last a lifetime."

She caught his hand and pulled him with her along the hall to her uncle's old bedchamber. Lord Wade looked around as they went. "You haven't gotten very far since I was here last."

"It's slower now that it's just me."

Wade stopped abruptly at the doorway, and then strode into Uncle Oliver's bedchamber to peer closely at the scandalous painting Portia had found recently. "Have I seen this before?"

Portia settled against the doorframe. "I don't think so. It's quite old, actually. I found it hidden behind a large cupboard in the drawing room. Mother took one look at it and fainted. Father had to catch her. I like to imagine the lady was important to my uncle. Why else would he keep it?"

"There could be many reasons. Have you found anything else like it?"

"Not so far. Why?"

He ran his finger over the artist's inscription at the bottom left corner. "It's remarkably good and probably quite valuable. There could be more around."

For a moment, she wondered if he was about to volunteer to help her search, but then he shook his head. Having him here without his aunt as a chaperone was not a good idea for her reputation, should anyone learn of it. But he had been vastly helpful in the past. She would give anything to have his help again if she could.

Wade shook his head again and moved away from it, glancing over his shoulder a time or two to check where she was standing. Portia remained by the door, watching him move objects out of his way until he finally pulled a box from beneath the head of the narrow bed and placed it beside the pillow. He put his hands on top of the item, fingers spread. "I put this here so you might never look at the contents."

Portia nodded. "Well, go on. What are you waiting for?"

"Just remember, you asked for this." He opened the box, lifted out a pile of yellowed old letters, and stared into it. "I'm sure this has to be the one."

He placed a piece of dark wood on the pillow and returned everything else to the box.

Portia squinted in the dim light. The item was perhaps eight inches long but from the door, she could not be certain what it was. She took a step farther into the room as Wade turned his back and tucked the box away back under the bed.

She leaned across the dusty comforter and picked it up. "It's a stick."

Wade choked out when he saw it was in her hands. "Put that down!"

"What would my uncle want with an ugly, lumpy stick?" Portia held it up to the light and turned it slowly. She knew what it was, of course, but had never seen one up close—living or made of wood. "This is not what I was expecting. I thought it may be a jewel or something valuable."

"Dear God, put that down at once! I'd hate to think where that's been, or in whom."

He snatched it from her and put it behind his back.

"What do you mean *in*?"

Portia moved to the foot of the bed, and Wade did too. "It is not a stick. It's a man's," he sputtered and gestured to his trousers, "you know."

"Oh. Really?" Portia craned her neck, hoping for another peek. "I'll have you know I have viewed Elgin's Marbles, and I have studied depictions of male anatomy in books, but that is not at all the same."

"Not all are." He rolled his eyes. "This object is used for pleasure, not for study. It is said to be a replica of a certain gentleman's cock."

She flinched a little at the forbidden bold word but did not chide Lord Wade for using it. They got along much better when she ignored his little slips of the tongue. "Whose?"

"I've no idea or desire to find out." He shook his head, scowling at the thing. "I don't want to know, and nor should you. If I'm going to have trouble looking at the fellow, should I one day learn his identity, you certainly should be spared the embarrassment."

Portia smiled at how flustered Wade was becoming. "You are very considerate of my feelings."

"Flattery will not grant you the name when I learn it, either." Lord Wade was unlike the suitors she'd had before her engagement. He questioned her decisions, warned her away from temptation, but he had never truly refused her anything.

Portia grinned even more. "Are you sure I couldn't tempt you?"

"You could, but for anything but that name." He drew closer suddenly and looked deeply into her eyes. For a moment, she thought he was about to kiss her…but then he looked away and the moment passed. "So about the wager. If this is the right item, I've been promised a share of the winnings, which must really be given to you."

"I don't want the proceeds of a scandalous wager for that thing."

"Are you sure? It could be five and twenty pounds. That's a

lot of pretty ribbons for your garters."

Portia considered the matter. She had always known Lord Wade was not wealthy, but lately she'd been hearing more whispers that Wade was desperately short of funds. Winning a wager like this would be of more help to him than to herself. As she looked upon his lean face, she wanted him to have the money. "You should keep it, and spend some of it on ribbons for your *aunt's* garters."

He grimaced a little. "You are very kind."

They both heard a key inserted into the front door lock at the exact same moment.

They looked at each other in shock as the screech of protesting hinges echoed through the house. "Someone's here," she cried.

"Quickly, we have to hide."

Portia grabbed Lord Wade's hand and dragged him from the room. They bolted for the front of the house together where there was a tiny room with a key for the lock—the only one in the whole house that they could safely hide in.

The screech of protest from the front doors hinges shutting again concealed any sound their feet might have made. They rushed inside and locked the door tight.

The little room was not entirely empty but there was room enough for two if they stood very close to each other. A tiny window set high in the wall kept them from total darkness. Portia had once promised to hide here if she ever thought herself in peril.

Lord Wade pulled her toward the window urgently and then laced his fingers together. He lowered them so he could boost Portia up to look outside. "My father's carriage!" she whispered in a panic.

"You cannot be found with me," Wade whispered back, glancing round the space with wide eyes as he lowered her quietly to the floor. "There's no way I can reach the rear door without alerting him to my presence."

"We'll have to wait him out. Together."

They bumped against each other awkwardly in the small

space, and then Portia had no choice but to lean against Wade, making the best of the cramped conditions. Her father's steps grew louder and louder, coming ever closer to their hiding space.

Wade put his arms around her, and that made their predicament very much like her dream. Wade was quite the right height for this sort of thing, and she lay her head on his chest with a soft sigh. There were worse places to be trapped, after all, and Lord Wade was very familiar and comfortable.

He settled his chin on top of her head and must have had his eyes on the door, judging by the direction they were standing. If they stayed quiet and still, they might remain completely undetected until father left.

Portia jumped as her father's voice rang out. "As you can see, the place is fully furnished."

Lord Wade smoothed his hand down her back. She found his touch highly distracting, and quite lovely, too.

"More than fully," Montrose complained, and it seemed he was on the other side of their door. Portia held her breath, trembling in Lord Wade's arms.

"Ample choice then in what is kept or thrown out," Father insisted with a laugh. "We are not sentimental about any of it, so feel free to expel anything you do not need to the street."

Wade seemed to press closer to her body, then his lips grazed her ear. "What is going on?"

She wriggled a hand free of his waist and lifted her finger to his lips to silence him. She'd explain later, after father had gone on his way home with Montrose.

He nodded, and his warm breath on her fingers sent a shiver rushing though her. She let her fingers scrape lightly over his chin as she lowered her hand, and then rested it over his heart. They continued to listen in silence as father extolled the virtues of Soho Square and the house to Montrose.

She caught Wade's eye as Father's voice grew softer, coming from further away and when she could not hear either of them she took a deep breath. "Father will lease the house soon."

Wade shook his head. "But I thought you were going to keep it as is."

"A few things must go."

"I suppose," he murmured dubiously.

"Montrose has no real interest in the house," she confided as her father's steps returned suddenly, thudding loudly past their tiny hideaway. At last, the front door opened again with a terrible shriek, and then another as it closed.

When all was quiet again, she risked another few words. "They've made a bargain to begin a lease now, and then Lord Montrose's man will take over the management of the place once I'm married to him."

"I'm surprised Montrose didn't want to sell it."

"He did, but it cannot be done. My uncle's will forbids any sale."

"Ah," Wade said as he sighed. He pulled away from her, jumped up to grab the window sill and pulled himself up. Portia was impressed by his unexpected display of strength and agility. He hung there, feet dangling, for a long moment before he dropped lightly to the floor. "Still on the pavement outside. So the house cannot be sold, but you cannot live here."

"Unfortunately not. I wish there was some way to save everything, though."

Wade looked about the room. "Perhaps not everything must be hoarded. A family would need some of the space to live in, to grow."

"True, but…"

He took another peek outside then dusted off his hands. "They're gone," Wade said in a normal tone, and then sighed. "That was damn lucky for us."

Being caught alone with a gentleman, being compromised, was something that Portia had done her best to avoid. Yet looking at Lord Wade now, she realized that if it had been him, she might not have cared so much. A few months ago, she had felt differently.

He smiled suddenly. "So, tell me more about your uncle's

unusual will."

"It is not that unusual. Uncle Oliver died without a son or other male relative living, so he drew up his will to leave his money to my mother and me and to my sister. This house forms part of a trust for my son when I have one, and it cannot be sold until he has reached his majority. There are similar provisions for Lavinia, but her property is a small estate in the country."

Lord Wade nodded, his expression speculative. "A forward-thinking man. I never would have guessed. Would that my own family had given a thought to the future and made sensible decisions," he muttered.

Lord Wade fished the key out of his pocket and squeezed past her to reach the door.

Portia watched in silence as he unlocked it but to be honest, she rather thought she'd like to stay right where she was. It had been nice being held, and Lord Wade was always protective. She also liked that he was always interested in her family and her opinion too. "My father would disagree with you about the practicality of leaving property to females. He and Mother argue about what must be done with this place, and the other, all the time and never decide on anything in the end."

He eased the door open and peeked outside. "It really cannot be sold? That must have put a damper on Montrose's plans for the money he might have made from the sale."

"I suppose," she said evasively. "I don't know what might have been discussed when he learned of the restriction."

"Or what plans he's already made to spend your dowry, too, I suspect. He's always been a secretive bastard," Wade complained.

"You're a lot like him in that respect," Portia noted, thinking about his lack of funds and the way he avoided talking about the matter. He never acted like he had any concerns.

Wade said nothing as he stepped outside.

She sighed, a little bit ashamed of herself that she would

really rather stay here—alone with Lord Wade than face the future. She'd begun to worry about Wade and what the future had in store for him and his aunt too.

Wade reappeared a few moments later, his expression rather curious as he gazed at her from the door. "Your father and betrothed have gone. Are you coming out of there or do you plan to spend the night?"

"Oh, yes. I'm coming." Portia exhaled and walked out. Lord Wade backed up a few steps as Portia brushed off her skirts and looked around. "I can't bear the thought of strangers living in my house."

He nodded. "Perhaps a friend of yours might be interested in the lease."

"My friends know that I want this place for my own. That cannot happen unless I marry."

"And even then, you could not live here as a duchess. It would embarrass Montrose." Lord Wade grinned widely. The prospect of Montrose put out must have appealed to him greatly.

"What really happened between you?"

"The usual. A few harmless pranks and we became sworn enemies." Wade turned away, glancing up at the leadlight window above the stairs. "I want for you to live here. I know how much you adore the place, creaky front door and all."

"Don't forget the murderous wine cellar," she added. "I've not been brave enough to venture down there on my own since you were here last.

"An incentive to give up drink, that one," he said, and then chuckled. "I'd better not bring my aunt here again. She enjoyed the contents of that wine cellar a bit too much."

"She was a perfect guest and chaperone." Portia brushed her hand over his sleeve. "I suspect it would be impossible to convince anyone to move into this ramshackle place. No one would want to live among this chaos."

"It does have a certain unique charm," Wade noted, and then scowled. "He's always had a stick up his backside about everything, especially where he belongs and what he can do.

Personally, I like the place."

That pleased her. At least one gentleman did. "Tell me what really set you apart and perhaps I can find a way to smooth things over."

"Leave it alone, Portia."

"I cannot believe anyone could remain that cross with you for so long, no matter what you did to them."

A strange smile spread over his face. "What makes you think I was at fault?"

"Well…"

"I found fault with the way he treats those with less, and said so out loud," he told her. "Did he stand up and challenge me? No, he sent his friends to do his dirty work for him the next day. Luckily, Sullivan was with me, or the outcome would have been *me* beaten and bloody, instead of a fair fight."

He turned away. Portia did not like the sound of that, though she didn't believe Wade would lie to her. Montrose had demanded to know with whom she'd danced, and maybe it was a good thing for them that she'd kept quiet. Admittedly, she'd only had occasion to recommend an introduction to Sir John, but she'd planned to make her regular partners known to Montrose soon.

She rushed to catch up to Lord Wade. "I can accept that he might act superior sometimes," she agreed reluctantly.

Wade stopped and looked down upon her with a startled smile. "Always," he warned. "Keep watching him, and you'll see what I mean eventually." He looked about the place. "It will be a shame to know all this history is gone, and I am sorry that I cannot prevent it from happening now," Wade told her. "You belong here."

"Thank you for saying so." She smiled, pushing aside her troubles. "Shouldn't you be on your way to collect your share of that wager?"

"Indeed I should." He brandished the phallus, pulled a face as he realized what he'd done, and jerked his arm down to hide the thing behind his back.

Portia laughed. "I suppose I shall have to get used to such

matters soon."

His cheeks darkened. "But not with me standing in the same room."

"I should hope not. That would be a little crowded." She watched Lord Wade fidget. "I swear you seem more embarrassed than I am."

"I might be, too, but for different reasons. I had better go," he said. But he didn't move.

"You might want to wrap that."

"Good idea. I can't just waltz into an earl's house swinging this dreadful thing about."

Portia giggled. "So the wager involves an earl, does it?"

"Shh," he warned as he tugged a small dustcover off a vase and wrapped it up carefully. He glanced her way, and then held out his empty hand.

Portia shook it firmly. "Good luck. Oh, and Wade, if it isn't the item being sought, throw it away or burn it as soon as possible. I don't wish to ever see that again."

He drew her into him and pressed a kiss to her cheek. "Thank you," he whispered before darting off into the shadowy staircase to the kitchens.

Portia slowly straightened her toes, which had curled in her slippers when Lord Wade kissed her cheek. A good kiss tended to cause havoc with her senses, but until recently, she'd never suspected Lord Wade would be good at delivering one.

The kitchen door closed with a firm boom, and Portia sighed. She sat down on the cluttered staircase amid more boxes and put her chin in her hand. Her maid would return soon, and then it was back to being the future Duchess of Montrose, whatever that might mean.

For now, though, her thoughts traveled with Lord Wade as he headed toward an earl's home to win a share of a scandalous wager. It was really very sad that he must be so desperate for coin that he would traipse across Mayfair carrying a replica of a man's private parts. She'd always assumed Wade a fortune hunter, but his ambitions had just been revealed as far more modest than most gentlemen who called upon her.

To prove the point to herself, she put her hand out and picked up a silver butter knife from a nearby box—one of two dozen boxed-up sets to be found in all parts of the house. Silver went missing from grand houses all the time, and there had been many occasions when Lord Wade might have just taken something of value without asking. He knew where the key was hidden, but he'd never betrayed her trust.

"I misjudged him so badly," she whispered to herself in stunned surprise. "It's much too late to wonder if he'll ever kiss me…even if I think he should have by now."

Chapter Eleven

Julian laid the wrapped bundle on Lord Windermere's desk and stepped back in a hurry. He was extremely anxious to be rid of the object. Carrying around what was supposed to be an exact replica of another gentleman's cock was awkward, to say the least. It was very well done—lifelike. "As we discussed the other day."

Windermere grinned and unwrapped the object. He seemed to have no hesitation in inspecting it from end to end. "This is the one."

Julian frowned. "How could you be so sure?"

Windermere flipped it around and showed him the base. "See these little marks that go round half the end but no farther? He marked it himself as a way to keep score of his conquests."

Julian grimaced. "Charming."

"He isn't." He glanced up, his expression excited. "I have been waiting so long for this moment. I cannot thank you enough. I assume you had no problems convincing Miss Hayes to part with it when you met with her."

"I did not meet with her."

Windermere stood back with a grin. "I think you did. How else might you have gotten into that house so easily? Others have been trying since Oliver passed away, but Hayes always refuses. And the girl is to inherit the house upon her marriage. Besides that, there's a long-running rumor floating around that you have a soft spot for Miss Hayes. I very much doubt you would steal from someone you cared about, so it follows that she must be a willing accomplice."

Julian's cheeks warmed with discomfort. "She is engaged."

"Yes, yes. My wife believes Miss Hayes made the worst choice she could," Windermere remarked with a shrug. "This certainly proves she's not a lost cause."

Julian turned away so he did not reveal his agreement with that assessment. "I trust you will not hold her marriage against her in the future."

"I will not, but others might. Montrose isn't popular and has already thrown his weight around, putting noses out of joint left and right. At least now, we might knock him down a peg or two. Teach him some respect."

"How?" Julian stared at Windermere. "Wait. Who owns that thing?"

But he knew, even before Windermere confirmed it, that Montrose had immortalized himself in wood.

He felt ill. He'd touched that thing. Portia had…*would.*

"Come now. Do not pretend you don't like the idea of embarrassing the man." Windermere grinned. "It is remarkable that she would give this up so easily. I take it she has no idea?"

"None." What had he done? "Portia'd had no idea it was even there. She'll never forgive me. I didn't know who owned it, or I would not have asked."

"It's better this way." Windermere wrapped the piece again and tucked it away in the desk drawer.

"Give it back," Julian demanded as he darted round the table to retrieve it. He did not care to think of the trouble this would cause Portia. Montrose might lash out at her.

Windermere pushed him back, but not before Julian discovered the drawer was already locked.

"Please."

Windermere studied him, and then dug in his pocket.

"Your fee for services rendered."

Julian stared at the money held out to him then slapped it away. "If he flies into a temper and hurts her, I'll hold you accountable."

"What's going on?"

Julian heard Lady Windermere clearly but he didn't acknowledge her. "Give it back to me."

"No."

Lady Windermere rushed to her husband's side and grabbed his arm. "Richard, what is going on? Why is Wade so angry?"

Julian looked at the woman he'd called friend for a number of years. She was a good person, if a little calculating at times. Surely Lady Windermere liked Portia too much to put her in any jeopardy? But she might need an incentive to see things his way. Julian had the perfect lure up his sleeve, too.

"I gave your husband an item that will embarrass someone dear to me. I did not know it would at the time, and I need it returned. Now."

"It's about Montrose," Windermere murmured. "I told you my plans for him."

"Yes," Lady Windermere murmured back, frowning. "And I also told you I disapproved. What has that to do with Wade?"

"Portia Hayes is involved now, though she does not know it. But your husband certainly did." Julian turned to the countess. He liked her—but he would not allow Portia to be embarrassed for the sake of a wealthy man's amusement. "How old were you when you posed for Monsieur Pliat?"

The countess blinked. "Pliat? I haven't heard his name in years."

"No doubt a lot of people will hear the name again soon." He smiled grimly. "It's a very pretty portrait of you. Easily recognizable."

The countess paled. "What do you want for it?"

"Make him stop." Julian shook his head. "Once I have the object back, you'll have your painting."

The countess turned to her husband and started whispering quickly. Julian waited patiently. It did not take long before Windermere turned for the window, his arms crossed over his chest. There was a click…and he looked up in time to see the countess opening the drawer and removing Montrose's property.

She handed it to him, without unwrapping. "You must love her very much."

Julian nodded. He strode to the nearby hearth and tossed the phallus directly into the flames. It began to smoke almost immediately as it was consumed. He stood silently until it had burned enough not to be recognizable, should Windermere try to fish it out again.

Assured that the earl could not use it against Montrose, he strode to the door.

Windermere was waiting. "Have no doubt, *I* will remember this day in the future," he warned.

Julian nodded. "Just stay away from her, and you'll never have to see me again."

"Wade," Lady Windermere called. "You will return my portrait, won't you? In person."

He nodded quickly. "In person and without showing anyone, I swear. I've no desire to embarrass you."

"Thank you," she said, as she moved to her husband's side and removed him from the doorway by force.

Julian walked out, but the encounter left a sour taste in his mouth.

He headed out to the street and hailed a hack immediately, sitting on the edge of his seat until he saw the Hayes family dwelling ahead. He rushed up the stairs of her home and asked to see Portia, if it was convenient.

The Miss Hayes' were in the morning room with their mother and welcomed him with a happy smile. He felt his stomach twist with shame over his near miss. The ladies were surrounded by fabrics and ribbons, a familiar sight to him on his visits, and this was how he always hoped to see them. Happy together.

However, it was imperative he speak to Portia privately. When he'd decided to come here, he'd not realized getting Portia alone might be difficult. He bowed to them. "Ladies."

"My lord, how good that you have come to visit us," Mrs. Hayes exclaimed, curtsying, before exchanging a long glance toward Portia. "Isn't it, Portia?"

"Indeed." Portia frowned a little. "But we were just about to go out."

"Perhaps you would care to escort us for a stroll, Lord Wade," the mother asked.

Julian considered the request carefully. It might just be the only way to steal a few minutes. He had accompanied the Hayes family on their outings before but not since the engagement was announced. "I'd be happy to join you."

Portia flashed him a wary smile, and he wondered if she hadn't wanted him to come. Yet out on the street, Portia claimed a place at his side very quickly.

The sister and mother walked ahead a few paces. He began with pleasantries. "I trust your day has been pleasant, Miss Hayes."

"Yes, indeed it has been."

"It looked like you were in the midst of planning an amusement."

"Yes. Something for Lavinia. Mother wants to make use of my wedding to show my sister off." Portia suddenly took his arm. "I must warn you, mother might rope you into her plans to launch Lavinia too."

Julian nodded. "I'm not worried, and I have done similar before without being asked. For you."

"This is different," Portia warned.

He liked that she was concerned for him, but there was no reason for it. He could look after himself. His affection for Portia extended to her family, including the little sister more spoiled than Portia was. He sighed. "It will be a little different. I will help with invitations as much as I can, but if the hostess does not care to invite a connection of Montrose's, I will be able do nothing about that." He looked around and calculated the chance of Portia's mother hearing his words. "I have to tell you something, and you are not going to like it very much."

"Go ahead," she whispered.

"That item you allowed me to take." She nodded quickly. "I know who the owner is, and I want you to know that once I found out, I burned it."

"Why? What about the wager?"

"Under the circumstances, it was not right, because it might involve you in unpleasantness. It is very important that you say nothing about the item or that I took it from the house with your permission. Promise you will never tell anyone, least of all Montrose."

"Very well," Portia agreed. "I promise."

"Thank you." He winced then. "However, in denying the wager a successful conclusion, I had to pledge to return that painting you found in your uncle's home."

"The naked lady," Portia whispered. "You *did* know her?"

"I recognized a similarity and some conversation confirmed it. The subject desires its return, and I have promised her my discretion in doing so."

Portia nodded. "If you think we should, then yes, by all means make good on your promise."

Julian noticed Portia was still on his arm. He liked the feeling too much to remind her to let him go. "Before I discovered whom the first item belonged to, it was mentioned that many a gentleman hoped to visit your late uncle's house."

"Whatever for?"

"At a guess, I think your uncle Oliver may have made other bargains, or he was holding items for other people. His sudden death may have inconvenienced important people. Your father refused to help them, but you could win favor by doing so. But I want you to think carefully before you agree. You must be sure anything returned is not used to cause anyone embarrassment."

"The house is to be emptied before it's leased. There's little I can do to halt my father's plans, not when Lord Montrose supports them."

"Then we've no time to waste."

Portia grinned. "I'll be at the house the day after tomorrow, in the morning. We can explore the contents again together."

He shook his head. "I need that portrait sooner than that. Today, if possible."

"Very well," she agreed. "I trust you will let me know when it's returned to her, though."

"Of course."

Portia stopped. "What about the other items? The people you said may have been turned away before. How do we find them?"

"I'll drop by the club and check the betting book again, and start discreetly spreading the word about potential recovery of any lost property. Otherwise, they'll have to be disappointed."

She shook her head. "That's a shame."

"There's nothing more we can do."

Portia sighed and held his arm a little tighter. "You are a good friend."

Julian covered her hand with his. After Portia was married to Montrose, she'd be just another conquest for the man. She deserved to be so much more than that. He swallowed the lump in his throat. "Promise me you will never let on to Montrose that we met at your uncle's house. Not even when you were hiding from Lady Scott."

"I wasn't planning to, but why shouldn't I?"

Julian sighed, imagining how upset she might be to learn her future husband had owned that phallus and kept score of his women. Thank God it was ashes by now. "Just trust me on this. He will not be pleased to know we were meeting."

At least there was still time left where they might talk to each other. After she married, he would never be able to call on her again. He might not even see her for a very long time too. The thought was almost unbearable.

"Are you attending the King dinner tomorrow night?" she asked suddenly.

"Indeed I am."

"We did not receive an invitation," Portia said in a rushed

whisper. "Mother is miserable about the snub. She keeps hoping for a late invite anyway, and has taken to haunting the front hallway in the hope of being happily surprised."

Julian extracted himself from her grip. It had begun, the subtle decline in Portia's popularity because of her pending marriage to Montrose. He was helpless to stop it. Mrs. King was a great friend of his aunt's, and his aunt was not happy that Portia was marrying Montrose. Clearly some of that had rubbed off. He might be able to appeal to Mrs. King for a last-minute change of heart.

But did he really want to vouch for Portia when she would become a Montrose soon? He could end up having to eat his dinner across the table from a man he despised. He did not think he could stomach seeing more of Montrose's self-satisfied countenance.

They walked on a few yards more, side by side and silent, before Mrs. Hayes announced she was too tired to continue.

Julian offered his arm to the older lady. However, Mrs. Hayes tried to have him walk beside Lavinia instead. She claimed to have stubbed her toe and assured him that Portia's help was all she required.

That left Julian no choice but to walk beside Lavinia for almost a mile. He liked the girl because she was Portia's little sister, but that was as far as it went. Lavinia was young and enthusiastic and very spoiled. She peppered him with harmless questions about members of the *ton*, the events he attended, and Julian answered most when he could. When it came to anything at all to do with his opinion of Portia, or dragging him into an attempt to tease her, he clamped his lips shut.

At the bottom of the stairs to the Hayes family residence, Julian waited patiently to one side of the path as the ladies bid him goodbye to return inside. Mrs. Hayes grabbed her younger daughter by the hand and drew her away. He didn't look to Portia at first but when he finally did, she was watching him.

"Goodbye, Miss Hayes," he murmured, wishing he could stay by her side and never leave.

She stretched out her hand to take his and shook it. "Good afternoon, Lord Wade. Thank you again for your company today, and happy hunting later."

He smiled quickly when released then hurried off to Uncle Oliver's house for the painting he must return to Lady Windermere, to make good on their bargain. However, he thought perhaps it might be prudent to wait a few days before he saw either of the Windermeres again, so tempers could cool.

Chapter Twelve

An empty drawing room was a disquieting thing during the early hours, when callers were expected but never appeared. Portia exchanged a worried glance with her mother. The swift retreat of *tonnish* gentlemen from her company seemed to directly relate to how widely the news of her betrothal had spread. Portia had always enjoyed a vigorous morning exchanging quips and a good gossip with the gentlemen she'd danced with the previous night. Not so anymore. She'd been utterly abandoned in favor of other available ladies, she suspected.

Mother had so hoped that Portia's engagement to the Duke of Montrose would make her more popular than she'd already been, bringing new faces to meet her sister.

"More tea?" Portia offered her mother.

"No," Mother said as she stood quickly and crossed the room to where Lavinia sat at the pianoforte, fingers resting on the keys in preparation for a knock at the door or a sign of someone coming to call. It was a shame. Portia's sister looked utterly perfect today, her hair dressed to make her appear very elegant. Her gown was new, too, the latest fashion from France, and without a crease or blemish. "Lavinia dear, perhaps you should return upstairs. I'll call if anyone should come."

"Yes, Mother," the girl murmured meekly enough, but her eyes flashed with disappointment when she caught Portia's gaze.

Once Lavinia was gone, Mother turned on her. "What have you done to spoil your sister's chances of making a match?"

"I?" Portia reeled back. "Nothing!"

"Then explain why my drawing room is empty today," Mother demanded.

"I cannot imagine," Portia said as she put her needlework aside, calm and sure she'd done no wrong.

"This is intolerable!"

"Mother, please calm yourself."

"How can I do that?" Mother began to pace. "We had it all worked out, and now, something you've done or said has dissuaded gentlemen from calling upon us."

"Mother, you are being unfair. Gentlemen call upon the ladies they dance with, and it's only natural that, since you have reduced my outings following the engagement announcement, there must be a decline in gentlemen calling for that reason, too."

Mother digested that, and then grimaced. "I guess we will have to go out more often. Come, get your bonnet."

"What? Now?"

"Indeed now. Who do we know that we might have neglected?"

"I'm sure we have neglected none of our closest acquaintances."

"Then that must be the problem. We have not made enough new friends." Mother bit her lip. "I know. Lord Sullivan? Did he bring one of his sisters to Town?"

"Not that I've heard mentioned." She really knew little of him besides his connection to Lord Wade. She had not seen *that* man for a few days now, and she found herself unable to stop thinking about him…and how he'd never tried to steal a kiss from her until she was engaged to marry another.

Mother rushed for a side table and opened the deepest drawer. Inside that drawer was their edition of the Peerage.

Mother must be serious if she needed to consult that old thing again. She combed through the pages, squinting at the text. "Oh, if only Lord Wade were here *today* instead of the day before yesterday. He would tell us what we need to know."

Portia moved to her mother's side and took the book, missing Wade for an entirely different reason. Mother's eyes were giving her problems of late, and any small text tended to make her cranky if forced to read. Portia was more than happy to lend a hand while she still lived here. "He does seem to know everyone."

"And their secrets, too. A valuable acquaintance indeed."

Wade had been a font of knowledge for all of them, really, but he had saved Mother from social disaster time and again when they'd been drawing up their very first guest lists. "Here it is." Portia quickly read the entry. "Lord Sullivan has three sisters, Amelia, Caroline, and Lydia. I've heard nothing of them so far. His marriage is not shown in our copy, but I know his wife died last year sometime. He's only just out of mourning. Her name was Clare."

Mother snatched the book up, shutting it and dropping it into the open drawer. She kicked it closed with her foot for good measure, proving her mood severe indeed. "We will purchase a new edition as soon as can be."

Mother's answer to any obstacle was to buy a replacement. "We should invite Lord Sullivan to dinner tonight. And Lord Wade, too, and his aunt."

"Lord Wade is engaged elsewhere tonight," she told her mother quietly. "He's to attend Mrs. King's party."

Portia winced as mother shrieked in a very unladylike fashion.

There had never been an invitation for them to attend the King dinner, although they had every reason to expect one. Mother collapsed into a chair with another wail of despair. "I cannot believe Mrs. King simply forgot us."

Portia could not understand it, either, except that it could have something to do with her betrothal. Montrose had been very evasive about his connections, and because he'd been absent from London the past two days, she'd had no chance to quiz him about his friends still.

Portia was beginning to wonder if he had any, and if she was to endure an endless round of snubs in her future. If few of her friends liked Lord Montrose, would the feeling be mutual? If so, the dinners she'd hoped to host in the future as a duchess might be very awkward affairs, if they even took place at all. "I'm sure it's an oversight."

"I suppose it could be," Mother agreed but did not sound very confident that it was. "Perhaps she will host another entertainment soon, so we can show off Lavinia's pretty manners and accomplishments."

Catching titles for her daughters was all Mother had ever really cared about. Now that Portia was off the shelf, about to be married to a duke, she talked constantly of her hopes for Lavinia making a similar match. Mother and Father had both pushed Portia to seek the best marriage she could. But lately, she'd started to wonder if she might have chosen differently if they'd not been so particular.

"Mother, can I ask you something?"

"Anything, as long as it doesn't involve banishing your sister to her room again because she has annoyed you," Mother warned. "She cannot marry well if she is not seen."

Portia laughed. "Lord Wade. Did you ever think he might have been interested in me?"

"I suppose he might have, but it hardly matters."

Portia winced. "He has been very kind, helpful too, and we do like him very much. Did he ever offer for me, or ever hint that he might be considering it?"

"No. Not that I ever recall. Your father would never have allowed you to marry a fortune hunter, anyway."

"Is he really a fortune hunter? He's never acted like the other ones who came to call."

"My dear girl, the Wade family is virtually without a penny. I could never understand in the beginning how the *ton* continued to embrace the family."

"Perhaps he did someone a kindness."

"He must have done a great many kindnesses to be so supported. He keeps no horses or carriages and never entertains. But he is still on everyone's list when invitations are issued. How is that fair, when I have a daughter in need of a husband?"

"I don't know that much about his past, really." For much of her association with Lord Wade, she'd considered him a nuisance, intent on spoiling her fun. The way he had watched her, butted into her conversations while passing her by, had made her dislike his forwardness.

However, she had quickly appreciated his loyalty when there had been a murderess hunting down debutantes of questionable virtue. Portia might have been slain if not for Wade's constant presence near her.

She had not asked him to watch over her. He had taken it upon himself to be her protector. Out of the goodness of his heart, despite his argument that he'd done nothing extraordinary. He'd become her friend, an adviser she'd come to rely upon. She probably owed him her life.

At least now she had a means to repay him through her uncle's eclectic collection. Allowing him permission to take from her uncle's house might even help his finances in a small way, too. Those small wins might prevent him having to sell the lease on his Hanover Square home this season. She didn't like to think of being in London without his steady presence.

Portia poured herself a cup of tea but found it cold. She set the cup aside and stood.

"Where do you think you're going?" Mother demanded.

"I think I am done for the day, too. I was going to go up to my room and—"

"No, no, no!" mother cried. "We must wait until three for callers."

"But you sent my sister away."

"That is part of my plan, dear. She comes and goes so her arrival will seem unplanned. Fated. Who knows what might happen under the right circumstances?"

Portia's heart sank. At the beginning of her first season,

Mother had attempted to orchestrate several impromptu introductions. A dropped handkerchief in the park, a twisted ankle once next to a grand carriage. In retrospect, her behavior then was mortifying. She'd hoped Lavinia would be spared such nonsense

Now she thought about it, Lord Wade had been around in the early days when Mother tried to ingratiate herself with strangers, and had always shaken his head before stepping in to perform introductions. It was surprising he'd not run away from them, really. She knew a great many people in society because he had not. As a consequence of those early introductions, her family had been assured of an interesting evening of varied conversation whenever they went out.

And now, perhaps because of Montrose, they would not keep those friendships.

She glanced at her mother in consternation. "The best introductions have never happened in our drawing room, Mother."

She had first bumped into Lord Wade on foot in Green Park. She remembered the moment clearly, because he'd opened his mouth and swore out loud for no good reason. A proper introduction had come a few days later at a ball. She'd been very surprised to see him again; she'd not known they'd had acquaintances in common at the time.

"We should go out," Mother declared. "Your future may be settled, but we must think of Lavinia, too. Fetch your shawl and have the carriage brought round."

Portia rose, knowing she must obey her mother for the sake of any peace. "Yes, Mother."

"While we travel, we will give some thought to our circle of acquaintances and see who we can call upon. We cannot rest on our laurels. We must strike while the iron is hot, so to speak."

"And try not to singe our garter ribbons in the process," Portia quipped.

Mother glared. "Try to think of someone besides yourself for once, Portia Hayes."

Portia moved to the window on her way to the door, just in time to see her intended's carriage stop before their house. Grooms swarmed down from the gleaming black town carriage and smartly snapped out the carriage step. One opened the door and held it, standing at stiff attention. Montrose, however, took his time to exit. Once on the pavement, he looked up and down the street, and then strode purposely up the stairs to her front door. "Montrose has come," she whispered urgently.

"Oh," Mother wailed. "Oh my! Now we must stay to welcome him."

Portia rushed to sit again, fluffing out her skirts then picking up her needlework.

She held her breath, glancing at the closed drawing room door—but soon realized Montrose had been shown to her father's study, instead. Portia lowered her needlework when the distant door shut with a loud crack. It opened soon enough after, though, and then her father hurried in, followed by the duke. Montrose was still carrying his hat and gloves and, by the way he glowered at everyone, seemed very upset.

Portia hastily dipped into a curtsy. "Your grace. What a pleasure to see you."

"Miss Hayes," Montrose said as he bowed smartly, and then looked at her father.

"Yes, yes, of course." He hooked Mother by the arm and dragged her from the room. "Come along, my dear."

Surprised and pleased to be left alone with her betrothed, she smiled warmly up at him. "We were not expecting you to call today, your grace."

"Needs must."

She stared at his face and saw not an ounce of pleasure there for her warm welcome. She gulped. "Is something wrong?"

His eyes narrowed. "Why do you ask that?"

"You appear most upset."

"I am not upset."

Portia nodded quickly. The man was lying. He was

incredibly angry, she thought. What about, Portia could not imagine, but she decided that jollying him out of the mood was to be her first duty as his future wife. "Perhaps we might sit and talk. It has been a few days since we have seen each other. I trust you have been in good health and that your business went smoothly while you were away."

He nodded and sat in an opposite chair, flicking out the tails of his coat. He leaned forward, studying her face. "I have not known you very long, but I believe you to be an honest woman."

"I am," she assured him.

"Your father has made me aware that the house formerly belonging to Oliver Quigley is part of your dowry."

"Yes. I used to visit Uncle Oliver as a child, and since he did not have children of his own, he left it to me when he died. He was the best of men."

"An unusual decision, but I assumed your father had the managing of it."

"Until I marry, yes. Afterward, I hoped to have a say in what was done with it. My son will, after all, inherit the house. I want it to be left to him in a proper condition."

His stare became hard. "Your father had intended to clean out the house completely and to lease it before we married, but it seems someone else may already be doing so for him. Without being asked to."

Outside of family and servants, only Wade and his aunt and brother had been in the house since Uncle Oliver's death, and Anna and her husband, too, but they were far away right now. She remembered Wade's warning to hide their friendship from the duke very clearly and did not want to stir up trouble for anyone, including herself. "That cannot be. Nothing has been removed without permission."

"I see." He squinted at her. "And yet, an item known to be in your uncle's possession before his death has reappeared in a most unseemly fashion."

She blinked several times. "I beg your pardon."

"I will not burden you with the particulars, but suffice to

say it caused considerable embarrassment to a number of acquaintances of mine." He tilted his head, his expression hard as ice. "How recently were you at the house in Soho?"

Several things suddenly clicked into place, and she almost groaned aloud. *Oh, Wade. Why didn't you tell me Montrose was involved in the wager?* Lord Wade had taken two things from Uncle Oliver's house. Both were scandalous. He'd claimed to have burned one and would return the other to the painted lady soon, if he hadn't done so already. But which item was Montrose talking about now? The portrait or the phallus. It did not please her that he might want either one of them in his possession. Especially the latter.

"Sunday," she said, lifting her chin, determined not to leap to conclusions. "I was looking through some old sheet music in Oliver's collection to give to my sister."

"What time of day was this?"

Portia lifted a finger to her chin, pretending to think about her answer. But her mind was racing. What did it matter when she was there or what she did with anything she found? The contents of the house would be disposed of anyway. Surely he couldn't want a painting of a naked woman to hang on his walls, a replica of another man's cock. Her cheeks grew warm that she'd even thought that word to herself. "It was after my visit to the dressmaker you recommended, but before luncheon."

"Did you meet anyone at the townhouse? See anyone leaving or acting suspiciously nearby?"

She'd met Wade there, and he'd made her promise never to mention that to Montrose. "Of course not. I was with my maid."

And thankfully, Mary would keep her lips shut about the hours they had been apart in between. Father would dismiss Mary if it was ever known she routinely visited her sister, who lived and worked a short distance from Uncle Oliver's home. It was their secret, and Portia wanted it to remain that way forever.

Montrose nodded slowly, then his features softened. "I

would appreciate it if you would keep the topic of this conversation between us."

"Of course," she promised him.

His gaze swept over her body then back to her face. There was a glint in his eyes she'd never seen before. "You look very pretty today," he said suddenly—before darting forward and planting a hard kiss on her lips.

Startled, Portia did not immediately respond to the kiss. She was too busy keeping to her seat. Montrose swept his hands over her back, and he locked her into his arms. Portia pressed her hands to his shoulders, but never considered moving them up to embrace him. She shoved a little when the kiss went on too long and she needed to breathe.

He drew back with a grunt. "Forgive me, it has been a trying few days."

"I'm sorry to hear that," she whispered, and then tried to smile as she comprehended the man kneeling before her did not kiss well. He took and plundered, and she felt very unsatisfied. "I'm very glad you came today. Please, won't you sit and talk about your trip. Where did you go so suddenly?"

Perhaps if Montrose was calmer, more in control, he might present her with a much better kiss if given a second chance. She licked her lips but he frowned instead of obliging her with even a smile.

"I must go, unfortunately," he said as he gained his feet.

Portia jumped to hers. "Already? But you have only just arrived."

He shook his head firmly. "I'm afraid I must pay a call on an old acquaintance that cannot wait."

Portia swallowed at the hard edge that had crept back into his tone. "Who?"

But Montrose shook his head again, planted another, somewhat gentler kiss on her lips and drew back.

Neither kiss stirred her passions in any way, she realized.

"Wear white the next time I see you," he demanded, before striding out of the room.

Portia glared after him, but Mother swept into the room

the next moment, holding up a letter and smiling widely. "I knew it must have been a terrible mistake!"

"What?" Portia snapped.

"Mrs. King has sent us an invitation to join her tonight, with her most humble apologies for the oversight and late delivery of the mail. It seems Lord Wade called upon her and mentioned in passing how disappointed he was not to have us there, too. A search was conducted, and our invitation found in her morning room. How wonderful that we have such good friends! Oh, has Lord Montrose gone already?"

Portia nodded, unwilling to speak of the duke right now.

"Well, no matter, he'll find his invitation soon enough."

Thankfully, Mother left her to begin her preparations for the coming evening.

Portia covered her face when she was finally alone—horrified and deeply troubled by what she had learned of Montrose today. That thing Wade had taken must have belonged to Montrose and been returned despite Wade's promise to the contrary. What else could have angered Lord Montrose more?

Wade! she shrieked silently, wishing he was here to rail at.

If Montrose ever learned who had been responsible for his embarrassment, she feared how he would react. She hoped the person Lord Wade had given that object to could be discreet about the viscount's involvement—and hers too. She couldn't bear it if Montrose and his friends ever caught Wade alone again. They were no longer in school. Disagreements between gentlemen were often settled by duel—with pistol or sword.

Chapter Thirteen

---◆---

Julian kissed Martha King's wrinkled cheek. "You're looking lovely tonight, Martha," he promised.

"That is what you said to me yesterday." Martha King wrinkled her nose. "Sweet words won't change anything. You owe me for this."

"I will owe you if you smile and say nothing about it to anyone."

The lady scowled at him. "It's a good thing I like you so much. You know it's not too late to put you over my knee again."

Martha had been Julian's family housekeeper when he was a boy, but had married very well for herself. "I'd like to see you try."

Martha laughed and sent him on his way to greet the next couple coming through the door.

Julian had liked Martha very much, and he'd been pleased when she had married a man who adored her and given her children of her own. The families had kept in touch over the years.

She was influential now, too.

Julian escorted his aunt into the drawing room. "She will hound you until you give her what she wants," Aunt Hesper warned in a low tone.

"Don't you dare tell her, but I like the opera. She thinks I'll be pulling out my hair."

Auntie looked at him with a worried expression. "Have you given any thought to how you'll pay for the box?"

"Not yet, but I'm sure I'll think of something eventually." There had been no fixed date when he must take Martha to the opera, though, so he had some time to work everything out.

"I hope the Hayes family appreciate your sacrifice," Auntie complained.

"I'm sure they would if I planned to tell them. You keep your lips buttoned about it, too."

Aunt Hesper grumbled and wandered off to speak to friends nearby.

Julian saw Sullivan not far away and strolled over to him. They shook hands. "I wasn't expecting to see you tonight."

"Your aunt said I had to come, or she would never speak to me again," Sullivan complained.

Julian grinned at his friend. "Some men might have welcomed that silence from her."

"Nonsense, I like your aunt. She's not the same battle-axe she used to be, though."

"The years have definitely mellowed her, that and the wine she constantly consumes," he grumbled quietly.

Sullivan laughed. "She used to lecture us about the perils of overindulgence. I should send her a barrel of it to see what she says in response."

She'd probably thank Sullivan, and mention she'd be happy to receive the rest of his wine cellar as well. "I'm pretty sure she'd blister your ears," Julian murmured as his eyes snagged on a welcome sight—new arrivals.

Mr. and Mrs. Hayes had arrived, Lavinia standing between them. Following was Portia, looking as lovely as ever…on Montrose's arm.

Julian stared across the room in consternation. "What the devil is he doing here?"

"Mrs. King neglected to mention he was coming, but this

should make for an interesting evening," Sullivan murmured. "She could have warned us."

"She certainly should have," Julian agreed. He hoped he could keep his dinner down. He was very hungry tonight, but looking at Portia's hand anywhere on Montrose made his stomach rebel.

Aunt Hesper was suddenly at his side. "What is he doing here?"

"We were asking ourselves that very same question," Sullivan suggested. "Perhaps he's come in the hope of being laughed out of *this* dining room, too."

Julian kept track of him and Portia, mostly. "What are you talking about?"

"Surely you heard the latest on-dit." Sullivan leaned close to whisper. "Last night, Lord Windermere served up Lord Montrose on a platter. He found it, Wade! He found the wagered item and gave it back in front of *everyone*. Montrose was so embarrassed and stormed off."

Julian gaped. "No, he couldn't have."

"I tell you, it was the most enjoyment I've had since school when he tripped over his own feet and fell headlong into that mucky pond they have."

Julian stared at Sullivan with a sinking feeling. "You saw it? Saw it given back. In public."

Sullivan nodded. "Windermere was in his element. The whole table was in an uproar. I've never laughed so much since my Clare died."

Julian swore under his breath and looked again in Portia's direction. She stood alone now and was staring at him, a question in her eyes. Did she know? Had she heard about the incident involving Montrose? He shook his head, trying to convey a thousand apologies at once.

Aunt Hesper laughed softly. "What a lovely evening this is turning out to be. We should speak to her now before dinner is announced."

Auntie latched on to Julian's arm and practically dragged him across the room to speak to Mr. and Mrs. Hayes. Sullivan came, too, and was enthused over as he was presented to the younger girl. Lavinia wore a pretty blue gown and a welcoming smile, but Julian only had eyes for Portia.

Tonight, she wore a white gown, one he'd seen and admired many times before. In that dress she had laughed and danced, pretending she'd not a care in the world, and later she'd clung to him, worried about him fainting at the sight of someone else's blood. It was a gown he was very fond of because, from a certain angle and with the right amount of light behind her, it revealed the long, lean form hidden beneath.

He stuck his finger under his cravat as she moved between him and the distant fireplace, allowing him a brief glimpse of his fantasy. "Lord Wade, so good to see you again," she murmured.

"Likewise, Miss Hayes. I see you've brought your betrothed with you tonight."

"It was Mother's idea to have the duke bring us here," she whispered, casting a troubled glance over her shoulder. "I didn't know about that when I saw you last."

Well, at least he wasn't alone in being surprised. "I see your mother worried for nothing about her missing invitation."

"I know you fixed it for us," she murmured. "But I don't understand why you would."

"You did want to be here, didn't you?"

"Yes but—"

"That's all the incentive required to make things right."

A fleeting smile crossed her lips as Auntie butted in. "Ah, there you are, gel."

"Mrs. Lenthall. So good to see you again."

Auntie smiled and cupped Portia's cheek. "It's been too long, my dear. You look lovely as ever in that gown."

"Thank you," she murmured before being called to her mother's side.

Lavinia Hayes remained and dipped Julian a curtsy. "It is good to see you again, my lord."

"It's good to see you again, Lavinia," he murmured. "How

have you been?"

"Very well, thank you. I wonder if we might have the opportunity to continue our recent conversations tonight."

"I'd like that," Julian murmured noncommittally, looking around the room. He did not want to become stuck conversing with Portia's little sister all night long if he could help it.

Lavinia suddenly slipped her arm through his. "Are you acquainted with the Plumptons?"

"Indeed I am. We sat down to dinner together not so long ago."

"I have not been so fortunate. Would you be willing to introduce us?"

There could hardly be any harm in it. The Plumptons were sufficiently well thought of, and they did have a son about the right age to consider matrimony.

Julian drew her there and held out his hand to Mr. Plumpton. "Sir. Madam. How have you both been?"

"Very well. Very well indeed." Mr. Plumpton grinned. The older man was close in age to his host, Mr. King, but he had long since lost any scrap of hair upon his very bald head. Loss of hair notwithstanding, he was a fine fellow and obviously very sharp. "I must thank you for the information you gave me at our last meeting."

"Helpful?" Julian asked, although he already knew the answer.

"I am indebted to you for your timely intervention. You saved me a great deal of trouble."

Julian nodded. "Think nothing of it, sir. It was providence that brought the matter to my attention and damn fine timing on meeting you at dinner the very next night."

Plumpton laughed. "If all my encounters with titled gentleman were so well timed, I'd be a richer man than I already am."

They both laughed, and Julian offered to introduce Lavinia Hayes to them both. Mrs. Plumpton was a kind woman, and both soon became engaged in conversation with the girl. He stepped back slightly and looked around as Mrs. Plumpton sang his praises, too.

Portia moved to join him, standing close to his side and listened in. "What has Lord Wade done now?"

Mr. Plumpton laughed. "Do you remember we had a little farm between here and Nottingham?"

"I think so," Portia agreed.

"The one nobody seemed to want to purchase," Mrs. Plumpton added. "It was in the middle of nowhere."

"Oh, yes, I remember it now."

"Well, someone has purchased it…and not just anyone, too."

"Daventry bought it," Julian told her before Mrs. Plumpton could drag the revelation on all night.

"He is the strangest fellow. Purchased it for his wife, of all things, and more than I asked for, too." Plumpton shook his head as if baffled. "More money than sense. It's nowhere near his other holdings. Excuse me. I must speak to Lord Montrose while he is free."

Julian was left standing alone with Portia for a moment as Lavinia continued to talk Mrs. Plumpton's ear off. He inhaled her perfume and smiled. "Daventry's purchase made perfect sense when you know the particulars."

"Oh?"

"The property was exactly halfway between his country estate and London. They break their journey there so his wife will be spared the rougher accommodations found at an inn."

"That is very sensible of him," Portia murmured. "The journey is a long one, and Lady Daventry is said to find travel difficult. I wonder how she will manage the trip to Exeter's estate? It's twice the distance."

"We will see," he murmured, looking at her at last.

"You will have to let me know after Christmas," she murmured, looking away quickly.

She seemed troubled. She must know what transpired had not been intentional on his part. Windermere, though, was another matter.

It was on the tip of his tongue to offer to speak to Exeter

on Portia's behalf, too, but then Montrose arrived at her side, and one glimpse of his toplofty expression stilled Julian's tongue. He would do anything for Portia, but only if Montrose wasn't involved with her.

Julian suddenly noticed a pair of sizeable footmen in livery standing in the background. Their hulking presence was unusual, even for a duke. Many a guest cast uneasy glances in their direction.

"My men," Montrose announced.

"You would bring your own servants to sit down to dinner in a friend's home?" Sullivan exclaimed. "My word, you've some nerve."

"It seemed prudent."

Montrose suddenly noticed Julian standing beside Portia, and he frowned severely. "I was not aware you had an acquaintance with our hosts or my betrothed."

He must be blind as well as a fool, then. "We have been acquainted for some time now," Julian admitted, noting Montrose did not look pleased to hear it. That was just too damn bad.

"Excuse me," the duke murmured. "Miss Hayes, you will come with me."

Portia left with the duke but she did not look happy to go with him. That was small comfort for Julian, who would never have spoken to her that way.

The duke marched over to their hosts and began talking to them in low tones. Julian discreetly followed…and caught his own name mentioned, and Sullivan's, too. Mrs. King cast Julian a look that spoke of extreme discomfort then.

Julian smiled and nodded to reassure her that everything would be all right.

Sullivan leaned close. "I don't think he likes us still."

"You more than I," Julian suggested, looking around the room with a frown. "It wasn't me who pressed sheep dung into the pages of his books at school."

"That was only after he'd stolen all the new boy's clothes and carried him outside while he slept. Well-deserved retribution for such an act," Sullivan said with a soft laugh. "I wonder if there is anything we can do to compel him to leave early tonight."

"Don't," Julian murmured, noting Mrs. King was starting to look very distressed indeed. Montrose had upset her, and Julian scowled at his broad and expensively clad back. "Schoolyard pranks should be far behind us."

Sullivan heaved a heavy sigh, and then one last couple arrived, tardily, and Mrs. King visibly relaxed. Once introductions were performed it was time to go into dinner.

Julian escorted Mrs. Plumpton into the dining room, which had been stripped of all but the bare necessities to extend the table to accommodate all the guests. Julian took his place at one end, noting he'd been placed far from Sullivan, Aunt Hesper, and Portia, too.

He allowed a servant to settle a napkin on his lap, noting Montrose gestured for his own man to do it instead of one from the King household.

As the first course was placed in front of him, Julian strained to hear Portia's voice. She was unusually quiet tonight, but her betrothed was talking enough to fill any silence. Julian turned to Mrs. Plumpton and smiled. "Did you have any luck with training your dogs, Mrs. Plumpton?"

"Indeed I did. Patience was all that was needed. A few months and the little beast ceased snarling at poor Plumpton and now follows him about—utterly devoted to his new master." She leaned closer. "It did help tremendously that he kept dropping chopped liver slices everywhere he went."

"Animals learn who will look after them best." Julian smiled, even as noted that Portia appeared fascinated by her dinner. She usually talked more. "It's the same with people sometimes."

Mrs. Plumpton agreed. They talked of the weather, travel and events in her neighborhood for the rest of the dinner. Their street was a lively place to live, apparently. There had been warring neighbors, marital spats, and misbehaving children to hear about. Julian kept quiet about his own life and had little gossip to share from Hanover Square.

At the end of the table, though, Aunt Hesper's voice rose above all others. She raised her empty glass to her lips, and then frowned to find it empty. Julian sighed as a footman rushed to refill it. Once reinforced, she started talking again. Loudly. Even more excitedly than before.

Dear God, he hoped she would not drink so much. His back had hardly recovered from the last time he'd had to put her to bed because she couldn't climb the stairs on her own.

She caught Montrose's attention. "This reminds me of another dinner. Dear Oliver Quigley, may he rest in peace, hosted the most amusing get-togethers, and your father, dear old Montrose, was there—standing on the table in just his undergarments," she said with a loud laugh, glancing along the table and nodding.

Montrose turned a withering glance on Aunt Hesper. "You must be mistaken."

"No indeed. It's not a memory a lady is likely to forget. He was even… Well, you know." Although she laughed, Aunt Hesper seemed to realize she'd said something very wrong and coughed a number of times. Julian was simply too far away to offer any assistance in deflecting the conversation. He winced.

Tomorrow, she would be full of regret and most likely fall into another sad spell. She missed the days of her youth, when she'd been firsthand witness to her friends and their scandals. Most of them were gone now, though.

Sullivan smoothly redirected conversation to horseflesh and the latest offering at Tattersalls. He talked of a particular horse he had his eye on and hinted he would purchase it soon.

Montrose's gaze swung in Julian's direction suddenly. "And what of you, Wade? Do you still play billiards?"

Julian held his gaze and tried to keep his expression neutral. Someone had talked. Montrose did not live in Hanover Square. "Not lately."

"Oh, that's right. I heard you sold it. Caused quite the commotion in Hanover Square. Everyone has been talking about it, too."

Not friends of mine, as far as I know. Julian shrugged away the discomfort. "It was only collecting dust."

Montrose's smile grew. "That's why a proper gentleman employs enough servants to take care of those tedious matters beneath his notice," he sneered. "You do still have the odd servant lying about the place, don't you?"

"Of course."

"But no horseflesh, carriage, or billiard table now."

"He's awaiting a new one and a matched pair," Sullivan remarked, quite incorrectly.

Julian groaned under his breath at the gross exaggeration. How the devil was he supposed to pay for something like that, or pretend he'd changed his mind? He paid attention to his dinner which was quite to his liking and plentiful.

Mrs. King came to her feet immediately after he'd finished the last mouthful on his plate, her expression one of disapproval for the duke.

Portia joined Aunt Hesper and the pair strolled off toward the drawing room arm in arm.

With the ladies gone, and the doors closing, Montrose's smirk grew worse. The bastard knew Julian's finances were in bad shape and was not above rubbing his nose in it. There was nothing he could really do to retaliate besides mentioning the return of his phallus. Doing so would end up embarrassing Portia so he had no choice but to bite his tongue.

Sullivan sauntered around the table, cigar in hand, passing close behind the duke's back.

Montrose flinched, swatting at his neck with an oath. Sullivan just kept walking by, a small smile playing on his lips. Sullivan had never been impressed by Montrose, nor his lofty title, not in school and not now either, apparently.

Montrose shot to his feet and looked at his footmen harshly. "Did you see what he did?"

Both shook their heads, shamefaced.

Sullivan took the chair next to Julian, held his cigar between his teeth and folded his arms across his chest. The pair glared at each other—and it was Montrose who backed down first. He went to speak to Mr. King.

Julian sighed. "I asked you not to provoke him."

"He started it. Since when do you care that Montrose is unhappy?"

"My aunt started it by mentioning his father dancing on tables," Julian whispered. "It may be true but stories only get more lurid the more she drinks."

Sullivan scoffed. "I've found myself in that condition a time or two. Don't be cross with her for having a bit of fun."

"I'm not. I just worry about her."

"Very well," he promised. "I'll not dare her to drink me under the table tonight then." Sullivan clapped a hand on his shoulder then drew on his cigar. He inhaled and blew a perfect ring across the dining table. "These are excellent."

"From Friburg and Treyer, I should imagine. King always goes there."

"We should visit sometime," Sullivan suggested. "Make a few purchases of our own."

"You can visit. I don't care for cigars anymore."

Sullivan met his gaze, his expression full of curiosity. "Is that another indulgence you had to give up recently?"

"No. It's been a few years now."

"My Clare could blow one ring, and then another to float through the first." Although Sullivan made several attempts, he could not do it himself. "She had talent."

"Indeed she did."

Mr. King returned and started moving about the room, inviting them to make their way to the drawing room. In passing, he mentioned Montrose regretfully had been called away.

Sullivan started chuckling evilly, but then schooled his features once he saw Julian's scowl. "It looks like the evening can be salvaged after all. Let's go and enjoy the ladies."

"Yes," Julian agreed, following behind his friend.

Sullivan had actually changed a bit since his marriage to Clare. He seemed a great deal more comfortable about everything that had once terrified him. However, missteps and scandals were long remembered by the *ton*. Montrose would remember tonight, and one day no doubt try to cause trouble for Sullivan, and Julian, too, most likely.

Julian breathed deeply, pushing aside those worries for another day. He had another few hours in Portia's company, which would do him no great harm. He could even try to forget she was betrothed to another for one more night.

But as he entered the drawing room and looked around, he discovered the Hayes family were already gone. He had forgotten they had traveled here with Montrose and of course would leave with him too.

Chapter Fourteen

———◆———

"No thank you," Portia said again. "I am not at all tired or in need of a chair."

What she was tired of was Montrose hovering at her elbow and spoiling her fun tonight. She was no wilting wallflower who needed constant rest. What drained her energy were his attempts to coddle, and his scowl that was driving her good friends away. She hardly had a name on her dance card tonight, thanks to his behavior, and she was very disappointed in him.

"Would you like a glass of punch?"

"That would be lovely, thank you." She smiled at him, grateful for the suggestion, which would take him away. She needed a reprieve from his attentions. Not that there had been anything much since he'd kissed her on Tuesday. A few bows over her hand, a brief touch upon her back, a softer smile than he bestowed on anyone else. He was not a demonstrative man by any stretch of the imagination.

And that would not do at all.

For the moment, though, she was glad to watch him walk away. She whispered to her mother that she would be right back.

Thankfully, Mother wasn't a woman who paid attention to every minute of Portia's existence. She weaved her way through the crowd, steering clear of the refreshment table where her betrothed was standing, and slipped out into the hall. Technically, she was on her way to the ladies' retiring room, but she'd make a brief stop at the library first.

Portia pushed open the doors and slipped inside. She glanced around somewhat nervously, making sure there were no lingering figures hiding in dark corners or behind doors or curtains. The last time she had been in a gentleman's library, a murderer intent on destroying young women in search of harmless adventure had been on the prowl. Lady Scott was dead but the memory of her lived on. It was not a night she'd ever forget.

She shivered as the door opened and shut quickly, and a familiar figure joined her.

Lord Wade's expression was hard to read, but he was unsmiling, so that gave her a fair indication of his mood tonight. "Haven't you learned your lesson about slipping away on your own? Especially to a library."

She grinned up at him. "I knew you'd follow."

He frowned even more. "Not forever. What do you want tonight?"

Undeterred by his irritation, Portia laughed softly. "I have a favor to ask?"

One brow rose. "What is it this time?"

Portia moved closer to him. "Miss Regina Waters."

Confusion flickered in his eyes. "I don't know her."

"She's a lovely young lady. Very sweet and gentle."

Wade crossed his arms over his chest. "You mean she's another wallflower, hugging her mother's skirts and drooling for a title, starry eyed at the choices before her."

Portia scowled. "That isn't nice to say of anyone, especially someone so new to Town. She does have a dowry, and she's very pretty. With a little bit of masculine attention, she is sure to shine."

Wade glanced heavenward. "What do you expect me to do with her? Polish her like a bit of silver?"

"Introductions must be made first, and then you should ask

her to dance." Portia beamed again. It wasn't too much to ask of any gentleman, really, but she trusted that Miss Waters dancing with Lord Wade would draw lots of attention from the other guests. The right kind would ensure Miss Waters caught the eye of the right people.

He gave her a suspicious side eye. "How am I to accomplish the introduction when I don't know her or her connections?"

"Oh, that's easy," Portia told him. "She has an acquaintance with Lady Ettington, as do you."

Wade began to shake his head. "Impossible."

"Why?"

"Because I simply cannot do it."

"But why will you not even ask for an introduction?"

"I'm not exactly on the best of terms with the marchioness," he admitted. "Ettington is particularly sensitive about his wife, too, so I have kept a distance."

"But you are spending Christmas with them?"

"A tricky proposition indeed," he mused. "I had planned to keep out of their way as much as possible."

His stance relaxed a little, and she forged on. "I'm not asking you to do anything improper with the marchioness, or Miss Waters, either. Just say hello, and chat for a bit, and ask if she knows who the new face in the crowd is. I'm sure she'd be happy to introduce you if you indicated you have an interest. She'll think you a potential suitor."

Lord Wade met her gaze, his expression unreadable for a moment. "No one would believe that." But he nodded, and she knew she had a chance. "What's in it for me?"

She balked at his question. "Well, it would make me happy, for one."

"Not enough of a reason." He scowled and folded his arms again. "You have other swains here tonight. Beguile one of *them* to do the job you want done."

Floored that he'd refuse so absolutely, Portia cast about for a better inducement. She had really liked Miss Waters from the moment they'd met tonight, but Regina was so shy and her aunt was so overpowering—not just in her perfume, either.

Portia feared Regina might never have any fun. She'd be married off to the very first man who asked for her hand, no matter if he were sixty!

But what could she give Lord Wade that might tempt him to agree? She'd never needed to do more than ask for a favor before. She probably owed for those past favors, too. She smiled suddenly as the perfect form of payment came to mind. "Would you do it for a kiss?"

Wade laughed harshly and shook his head. "Not a chance. The value of that currency has declined sharply since your engagement."

"Oh," she whispered, deflated. She had assumed after their encounter the other day that he'd be as eager as all the other gentlemen who had stolen kisses from her. "Something else, then?"

She had pin money enough on her person to exchange tonight, if need be. It would be extremely awkward to give a gentleman money, though. Lord Wade keeping the proceeds of a wager was one thing. Accepting cold hard coin from a lady was quite another. But he did need money more than anything else. She lifted her reticule, ready to count out what she had.

His eyes narrowed suddenly, and a bitter smile twisted his lips. "Your garter."

She blinked and the bag slipped from her fingers. "I beg your pardon."

Wade came closer, his voice lower. "I'm risking my health approaching Lady Ettington. If I do this, I could very well find myself on the receiving end of the marquess' displeasure again. It is not inconsiderable, let me tell you."

Portia had not known Lord Wade was at odds with the Ettingtons or she would not have pinned her hopes on him. There was no one else, though, she would dare ask. Every other gentleman she trusted appeared to be keeping a distance. However, enlisting Lady Ettington's help was the only way to draw Miss Waters from her dark corner tonight.

She would definitely owe him a boon for his efforts. The

more personal the better. "Very well."

His brows shot up. "Very well what?"

"My garter. I'll show you. Just one, mind you."

He blinked and took a pace back, glancing down. "For how long?"

Portia considered. "The count of five."

"Twenty. Do remember, I could end up with a bloody nose."

She gaped. Lord Wade fainted at the sight of his own blood, unfortunately. "Ten, and not another moment longer."

"Done," he said eagerly.

Portia took a few steps away, and then spun about. She caught up one side of her gown and inched it higher as she thrust one leg forward. She stood in that awkward position, her gown bunched higher than could ever be considered ladylike. "Ten, nine…"

Wade exhaled slowly. "And the rest."

"I beg your pardon."

"I can only see one small part of the garter. All or nothing."

She rolled her eyes and adjusted the gown so he could see all of her knee and lower leg. She stood there, continuing to count down in low tones until she reached the end. Then she released her gown and smiled. "That was even longer than our bargain."

"But worth every moment." Wade sighed. "You're a determined woman, Portia Hayes, but you will have your wish."

Portia clapped her gloved hands, knowing the sound would not travel. "I knew I could count on you to help her."

Lord Wade approached, his eyes lingering on the bottom of her gown. His attention rose slowly until he finally met her gaze. Portia experienced a little thrill at the heated look in his eyes. Many men had looked at her in such a fashion, but for a change, her first instinct was not to back away to safety. She stayed…and couldn't look away herself.

"I'm helping you this one last time," he warned, the tip of his tongue flicking out briefly to wet his lips before he continued. "There are limits to my generosity."

"I know," she promised, studying the fullness of his lips. A pity he wasn't interested in kisses. She suddenly wanted to know whether he was any good at them. Some gentlemen needed practice, some seemed born to sin. "Thank you," she whispered, inching closer to him.

He gestured to the door suddenly with an angry flick of his hand. "You'd better go back, and make sure no one sees you."

"I need to point her out to you," she said, grabbing his arm. "We can go this way and no one will see us. I promise."

He uttered a small protest but stumbled along behind her. Portia was sure of her path. She'd been to a ball in this house before and had used this route to avoid an unsavory suitor in hot pursuit.

They reached a spot where they could peek at most of the ballroom. Portia scanned the faces, and then found Miss Waters. She pointed her out to Wade, and his eyes widened in surprise.

"Please, Wade," she whispered, peeking around a curtain. "The girl is a hopeless case. Look at how she's hiding. She's been that way all night."

"Ah yes, that one." He nodded slowly. "It might look like she's hiding but her uncle is wider than a house and blocks that whole side of the ballroom."

Portia hit his arm with her fan rather hard. "You should have mentioned you knew who I was talking about."

"I've not been introduced but any fresh new face is gossiped about. On first glance I had assumed them country bumpkins, newly arrived to Town. A closer inspection when I walked the perimeter to meet you revealed their fashions are first rate, but they looked ill at ease in them. I concluded that the family obviously had money and an important connection in the *ton* if they are attending this ball. However, it seems they know only a few here so far. It might be their very first night at a London ball. They seem to be gawking at everyone who passes them by."

She clutched his arm. "That's what I had concluded, too.

You're the only one who can help her."

"Only you would ask me to." Lord Wade glanced her way, and then his lids lowered over his eyes. He had not closed them, but he seemed to be inspecting her gown anew. His attention lingered on her breasts for several heartbeats longer than could ever be proper and her heart rate leapt.

Portia's nipples hardened under his scrutiny, too, and she considered closing the gap between them to steal a kiss from him even if he didn't want one. Her cheeks grew warm as he met her eyes again and they stared at each other.

His fingers slid over hers suddenly. His touch was light, and her breath hitched again.

A teasing smile turned up his lips. "Do you really want people to think I'm interested in her?"

"We know the truth," Portia whispered. "You are just being a helpful gentleman."

He looked back into the room. "What if I'm not? What if I found I liked her enough to court her? Is that what you want to happen, too?"

Portia stilled, but studied his expression. He'd not spoken in jest. Portia nibbled on the tip of her glove as she remembered his conversation with Lady Windermere. She experienced uneasiness as she studied the distant family. Miss Waters could only benefit from Wade's introduction, and if more came of it…

She took a deep breath and let it out slowly. It didn't feel right anymore. "Obtain an introduction and ask her to dance. That is all you need to do."

Wade nodded slowly, jaw clenching briefly.

"I have to go back to my mother before she realizes how long I've been gone," Portia murmured, suddenly realizing Wade covered her hand still. She gently extracted herself from his grip. "You won't forget your promise, will you?"

"After that display of bravery from you, not a chance. However, I just need a few minutes to readjust my mind for the mundane act of dancing."

Portia frowned. "Why?"

"Your slender leg is far more enticing than Miss Waters could ever be."

Portia beamed despite the image he painted being scandalous. "That was a sweet thing to say."

Wade grabbed her shoulders roughly, turned her about, and marched her forcefully toward the distant doorway to the library. "Don't tempt me to say what I really think."

Portia slipped inside the room and found it still unoccupied. "I don't see anyone. Quickly now."

Wade caught her arm and drew her toward him suddenly.

They stood in the doorway inches apart, and Portia quivered in his grip. She wet her lips. "Mind your manners around the marchioness, *and* the marquess, too. I wouldn't like you to be hurt."

A tiny smile played on his lips, and he nodded. "By the way, I would have been happy just to have known the color of the garter you wore tonight," he whispered, before he darted around her. He walked backward a few steps, arms spread wide. "The leg was an unexpected treat. I do thank you for the pleasure."

Before she could smack him with her fan again, he was gone, racing for the far doorway.

Portia followed him, chuckling at his audacity and slipping out into the hall. She would boldly stroll back toward the ballroom as fast as was seemly and, since she had few dances tonight, keep an eye on proceedings.

Lord Montrose was coming toward her parents with a full champagne glass in his hand as she rejoined them.

Her parents were engaged in a vigorous debate over the value of keeping pheasants over rabbits as she returned to them unnoticed. Her father was strenuously opposed to rabbit, refusing to eat it, but mother was highly sick of pheasant and threatened never to serve it again. This was the type of scintillating conversation Portia had endured all her life. Was it any wonder she had agreed to marry so quickly?

She couldn't wait to escape her parents. They never agreed on anything. It was no wonder that Lord Montrose never stayed very long when he came to call, either.

Portia scanned the boundaries of the ballroom, looking for Miss Waters.

Once she was found, still hugging the shadows of her aunt, Portia looked for Lord Wade and found him not far away. His aunt was at his side, glass in hand as was often the case. He bent low to speak to her but she pushed him away, as if he'd told a rude joke or scolded her.

Lord Wade's attention flickered to where Miss Waters stood, and he seemed to study the air about her and the guests standing closest to the girl.

Portia discovered then that she was becoming anxious about their meeting. *She* had once been that shy wallflower, terrified of putting a foot wrong. Lord Wade had been the first gentleman to really try to make her feel she deserved to be here. He'd also asked her if she was as virginal as she appeared. Her outraged reply after a long moment of shocked silence had only made his smile widen. He'd told her then that it would be the question every gentleman she met was dying to know, simply because she possessed so large a dowry.

Wade had truly prepared her for the worst of society. She *had* been asked the same question in any number of ways, too, but none so boldly or immediately. Gentlemen—titled, wealthy or desperate fortune hunters—had been attempting to lure her away to dark corners to rob her of her virtue ever since.

If Miss Waters could survive a dance with Lord Wade, and his inevitable bold questions, she could do so with anyone.

Wade, despite her annoyance with him in past years, did have a fine eye for good women, especially those in the first all-important season. Portia wondered briefly what he had said to Lady Ettington to have upset her so thoroughly. Had it been that lady's first season, too?

She would have to ask him another day, because Wade had finally made a move toward speaking with the tiny marchioness, and she couldn't help but notice his bow was very low indeed. She really needed to find out what he'd done, and soon.

Chapter Fifteen

Julian winced. "I am sorry that I offended you the last time we spoke. I had hoped you might have forgotten, or if not, forgiven me."

Lady Ettington's stone-faced stare suggested she had not.

"In my defense, I knew you could not be the least bit right for Lord Louth, although I should not have expressed that sentiment in the manner that I did. Not when Ettington was looking daggers at anyone who admired you for too long. Anyone with eyes and a mind could see how right you were for each other from the start."

She scowled even more. "That is a Banbury tale."

He shook his head. "No. Not at all. Ettington and Louth are friends, and if you had set your cap for Louth, you would have come between them. Trust me, all gentlemen should avoid provoking a territorial fellow like your husband." He widened his hands. "And I see it has all turned out for the best. You are married, and now he may openly threaten anyone who gets too close to his heart's desire."

Her eyes narrowed on him. "You were friends with that atrocious woman, too."

He sighed. "I did try to warn Miss Scaling that her ambitions involving the marquess were bound for naught. Repeatedly, in fact. She wouldn't listen."

"And the pond? You played a role in my dunking."

"Unwittingly, yes." He winced again. "Unfortunately, I was distracted that day and made clumsy. I had meant to tap Miss Scaling's foot to back her up, away from you, and instead I—"

"You tripped me. I fell back into that filthy pond of water and ruined a perfectly lovely day. You both made me look a fool, just as she wanted. I was made sick from the chill I took."

Wade shook his head. He was in the wrong. Utterly. Completely. Not all of his early matchmaking attempts had been subtle or successfully carried out. He glanced around quickly, noticing they were drawing attention. The Duke of Exeter, her husband's uncle, was watching him through narrowed eyes. Thankfully her protective husband hadn't noticed them talking as yet.

Ettington had quickly made his displeasure with him known shortly after the marriage had taken place, but that had been some time ago now. He hoped the man had forgotten he existed. "After the events of that day, I feared there would be worse to come. I only kept the acquaintance, acted as her friend, hoping to learn ahead of time what her plans might have been next. I had not counted on her being more devious than myself."

The marchioness eyed him with suspicion, and then nodded. "You are forgiven."

"Thank you." He smiled quickly in relief. The Marchioness of Ettington had completely won over the *ton* since that long ago day. Now people came to her for help quite often. "About the favor I asked for…"

"You want me to introduce you to a young lady."

"Indeed. Her name is Miss Waters. She is new to Town. I believe you have an acquaintance with her, and her aunt and uncle."

"Mr. and Mrs. Lowell are old acquaintances of mine from the north." Lady Ettington glanced past him, and her brow furrowed. "Oh dear. Regina is hugging the shadows behind her aunt again. No one will notice her there. But tell me, why have *you* noticed her?"

The marchioness was perceptive, which is what had made her a perfect partner for the marquess. "I made a promise to a friend to dance with Miss Waters, but it must be tonight," he quickly explained.

The marchioness looked him up and down, then smiled. "I would be happy to. How would you like to proceed? It would look odd to just march up to her."

He thought so, too. Rushing at her would be unseemly and suggest he was desperate to win her favor. "Perhaps you'd care to take a turn about the room, so our introduction does not look so obvious," he said quickly.

"You've done this before," Lady Ettington murmured as she slipped her arm through his. "How many times have you danced with a wallflower to make them seen?"

He shrugged. "Once or twice."

"Oh, more than that I would wager." She laughed softly. "Since our last conversation all those years ago, I've made a point of paying attention to where you are—for safety's sake, you understand."

He nodded, but wondered how long she'd hold his prior behavior against him. "I'll never harm you again, I swear. I never meant to in the first place."

She glanced up at him, her eyes boring into his. "You dance with a lot of wallflowers but never end up married to any. Why?"

He shrugged again. "What can I say, their taste in men is appalling."

The marchioness faced forward, nodding to acquaintances as they passed. "The ones I noticed you spending the most time with ended up marrying for love."

"Foolishness," he murmured, hoping the lady would not question him so closely about his business. He was usually very quick to spot the signs of an ardent infatuation in his friends and acquaintances. He might have even nudged more than a few along to a satisfying conclusion. It was a family habit. Aunt Hesper had it down to a fine art.

"I knew Miss Waters' parents very well. They were

neighbors to my childhood home but both died last year in a carriage accident. Regina is of age, but remains under the protection of her maternal aunt and uncle. They are good people, but not familiar with the ways of the *ton*. She has a dowry, of course, enough to interest a great many gentlemen who might court her. She is staying with us as our guest for the month."

"Having the Marchioness of Ettington's stamp of approval will ensure she is married quickly," he murmured.

"Speed is not important so long as she is made happy," Lady Ettington replied. "I trust you will keep that in mind and not lead her to imagine you have intentions when you do not."

"I would never do so," he promised. He glanced down at the lady on his arm and smiled. "You are very wise."

An impish smile crossed her lips, and then she laughed. "I know."

Julian laughed along with her and looked ahead with newfound excitement for the evening. If he had just reclaimed the marchioness' approval, he may find that her help might see *him* happily matched one day, too. At the moment, he was more interested in this new matchmaking scheme. He had no idea who would do for Miss Waters but by the end of the night, he might.

They finally reached the location of his quarry, and the aunt was very quick to catch the marchioness' attention and begin talking. The marchioness was very gracious and kind to a woman clearly out of her depth in such company.

Lady Ettington patted the woman's arm and smiled. "My dear, I trust you are enjoying the party."

"Indeed we are," the uncle enthused, looking around with wide-eyed wonder.

Wade kept his place, striving to seem bored but noticing everything. The debutante blushed at the first mention of her name in the conversation but spoke well for herself. When finally Lady Ettington introduced him to them, describing him as a fine gentleman and a close friend, Regina Waters reddened quite a bit.

He bowed over Miss Waters' hand to hide his amusement. Virgins were so easy to spot in a room with more experienced and bored women for comparison.

When he asked her to dance, Miss Waters looked to her aunt for permission.

"He is a friend of the marchioness, so of course we are delighted," the aunt said boldly, winking to the marchioness.

Julian shifted uncomfortably. He was only trying to dance with the girl, not commit to marry her. She had a good-sized dowry, and if that had been all important, he might have done his best to sweep her off her feet there and then.

They said their goodbyes, promising to return for the dance before supper, but after a few steps on his arm, Lady Ettington began to chuckle.

Julian glanced at her inquiringly. "Did I miss the joke, my lady?"

Lady Ettington's grin grew positively evil. "Oh, forgiving you was well worth witnessing your terror just now."

He sighed, which made her laugh all the harder.

As they continued their saunter about the room, pausing to speak with mutual acquaintances, the marchioness slowly settled. "It's not like you've never known that one day you'd marry. I swear all men think it's so far in their future it doesn't concern them at all. However, when faced with a lady they find interesting, they get tongue-tied. You used to talk more."

"Did I?" He glanced back over his shoulder, noticing Miss Waters watching him. He nodded and looked away. She was pretty but...she did not stir his blood. Not the way Portia always had. Perhaps a longer acquaintance would improve his attraction to her. "Perhaps next time."

When they reached the Marquess of Ettington, Julian's stomach fluttered momentarily with anxiety. The marquess' expression was utterly frosty tonight. Ettington was not a man to offend, and everyone knew that. However, his wife rushed to her husband and pressed a quick kiss to his cheek. "Be nice. We are friends again."

"If you say so," Ettington murmured, and the frost melted

away as he smiled down on his wife. "What have you been up to?"

"A bit of this, a bit of that. I'll tell you all about it later," she promised, patting Ettington's expensively tailored chest.

Julian bowed deeply and excused himself just as quickly. He sauntered toward the nearest servant holding champagne and took up a glass from the tray. He found a quiet spot to wait his turn dancing with the wallflower and watched the ball progress in silence.

Although Portia Hayes took to the floor with a distinguished rogue, Julian studied Miss Waters instead. She was pretty, despite her blushes. She was introduced to another gentleman then, and added another dance partner to her card.

Her eyes sought his suddenly, and Julian nodded, encouraging. Her shoulders rose and fell, and she turned away to bid farewell to her new acquaintance wearing another blush.

He chuckled to himself. Virginal girls were a continual source of amusement. He only hoped that when he finally reached the dance floor with Miss Waters, that the poor girl didn't faint from overstimulation of being seen.

There was something of a stir behind him, and he glanced over his shoulder briefly.

The Duke of Exeter had moved.

Julian chuckled again and paid attention to those guests standing around those nearest to himself. The ladies, young and old, had their eyes practically glued to the Duke of Exeter's location. But it wasn't due just to the title his grace possessed or his bottomless pockets; it was the ageless quality of his face and form that kept the ladies panting after him. When he stood close to his nephew, the Marquess of Ettington, Julian swore some of them swooned.

They were probably hoping they'd be lucky enough to be asked to dance by him. Julian didn't like their chances. The duke was particular and had never married, or seemed likely to do so at his age. He was over fifty years now, but still appeared a man in his prime. Some men never bothered with marriage, although the duke was devoted to his family.

A nervous twitter swept through the crowd and a presence stopped at Julian's side unexpectedly.

"Good evening, Lord Wade," the Duke of Exeter murmured.

Julian turned to face the duke and bowed deeply. "Your grace."

The duke gestured him up with an impatient sigh. "I trust you are having a pleasant evening."

"Indeed." He saw Portia watching him from across the room and smiled, remembering the events of earlier in the night. Unfortunately, everyone else was watching him now, too. His grace rarely prowled the ballrooms unattended. "And you?"

"Fair."

Julian winced. Their hostess would be crushed by that faint praise.

"I trust you are still coming to visit at Christmas," the duke asked.

"Yes, indeed, and very much looking forward to the holiday," Julian promised. "My aunt is, too."

"Yes, she mentioned that last time we spoke." The duke sighed again and glanced over those present. Some noticed the duke's attention on them and fans snapped out as the ladies offered him every encouragement to come closer. Some even waved and primped their hair. The duke, however, shook his head and turned back to Julian. "Does this all seem as tedious to you as it always has to me?"

"Sometimes," Julian promised as a lady performed a perfectly artless swoon. She fell in a tidy heap on the parquetry, waiting for the duke to rush across the room and swoop her up. He did not, of course. "I obviously don't provoke the same level of universal adoration as you."

His grace barked out a laugh. "You are probably wondering why I really stopped to talk to you."

"I'm all ears," he promised.

The duke's expression grew pensive. "I'm afraid I have a favor to ask of you."

Doing favors for friends was not unusual for him, but he gave the duke his full attention now, because it was the first time Exeter had ever approached him for one. He sensed extreme discomfort in the duke—and that intrigued him. How often did a duke seem reluctant to demand anything of anyone and expect it done without question? "How may I be of assistance?"

The duke glanced around swiftly, his expression souring. "Not here or tonight. Would you ride with me in Hyde Park tomorrow morning?"

The duke rode every morning, but Julian did not. A year ago, he would have leapt at the chance, but he didn't own a horse anymore to take out. He winced as he realized he must refuse. "I'm afraid tomorrow morning is not convenient. Perhaps we could talk at White's later in the day."

"I have an engagement tomorrow afternoon that cannot be put off." The duke frowned. "Would it be possible to drag you away from all this merriment tonight for our discussion?"

"I only have a dance with Miss Waters coming up, second to last before supper," he told the duke.

"After supper then." He nodded, turning to go. "I'll be in Northam's study."

Julian was concerned enough about the duke's haste to detain him. "Is something the matter, your grace?"

The duke turned back, his expression troubled. "No. Yes. Perhaps. We'll talk later, and then you will understand."

"Of course. Until later then," Julian promised.

The duke pivoted and strode off toward his nephew, leaving a number of ladies sighing in his wake. Julian was clueless about what the duke could want with him, but he couldn't wait to find out. He rubbed his hands together. It must be something very delicate or very scandalous.

Chapter Sixteen

———◆———

Portia ran her fingers though the silk ribbons, admiring the array of colors a lady could choose from. She rested her fingers on a particularly lovely shade of soft blue, and Lavinia quickly snatched it up. "I like that one," Lavinia cried.

"We have remarkably similar taste," Portia murmured but hid a smile. She'd been leading her sister around by the nose in this shop for the last half hour, and was well pleased with the additions she'd made to her sisters wardrobe without the girl realizing she was being manipulated. However devious Portia's action might seem, they would both benefit—but mostly it was to keep Portia's possessions safe.

A quick glance across the room confirmed that their mother was well occupied, speaking to the proprietor. Lavinia was undoubtedly being spoiled but it was for a good cause. She deserved to be noticed. "Is that enough to wear with the new gowns Mother ordered made for you?"

"I think so. Do you think I need more?"

Portia considered her sister again. "Perhaps another length of white ribbon. White goes so well with everything and always looks lovely in your hair."

Lavinia moved back to the selection of white ribbon and selected a quarter-inch strip to bind around her head then showed her.

"A good choice," Portia promised. "We have plenty of the wider length at home."

Lavinia glanced at Portia's empty hands. "What are you getting today?"

"I need nothing, now my sister has her own ribbons." She put her hands on Lavinia's shoulders and squeezed. "I can always borrow from you if I need anything."

Lavinia held her selections tight against her chest, protecting them. "Oh, don't."

"I'm only teasing." Portia laughed softly and they returned to their mother.

The proprietor of Cabot's Haberdashery greeted her with a smile. "Miss Hayes, what a pleasure to see you visiting the emporium again."

"Thank you, Mr. Cabot."

"May I say congratulations on the occasion of your future marriage?"

Portia nodded. It wasn't the first time a business they patronized had made mention of her upcoming wedding that morning. "Thank you."

"If there is anything you might need, please be sure to send word. Day or night, we are at your service, and happily so." He smiled quickly, and then looked past her, frowning. He nodded and looked toward their mother. "Is there anything else you require at the moment, madam? I must see to another customer's needs."

"No indeed. We are happy to browse a little longer before completing our purchases."

"Thank you." He bowed. "Excuse me."

Portia glanced over her shoulder to watch him go—and saw Lord Wade enter the shop.

She turned fully to face him, watching him quickly conduct his transaction. He purchased something quite small but tucked it into his pocket before she could determine what it might have been.

Business done, he made his way to her side. "Good morning, ladies," he said with an indulgent smile. "You are all out bright and early today. Did you enjoy your evening last night?"

"Indeed we did, but I thought there were far too few chairs to sit upon."

"Ah, it is always so at the Northam events." He leaned close to her mother. "They do it so everyone must mingle rather than perch."

"Oh, that is so devious," Mother cried, but then she turned to Portia. "You must remember that trick, darling, for when you host your first ball as a duchess."

Portia noticed that Lord Wade's smile slipped a little before he spoke again. "I'm certain her dance floor will be a crush of bodies no matter how many chairs she puts out."

"I quite agree," Mother murmured, and then turned away to complete her purchases for Lavinia.

Portia was happy to be left with Wade to confide her fears. "I hoped that might be the case, but now I'm terrified I'll be abandoned."

Lord Wade's shook his head quickly. "No one will snub a duchess, but you might find yourself with an entirely new set of acquaintances."

She caught his eye, admiring his countenance. He was one of the few gentlemen she knew who seemed the same morning and night. She'd never heard him complain of being up too early or abed too late. "Did you enjoy the dance you shared with Miss Waters?"

"I did," Lord Wade promised. "She has a lively disposition."

"And Lady Ettington was happy to introduce you?"

"Indeed." He shifted on his feet. "The lady quite enjoyed my discomfort, too."

Portia gaped. "Was she mean to you?"

"No, nothing like that. She was very gracious and has forgiven me."

Portia settled quickly. "What other discomfort could you mean then?"

"I think she has it in her head that I lied about my reason

for asking for the introduction. I did tell her about the promise I made to you, without saying it was for you, but I'm afraid she imagines I'm truly interested in Regina Waters."

"But you're not," Portia replied quickly. "You were doing me a favor."

"That is not how she saw it, or probably anyone else. Miss Waters has a tidy little dowry and the marchioness' favor. Despite my initial reluctance to approach her, I did find Miss Waters very pleasing to dance with, and believe that the marchioness' drawing room will be filled with the cream of the crop today."

"I am so pleased for Miss Waters," Portia said, setting her hand on his arm. "Every lady should be overrun with choice when it comes to choosing a husband. Do you feel she favors any particular gentlemen yet?"

Wade squinted at her hand. "I've no notion, but I hope to learn soon when I pay my call upon her, and in the coming weeks."

"Good. Do let me know what you discover," she whispered, drawing her hand back. "Perhaps we could help make a match for her."

Lord Wade blinked. "I think Miss Waters has all the help she could ever need in the Marchioness of Ettington."

"True, but you never know. She might choose someone quite unexpected."

Wade shook his head. "If only. However, I suspect she will marry very sensibly in the end. Most women have already formed an opinion of the gentleman they want before their season begins."

"That is not true?"

"Isn't it?" He faced her. "Wasn't a title all your heart truly wanted in a husband, then? I would have thought love or even a little affection ranked higher on your list than the cold alliance you've chosen. Personally, I'd choose love over money and power any day."

Portia stared at him in astonishment. "You've never said that before to me. Do you truly believe it?"

"I do." He looked away. "It is possible to be happy when you have very little to live on."

An odd tension filled Portia. She'd no idea Wade held such strong opinions on marriage, or love for that matter. He never really spoke about his own plans for the future. She'd just assumed he'd be like all the rest. He *needed* money, but he claimed he wouldn't marry to get it.

Mother returned at that moment, and Lord Wade was pressed to join them in a way he couldn't seem to refuse. Mother claimed his arm as they left the shop together, and she dragged him along on their excursion.

They went next to a bookshop, and Lavinia disappeared between the first set of bookshelves with a happy squeal.

Lord Wade laughed. "When your family sits down to choose what sort of husband would do for Lavinia, make sure an interest in books is high on the list of essentials."

"There is no list but I'm sure Lavinia will make sure her husband reads."

Lord Wade moved to a shelf and tugged down a slim volume. He inspected it, read the introduction…and then she noticed his fingers drift over the pencil-marked corner, where the price was written down. Wade put the book back on the shelf with obvious reluctance and moved farther along the row.

He glanced her way as she followed him.

"What were you and the duke talking about last night?"

"Christmas at his estate."

Portia picked up a book at random, feeling upset that she couldn't be there with him. She didn't want a new set of acquaintances when she married, just because she'd married Montrose. She liked the friends she already had, including Wade. "Did you return the painting?"

"No."

"Why not?"

He turned and a look of annoyance appeared on his face. "It's complicated."

"Oh, and do you think I'm too dim-witted to understand?"

"Oh, I know you're as smart as they come, probably smarter

than I." He nodded. "You're in the middle of this, and you should hear it all from me anyway. I trust you not to repeat it."

"I would never betray you," she promised.

He beckoned her farther down the row of books, away from where her mother and sister were browsing the shelves.

"The item I took, the carved stick, it belonged to Montrose, though I didn't know it until the moment I handed it over. Once I found out, I refused Windermere's money and managed to make a bargain to get it back. Then I tossed it into the flames. Windermere must have fished it out again after I left and completed the wager the next night."

"Windermere betrayed you," Portia said slowly, and then grew furious on Lord Wade's behalf. "What does Windermere have to do with the painting you wanted?"

"The portrait was done of his wife, long before they were ever married. Lady Windermere was very keen to get it back, and we struck a bargain…or so I'd thought. I've no idea why your uncle had it, and I will deliver it, eventually."

"You should make the Windermeres squirm first," she announced. "Montrose came to my father, and to me, too, and demanded to know if anyone had been to Uncle Oliver's house."

"What did you say?"

"Nothing about you, of course," she promised. She had not liked the way Montrose had questioned her about the house or its contents. "It was an innocent mistake we made."

"Truly, it was." He pulled a face. "He's not likely to forget it, though. I know I should have told you all the particulars sooner but, well…because you are going to marry the duke, I thought it best to keep you in the dark. It is easier to deny something when you've no knowledge of it."

"I had figured it out before I saw you at the King dinner." Portia shivered. "Why would he have had such a thing made?"

"It is not unusual for lovers to use such implements to heighten their pleasure. For Montrose, though, it's… No, never mind that now."

Indeed, Portia did not want to know about Montrose right

now. She was already doubting her decision to marry him every other day, it seemed. They turned into another aisle where Lavinia was feverishly searching the shelves, and the subject was dropped until they were more or less alone again.

"There is another reason why I've held on to the painting in my possession," he admitted.

She looked at him quickly. Portia had thought that one day she, too, might like to pose upon a long chaise and wear almost nothing. "Admiration?"

"Montrose has been to your house and may have seen it. If he recognized Lady Windermere in the painting, he could want to use it to extract revenge. If I return it to you, he'll own it eventually. I might be angry with Windermere, but I won't be a party to Lady Windermere's humiliation if I can help it."

She smiled at Lord Wade, admiring his resolve. "Even though they have betrayed you, you would still protect them?"

He nodded. "Her mostly."

Portia turned away, unable to stop grinning. There was much to like about Lord Wade, now she had finally put her prejudices aside about the reasons he was always around. "Did you find another wager to complete in the betting book at White's Club?"

"No, and I won't need to look for one, either," he admitted.

She looked at him in surprise. "Why not?"

"I've finally had a stroke of good fortune, and will be coming into some money soon."

"Don't tell me you sold the lease on the Hanover Square townhouse at last."

"No," he promised, his expression quizzical.

She winced. "Was I not supposed to know about that?"

"I assumed you didn't."

"People talk."

He shrugged. "I have taken on a commission that should stop further gossip on the subject of my situation in the near future, thankfully."

The idea that he'd leave London tore at her heart. "You'll break your aunt's heart when you leave her behind like your brother has."

And mine, too.

He laughed softly. "I'm not for the army, if that's what you fear."

She gasped in relief and grinned at him. "Then what?"

"It needs to stay a bit of a secret, actually," he warned. "I've been asked to help a fellow find a wife."

"What?"

"I'll be paid to be a matchmaker," he said with a laugh. "Believe me, I know how ludicrous it sounds, but he trusts my judgment for some reason, and I think I can help him."

"And he'll pay you what you deserve?"

He nodded. "And then some."

Portia clutched his arm. "You've a good eye for people. When do you start?"

"I already have."

Portia was so pleased for him that she couldn't stop grinning. "Will I see you tonight at the Marks dinner?"

"No, unfortunately. I have a dinner at Lord Sullivan's residence tonight."

Portia narrowed her eyes on him. "You mean you'll get drunk with your friend again."

"It was one time," he protested, sliding another book back onto the shelf. "I haven't seen Sullivan for years."

"I thought you were friends."

"Old friends." Lord Wade moved to the next aisle and picked up another volume. "When he married, we parted company."

"Did you not like his wife?"

"No, I liked her very much." An odd look came to his eye, and then he shrugged. "Too much, perhaps, at the time…and they were in love so."

And Lord Sullivan was a higher-ranked earl.

Lord Wade turned away suddenly, and Portia followed him about the room. He certainly had an eclectic taste in books but she noticed he purchased none in the end. Her heart ached for him when she thought about his situation, and what this secret arrangement to make a match could mean for his future. He was quite clever and smart. He'd missed out on marrying once already, and that pained her, too. Yet she had no idea how he'd come to have so little money. He had never seemed an extravagant man. He was too sensible in his habits for that.

"What were your parents like?"

He seemed very surprised by her question. "My mother died when I was quite young. I've little recollection of her at all."

"And your father?"

A look of disgust crossed his face. "A wastrel. He gambled, made foolish wagers, purchased expensive things we hardly needed. He was hell bent on keeping up the appearance of having it all even when the coffers were full of dust."

There was a tight edge to his words—and Portia finally understood Lord Wade. He was embarrassed and disgusted by what had gone on before he'd taken the title.

She put her hand on his arm again and kept it there. "When did your aunt come to live with you?"

"After my father died, we decided that one household would suit us better. She'd been widowed for a while and was struggling with being alone in an empty house. She longed for family to fuss over. She mothered my younger brother a bit, managed the household, and all I had to do was pay the bills. I've no regrets about that decision."

"I'm sure you've done your best. She is a wonderful aunt to have."

"She drinks too much when she's lonely," Wade complained. "Which seems to be a lot lately, as you might have noticed."

"I didn't notice," Portia lied, and immediately saw that Wade did not really believe her. "I like her a great deal."

"She likes you, too," Wade promised.

She *had*, but Portia kept that thought to herself. Wade would only deny there was anything wrong between them. It all came back to her decision to marry the Duke of Montrose. The changes in her popularity had been subtle at first, but the closer the wedding date became, the wider the chasm between the life she had and the one she was headed for. People were already expecting her to behave in a different fashion.

Well, she was having none of that.

Portia turned around and marched back to the shelf where Lord Wade had admired that first book. She carried it to the shop counter and paid for it out of her pin money.

When she turned around, Wade was standing a few feet away, his expression slightly alarmed.

She held out the book to him. "Would you carry this for me?"

He nodded slowly, and by then her mother and Lavinia were ready to move along to the next shop on their trip.

Once outside, Lord Wade turned the book over in his hands. "I thought you did not read French very well."

She affected surprise. "Is it in French?"

He scowled. "You know it is."

"Well, I do read French a little," she murmured as she raised her parasol over her head. "Perhaps you could read it for me first and decide if I have any chance of understanding it."

His eyes narrowed. "Portia," he growled. "You should not do such things. Montrose would not approve."

All the more reason to have done the unexpected. "I trust you will provide a full report by the end of the month at the very latest, Lord Wade," she said to end the discussion.

She would enjoy hearing Lord Wade's account of the book, but could care less if she saw it returned to her in the end. It was a gift for her friend because he could not afford to purchase it himself yet, and because she wanted to spoil him.

Portia bit her lip as he stared at her too long, obviously debating whether to accept the present or not. He appeared about to protest, but when she linked her arm through his and pulled him along after her mother, he fell blessedly silent.

They passed the rest of the morning in each other's company, looking on as Mother and Lavinia depleted the shops of their goods. But it felt like something had changed between them. Something significant. Something she knew she had to keep to herself for a while.

Chapter Seventeen

An empty house was a sorry view, but not so the one in Soho Square. Julian let himself into Portia's late uncle's home in the early Sunday afternoon and breathed a sigh of relief that he had passed no one he knew coming here. And then sneezed because of the dust his arrival had stirred. He listened carefully to decide if he was alone or not before he took another step.

Convinced there was silence above his head, he weaved his way through boxes and possessions littering the servants' quarters, and then started up the staircase to reach the front hall. This area was a little clearer of debris, but he kept well away from the windows in case someone happened to look in when he looked out.

He always worried he'd be seen here, coming or going. He did not want to be mistaken for a thief or for word to reach Lord Montrose now. No one would understand how difficult it was for him to stay away from Portia Hayes, and this house. She was usually here on Sundays, after services, and he planned to wait and hope to see her again.

He moved through the cluttered first floor, glancing left and right to see what had been changed or newly uncovered. He would be very sorry when he no longer had an excuse to come here. Portia's marriage to Montrose put an end date on their friendship, as well as these secret adventures.

He squeezed round some old tea chests stacked in the hall, wondering briefly what was inside, before he swept up the grand old staircase to the floor above. Sunlight pierced the gloom from a high window, bathing the path ahead in violet light. He turned and looked up, admiring the colors as he always did.

In many ways, he preferred this house to his own. It was a sound old building, full of nooks and crannies he longed to have leisure to explore.

He moved toward old Oliver's bedchamber and stopped at the doorway. The room was big, but not as cluttered as all the rest. Full of heavy mahogany pieces, he'd coveted this room for himself since the first day he'd come here. It would make a fine chamber for the eventual master of the house.

At least that would not be Montrose. He'd never lower himself to spend one night in this humble abode with Portia.

There was an adjoining chamber, a mirror image of this one. Oliver Quigley had never married but the state of the adjoining chamber made it appear so to Julian. It seemed lived in, like a woman's domain, though Portia had never mentioned the house's history beyond Oliver owning it.

Perhaps it had been in the Quigley family for several generations.

Wade clearly heard the front door open and shut beneath him, and he rushed out to the rail. He glanced down, expecting Portia and her maid—but saw men, instead.

When they instantly began to mount the stairs, he fled back into the room adjoining Oliver's because there was not enough time to reach the little room with the key this time, and then quietly rolled underneath the old bed, stirring up a cloud of dust.

He lay flat on his stomach, peeking out under the comforter, as whomever it was entered the adjoining bedchamber.

There was a brief moment of silence, before, "Where the hell has it gone?"

Montrose.

"I've no idea, your grace," Mr. Hayes apologized. "Perhaps my wife has removed it."

"Removed it to where?"

"I can ask her," Mr. Hayes promised quickly.

"Do that," Montrose bit out. "I'm late. Send word when you find the painting. I'll come fetch it personally."

So Montrose *had* noticed the painting on his last visit, and obviously recognized Esme in it. He'd clearly had plans to use it, too.

Julian hated when he was proved right by very bad people.

Heavy footsteps raced away, pounding down the staircase, moving at a fast clip.

One set only, though.

Though his eyes watered and his nose tickled from the dust, Julian remained where he was until the front door opened and shut. Hearing nothing but silence, Julian rolled out from under the bed as silently as he could to investigate if Hayes had departed, too.

By now, Julian knew most of the spots that creaked, and he moved almost silently to the door.

He heard a noise in the adjoining room and quickly hid behind the nearest door and waited

After a time, Julian risked peeking out of the room again.

Mr. Hayes stood in the hall, looking into Uncle Oliver's room. Portia's father scratched his head. "I'm not going to miss this wretched place, but that painting I will. Damn woman. I hope to God she didn't burn it. Montrose will throw a fit if she has."

Julian smirked, very glad Montrose would never put his hands on Lady Windermere in oil. There was no telling what he might have done with it. It was safe for now, but Julian would have to let Lady Windermere know Montrose was after it as well.

Mr. Hayes poked around the upper floor a bit longer, completely unaware of Julian's watchful presence, and then he departed, too.

Julian considered what to do. It was not imperative that he

speak to Portia today. There had been nothing in particular he wanted to say to her that could not wait another day. He should, by rights, deliver Lady Windermere's portrait back to her. He'd no desire to remain in the middle of the growing feud between Windermere and Montrose.

He dusted himself off and left via the rear door as usual and headed home to collect the wrapped portrait.

Windermere did not live all that far away from him, but he hailed a hack so he might pass through the streets unnoticed. He had the carriage stop at their door and sent a man up to see if Lady Windermere would receive him.

As he waited in another unremarkable hack, he spotted the Duke of Montrose's crest on a carriage passing him by. Julian turned his face away to hide his identity, and then saw the man returning to his carriage. Assured she was at home and available, Julian exited the carriage with his package and rushed inside.

Lady Windermere had aged very little since the portrait must have been painted. There was a brightness to her eyes still and suppleness to her figure that few women kept so late in life. Lady Windermere eyed him warily, and then her attention dropped to his hands. "Have you finally brought it?"

"I have," he promised. "I never break my word."

"It's one of your most endearing qualities," Lady Windermere murmured approvingly.

He took it to her—but startled when a loud knock sounded behind him.

The lady sagged in apparent relief as she quickly glanced at the painting and then gestured behind her. "Good, put it behind that door over there. Quickly, and then come and sit down next to me and do not contradict me."

Confused by her demand, Julian did as asked.

And not a moment too soon. There was a tap at the door, and her husband joined them, followed by Lord Montrose.

The duke scowled when he noticed Julian sitting in the room.

Julian greeted Lord Windermere with a cool nod. "Good

morning, my lord,"

His eyes narrowed. "Is it morning still?"

"I would say so," Julian confirmed.

Lord Windermere appeared unusually harried. He looked between Lord Montrose and Julian with a question in his eyes.

"We are acquainted," Lord Montrose informed him in repressive tones.

"School," Julian apologized.

"Ah, I see." Windermere gestured for the duke to take a chair.

Lady Windermere smiled. "Would you care for tea, your grace?"

"No, thank you," Montrose said, declining.

Lady Windermere called for tea anyway and, while she waited, began to discuss the weather. Julian added an opinion when required but spent his time watching Montrose's face grow steadily darker.

When the tea arrived, she poured for herself and for Julian, but ignored her husband.

When she offered cake to everyone but him too, Montrose glared. "This is not a social call. I was led to believe we were to talk. Alone. It is a business matter, after all."

"Oh, there's no need for that sort of talk now, your grace."

"There is every reason. Do not misunderstand the situation, or your choices," Montrose warned. "They are quite limited."

Lady Windermere smiled prettily at Montrose. "Oh, I am afraid you will find the situation has resolved itself without your assistance, your grace. There will be no scandal or shame involved here."

Montrose spared Julian a brief glance. "I do not agree. You would be wise not to doubt me on this matter."

"Agree or not, we really do have no business left to discuss." The countess blew to cool her tea and took a dainty sip. Julian could see the smirk on her face and knew she was definitely enjoying herself.

Had Montrose threatened the Windermeres, too? He seemed to be making a habit of upsetting quite a few.

Montrose glanced in Julian's direction again, and Julian schooled his features to show little understanding when their eyes met before leaning forward a little. "What business could you possibly have with this beautiful lady?"

Montrose's jaw clenched, and his eyes narrowed. He shook his head and stood abruptly. "None that concerns someone like you."

He strode out of the room...and Lord Windermere collapsed. "We are ruined."

"Nonsense. We are saved, no thanks to you."

The pair exchanged a long glance, and then Lady Windermere turned his way. "Lord Wade, would you mind setting my husband at ease that the situation is as promised?"

"Only too happy to," Julian murmured as he quickly retrieved the painting.

He uncovered it and showed the earl.

The earl pressed his hand over his heart. "My darling. You look just the same!"

Lady Windermere giggled. "I only wish." She schooled her features, appearing suddenly cross as she looked at her husband. "You can go."

"But Esme..."

"You lied to me, and Lord Wade too. You never had any intention of keeping that promise," she argued.

"I did," Windermere protested. "Yes, I fished it out of the flames and cleaned it off. It was only a little singed at the business end. I had planned to keep it as a private amusement. Then I saw him strut into Wilmot's dining room like he owned the place, heard him belittle Lady Sanderson's hospitality at her last ball, and other hostesses too. Your friends. Even Lady Birch was criticized. I sent a servant to fetch it by the time the dinner was half over."

Julian nodded. "Sounds like he hasn't changed."

Lord Windermere crossed to sit beside his wife. "Montrose claimed to have the painting in his possession. Bastard was positively smug that I'd have to give in to his demands and exchange it for the land he wanted. Otherwise he was going to auction you off to the highest bidder."

"As charming as ever," Julian murmured in disgust.

"However did you get it?"

"I've always been able to rely on my friends for assistance." She gestured to Julian. "You owe Lord Wade an apology for breaking our arrangement. At least *he* kept his word."

Windermere stood. "I'm sorry."

"You owe me, Windermere," Julian warned. "I will come back to claim a favor from one day soon."

"Anything to have that painting hanging over my bed tonight."

Lady Windermere kissed her husband's cheek. "We'll nail it to the wall, too, just in case you start to wander about again."

"Probably a good idea."

Lord Windermere kissed her, and Julian turned away to prop the painting safely against a chair. When he turned back, the couple were still kissing. Although he cleared his throat a few times, Lady Windermere and her husband were too swept up in their passions to notice they still had company.

Julian backed from the room and let the door shut quietly behind him. The pair were worse than newlyweds. He hoped that never changed.

"I wouldn't go in there," he warned the butler as he arrived with Julian's hat.

"I wasn't planning to, my lord. Not till called in." The young man grinned. "Lord Montrose requests a word with you, my lord. He's waiting outside."

Julian glanced out the window and saw the duke's carriage drawn up before the house. He set his hat on his head at a jaunty angle and took his own sweet time readying himself to leave. The bastard was probably stewing in his own juices by now. He expected at least threats, probably worse. Julian did not care to be beaten to a pulp for helping a friend, but he had no choice. He was not a coward.

When suitably prepared, he descended to the street and stopped before the carriage. "What do you want, Montrose?"

A groom opened the door to Julian. "His grace wishes a

private conversation."

"Does he now?"

He peered into the dark interior and stepped closer, keeping an eye on the duke's servants in case they moved in around him. "I cannot imagine what you could have to say."

"You know what happens when people cross me."

"Well, you *used* to run to your three friends and set them to beat me while you watched. You always hated to get your hands dirty. Two of them are dead, and the other is probably drunk in a gutter somewhere. What will you do now? Glower at me some more?"

Montrose curled his fingers into a fist. "You should not have interfered with my business with Windermere."

"I have no idea what game you're playing, but my *friendship* with the Windermeres has nothing at all to do with you. In fact, I haven't a clue what your business is with them, and little do I care to know. If I got in your way, it was entirely by chance...or was it providence for the ill you do to others?"

Montrose's expression darkened. "I'll enjoy ruining you, Wade. Oh wait, I can't do that. You already have pockets to let."

He had already lost Portia, not that Montrose would imagine he had any chance with her. He'd been labeled a fortune hunter almost from the moment he'd met Portia's father.

"Enjoy your day, too, your grace," Julian muttered as insultingly as possible, and then turned his back on the angry man.

Chapter Eighteen

Lord Wade was dancing with Miss Waters again, and to Portia's keen eye, he looked to be enjoying himself, too. She felt a pang of envy that she wasn't enjoying herself just as much. Wade was smiling and laughing and obviously getting along famously with the pretty debutante.

Portia glanced sideways at her betrothed, who had finally put in a late appearance, and heaved a sigh. Montrose had promised to meet them here hours ago, and she'd left room on her card to dance with him earlier in the night. Because she had left space, and he'd arrived late, Portia had missed several opportunities to dance with her friends.

She stood beside Montrose now and desperately wished to be anywhere else.

Portia grew very still. If she felt this way now, what hope did she have for a happy marriage? He kept secrets from her, and she did from him, too. That did not bode well at all.

She cleared her throat. "Where were you earlier tonight?"

Montrose glanced down at her briefly. "With friends."

Montrose almost always answered her questions with breathtakingly clipped responses. She had at first assumed he disliked talking about himself, but she now suspected that his brevity was something else entirely, although she hoped to be mistaken. "Doing what?"

"Talking. You wouldn't be interested in the topics we covered."

"I could have been," she said under her breath. "Your grace, I have been patient but if I am to be your duchess, I must know who you trust. How can I plan dinners if I do not know who I may invite?"

"I seldom entertain, and never in London."

Portia blinked. "Are you telling me that out of all of London's residents, you have not one friend here?"

"My interests lie outside the metropolis. I hardly ever come here if I can help it."

Portia did not like how that sounded. She'd been looking forward to spending time here during the season, and she had assumed her husband would, too. Apparently a great many things had been assumed and were not to be.

"I should like to take a turn about the room, your grace."

"Of course." Lord Montrose held out his arm and they moved off at a stately pace.

"Will we stay in London long after we are married?"

"I see no reason to."

"And when will we return next season?"

"I have no need to return to the capital next year. I usually handle matters of parliament by mail or by proxy."

Portia licked her lips and glanced around at the happy, smiling faces. Those both dear and unfamiliar to her had no idea of her inner turmoil. She kept her voice low, so their conversation did not travel to other ears. "I have a sister who I am very close to. It was my hope to use my influence as your duchess to help Lavinia make a suitable match."

He sighed deeply. "You should not let others presume on your generosity."

"My family will do nothing of the sort," she promised him. She loved her sister, even if she wanted to strangle her occasionally. That was the way of sisters everywhere.

They walked on in silence a few more steps, and Portia chafed at the slow pace and Montrose's lack of communication. They were getting nowhere, and the wedding day was fast approaching. Given all she had learned of Montrose, and the few confidences he'd shared, she was just as quickly coming to realize there was little to recommend him but his title and wealth. "Tell me of Sherringford."

"I've told you before."

He had. She knew the acreage of the Sherringford Estate, the size of the house, number of rooms and windows, he might even have grumbled about taxes once. But it was bare facts without any feeling. She could not imagine living there. "Tell me what you love about your home."

"My ancestors built the place," he told her.

Again, bare facts and no substance. She tried once more. "But that is not why you love it."

"It is mine," he said shortly. They were at the end of the room, distant from her parents but not far from Lord Wade, she saw. "It is the one place I feel at ease."

"Well, that is good to know," she said, smiling when Lord Wade glanced her way. She looked up at Montrose. "Do you have any particular room that you spend the most time in?"

He looked at her sideways, a question in his eyes. "The bedchambers."

Portia's cheeks pinked and she looked down, gulping. "My sister likes to read. Do you have a large library of books?"

"Naturally."

"And your cousin's widow lives there, too. I suppose she is a great reader?"

"I wouldn't know."

Sherringford had not been described as a place so vast that one could become lost in it. Surely he knew, but why would he not say? "I look forward to meeting her. Her name is Ophelia, isn't it? Perhaps we will become friends."

"Mrs. Shaw acts as housekeeper and is kept quite busy."

"I see." Placing a cousin's wife into service was done, of course, but Portia hoped the woman was treated better than a mere servant. "And your other relatives? Where are they living?"

He shook his head. "I have a male cousin in Brighton and

another married female cousin living in the north."

Well, that was something. "How often do they come to the estate?

"They know better than to pester me every year. You will not have to entertain them very often."

"And what of your nearest neighbors?"

He stopped and turned around. "We should go back to your mother."

"But we were just starting to know each other," she protested.

"You know enough. The rest you will learn after we are married and away from this wretched place."

Several people nearby looked at them sharply. Montrose's criticism must have carried to their ears. Portia winced and fumed silently as they started back to rejoin her mother. She looked up and found Lord Wade coming toward them.

He stepped to one side to allow her to pass, but she felt his touch upon her hand, and then it was gone.

Portia glanced over her shoulder, wishing she could have stopped to talk to him.

They returned to her mother and stood around several more minutes until a waltz was called. "Ah, I believe this is our dance."

Portia looked up at him in shock. It was not their dance. She was meant to dance with Sir John next.

Montrose claimed her hand and drew Portia firmly onto the dance floor before she could protest.

Sir John stood to one side, squinting at her in confusion.

Portia couldn't even convey any sort of apology with her eyes that he would see or understand.

The duke caught her up in his arms and Portia stumbled. Montrose uttered a curse about clumsiness and forced her to dance with him, holding her fingers tightly.

She did her best under the circumstances to hide her shock, as she was almost brutishly manhandled around the dance floor by her future husband. Portia's eyes flew to the nearest exit, and she gulped.

She wanted to run.

And Portia had never once, not even on her earliest outings in society, been cowed by a gentleman's manner the way she was now.

She had always stood up for herself, made men treat her as their equal. Montrose had the manners of an ox.

Her mouth grew dry and she swallowed. Could she really marry such a man?

Montrose cleared his throat, and she looked up at him slowly. What possibly passed for a smile crossed his lips, and he raised one brow in question. Portia forced a smile but her thoughts were far from pleasing. She had aspired to marry a gentleman of position and wealth, someone she wanted to admire. Lord Montrose had a title, his own wealth, though his esteem in society seemed less than the best. He was handsome, and any lady might be glad to have won his proposal. Portia could go through with the marriage and become a duchess.

Her parents might disown her if she didn't.

Her legs felt wooden after their dance as she walked the length of the ballroom to her mother's side. She spoke automatically. "Thank you for the dance, your grace."

"Happy to oblige, Miss Hayes."

Portia bit her tongue hard as Mother babbled about how well they danced together. Clearly Mother needed to wear glasses as much as Sir John did. She looked for him quickly and found him with Lord Wade, not far away. The pair talked in whispers, and Sir John was nodding.

When he left Lord Wade's side, Sir John never looked back.

Portia shivered and wrapped her arm across her chest to hug herself.

Your grace.

Miss Hayes.

Two hard kisses and no conversation. They were a week away from the wedding and they were strangers to each other still. She felt closer to Lord Wade than to the man she would welcome to her bed.

Portia nearly sobbed at the thought of what was to come. She looked at Lord Montrose…and realized with shock that he repulsed her.

She'd made a horrible mistake in accepting him before getting to know who he really was.

Portia heard him apologize that he must leave them to speak with an old acquaintance, and she was relieved when he was gone.

Mother smiled, seeing nothing wrong at all. "Such lovely manners."

Polite now, but she'd seen a glimpse of his temper, and that frightened her. She rubbed her fingers to her brow and Mother saw the gesture. "What is it?"

"A sudden headache," she murmured.

"But you never suffer headaches."

"I know that," Portia snapped. "Forgive me. I think I am in need of some air."

"We'll go together. Indeed it is warm tonight."

Mother caught up her arm and led her through the nearest set of open doors. It was just as muggy outside as in, and Portia beat her fan before her face, looking up at the cloud-filled sky. "I just need a moment."

She felt as if she couldn't breathe properly. How could she pass up the opportunity to be a duchess? She rubbed her brow again and nearly cried in frustration. For two years, she'd been working toward marrying well, above her station, to improve the lot of her family. To make sure Lavinia could marry whomever she pleased.

What about my life, she cried silently to the night sky. She was already miserable and the vows hadn't been spoken yet. Marriage just might make her more so.

A footman passed close to the door and Mother acquired a pair of champagne glasses. Portia took a sip of hers, and then another, draining the glass quickly. To her considerable disappointment, the beverage did not make her feel much better about her situation, and her head only ached worse.

She turned to look back into the ballroom and saw Wade

cross the dance floor. "What did you want for your life when you were young, Mother?"

"Oh, a great many things, I imagine."

She looked at her mother, who was always happier when Portia's father was elsewhere. "What were they?"

"A home, a husband, and my beautiful daughters."

"Love?"

"Yes, I suppose I wanted that, too."

Portia wanted all of that. Especially love, but that seemed even further out of her reach than it had before she'd accepted Lord Montrose. She didn't want to live a life of regret or doubt. She had given her word to marry, but she never imagined the promise meant sacrificing herself.

A tear rolled down her cheek and she wiped it away swiftly.

Unfortunately, Mother saw. "What is wrong with you?"

Portia turned to her mother and hugged her tightly. "I'm so sorry. So very sorry."

"Here now," Mother chided, cupping her face gently. "What's gotten into you tonight?"

"I think I'm just tired, and my head really does hurt terribly." So did her heart. "Would you mind if we went home earlier than we planned?"

Mother studied her face, and then smiled. "The rounds are exhausting me, too. I'll inform your father and he can explain the situation to Lord Montrose after we are gone." Mother slipped her arm about her shoulders and turned her toward the ballroom. They did not cross it, but went around. The hall was cooler and quieter, and another tear slipped down her cheek before she could stop herself.

"It is quite natural to have doubts and fears get the better of you before you marry. I almost ran away."

Portia looked at her mother sharply. "Why didn't you?"

"The shame would have embarrassed my family."

Portia sank deeper into misery and left the ball without really seeing anything or anyone in their path. Once they were in the carriage, she curled up against her mother's side like a child. "I never wanted to embarrass you."

Mother hugged her close. "My dear, not a day has gone by without me being the proudest mother in all of England. Nothing you could do would change that."

Portia shut her eyes to blot out her certainty that she would do just that. Even suggesting she might end her engagement to the duke would undoubtedly upset both her parents. She needed to think, decide how it might be done as painlessly as possible, and the only place she thought she might make sense of her conflicted mind was away from everyone.

She raised her face slowly. "Mother, I'd like to spend tomorrow at Uncle Oliver's house. It might be the last time. Can I go there alone for the day?"

Mother nodded. "Just take your maid and perhaps a little picnic basket, too. You know how you lose track of time when you are rummaging around. We need you in good health for when you become the Duchess of Montrose."

Although Portia tried with all her considerable imagination, she couldn't picture it. She settled against her mother again with a weary sigh. "I'll go very early and return just before we will sit down to dine."

"Montrose promised to join us tomorrow night."

"Good." But that left her with just one day to decide the depths of her madness, and she wasn't sure it would be enough.

Chapter Nineteen

——— ♦ ———

The next morning offered drizzle to dampen Portia's growing sense of impending doom. She and her maid hurried into their waiting carriage despite the early hour and shook off the raindrops from their cloaks once inside. As they drove off, Portia leaned close to her maid. "You are free to do as you please today, but do return by four o'clock in the afternoon."

"Are you sure you don't want me to stay awhile, miss? You look terribly pale."

That would be because she'd barely slept a wink last night. "I'll be fine on my own. I'll keep all the doors locked, and stay away from the windows, too, until you return. I have the picnic basket, don't forget."

"Very well, Miss Hayes," the maid sighed.

Portia chewed on her lips as they turned into Soho Square and the carriage drew to a halt before the house. It was not the best address in London but the dearest to her heart. She couldn't bear to give it up.

She stepped out onto the pavement and together they headed in. Her maid carried in the hamper and set it down in the front parlor on a little table. They had cake and sandwiches and cold chicken, and some mulberry wine, too. Then the maid headed for the rear of the dwelling with a cheery wave. Portia watched her descend the servants stairs, headed for the abandoned kitchen and the rear door. She let out a sigh as the sound of the heavy door closing boomed through the house.

Finally alone, she dropped her smile and threw herself face down on the nearest chaise lounge and screamed. Nothing was going the way she had expected.

A step sounded behind her—and Portia instantly knew it was *him* before she turned over.

Lord Wade drew closer, eyes full of questions. "I saw you leave last night, and I was worried."

"I had a headache," she explained.

"You said they were missish nonsense and you never get them."

She gulped. He knew her, better than anyone.

And she knew him, too. By the rumpled state of his clothes and his messy hair, he'd been here for hours, just waiting for the chance to talk to her alone. It was just like him to notice that she hadn't been herself last night. She didn't deserve him, but she wanted him so very much to always be at her side.

Portia trembled as he sat down on the chaise next to her and took up her hand in his. He pressed a kissed to the back of it. "Do you feel better?"

"Not really. Why are you here?"

"I'm here because you are unhappy."

"I *am* unhappy. I'm miserable, and I don't know what to do," she admitted with an unhappy wail and threw herself against his chest. Tears filled her eyes. "What is wrong with me?"

His arms wrapped around her, and Wade held her tightly against him. "There's nothing wrong with you, Portia. Not now. You're having doubts about marrying Montrose," he suggested. "And you are trying to decide what to do about that, and whether your parents will forgive you if you don't marry the duke they picked out for you."

She nodded, and the tight band of anxiety around her chest exploded. "I can't marry him! I just can't!"

"There are others."

"I don't want them either."

"Thank God," he whispered.

Portia inhaled deeply and burrowed against the viscount's chest anew. The beat of his heart was quick, and she glanced up at him slowly.

There was a look in his eye that she'd never seen before. Longing.

Portia trembled now for all the right reasons. She knew exactly what he wanted—what he had *always* wanted from her.

And she wanted the same thing now too.

She smiled through her tears, astonished by how desperately she needed him and his remarkable love and patience. "I'm not mad, am I?"

"Not even a little."

Lord Wade captured her face and finally kissed her lips. Portia put up no resistance before raising her arms about his neck and kissing him back.

She found everything she'd lacked in her previous experiences with other gentlemen in his kiss, and she cried all the more. But they were happy tears, tears of joy so profound she felt herself changed. Not into someone new, but back into the person she'd always been.

She drew back from him, astonished that she had been so blind. So dismissive. She wiped away her tears quickly less he misunderstand and grasped the lapels of his coat and shook him. "Kiss me again," she demanded.

Immediately, Portia melted under another tender assault on her senses as he kissed her so passionately, her toes curled in her slippers. He linked their fingers as he plundered her mouth until her whole body began to quiver. She let him have his way, because she wanted him too, enjoying every moment of his ravishment.

When he drew back, Wade was breathing hard. He peppered kisses on her brow, and then just held her close.

"I don't want to lose you," he whispered.

What a fool she'd been to deny herself the passion of a kindred spirit. Portia smiled up at him, and then she pushed his hair back from his eyes that seemed unusually bright.

"You'll not lose me. I'm giving myself to you."

He looked down. "But I cannot keep you. Your father will not allow you to marry a fortune hunter."

She lifted his chin, smiling still. "I don't think you were ever a fortune hunter. But I wholeheartedly believe you are a man interested in stealing my virtue."

Julian's gaze drifted down to her breasts then back up. He grinned slowly. "You don't make it easy to ignore what's been so close and yet so blasted far away. Damped gowns, low necklines, flirtatious smiles for everyone but me. It's enough to drive a man insane with longing for you."

Portia blushed but leaned back, raising her hands up in surrender. "I didn't mean to torment you, but I'm all yours if you still want me."

"Now there's an invitation I never thought to hear from you." Julian started to chuckle softly, and he shook his head. "However, we shouldn't stay in this room much longer if we're going to continue this conversation. This empty old house receives a startling number of unexpected visitors. We need a more intimate location if we are to decide what to do next."

"I know what I have to do. I have to speak to Montrose before dinner tonight. However..." Portia licked her lips, anticipating a great many things. "Since dinner is several long hours away, and my mother already knows where I am, I think I am happy right here. Alone with you."

He began to smile. "Is that so?"

"Indeed. We have all we could ever need under this roof, even food."

She lifted the basket to show him, and then passed it to him and stood. Portia drew him toward the staircase. "The master bedchamber has not yet been cleared out, but I'm sure we can find a spot where no one can find us."

"Not the room where we hid together." They started up the stairs. "What about the attic chamber? Its very private."

Portia nodded quickly. "We can see the sky from there."

"And the stars, too."

Portia's face fell. "I can't stay that long. Mother expects me home by the dinner hour."

He grinned. The stairs widened enough that he could put his arm around her shoulders. "I was referring to another kind of star. You'll understand what I mean in about twenty minutes or so, I expect."

She didn't understand but his eyes were merry with anticipation, so she believed him. She held his gaze as they walked along, knowing she would be forever changed by what happened next between them. "Will you still look at me this way when I am old and gray?"

He set the basket down and captured her hands, bringing them to his mouth to kiss. "Every day of your life."

Julian surprised her by sweeping her up into his arms.

Portia giggled. "So gallant."

"Also expedient," he murmured, as he jostled her and the picnic basket up the next flight of stairs, and then down a narrow hallway. "You know, in romantic novels, this always sounds like an easy business."

"Are you saying I'm heavy, my lord?"

He grunted. "I'm saying I wish I hadn't given up boxing."

He set her down on her feet when they reached the narrow attic landing. He bid her go ahead but reminded her to duck under the low door.

Portia looked around the small chamber in surprise. This was not how she remembered the state of the room. There was little in it now besides a mattress draped in fresh linens on the floor, plus a bottle of wine and two glasses.

At the window, a bunch of daffodils had been put into a short vase. Her eyes teared up again as she discovered Julian somehow knew her favorite flower. He'd never brought her flowers before, and she'd never told him what she liked, either. If he had given them to her sooner it might have saved them both a whole lot of foolish nonsense.

She turned to look at him, feeling very uncertain of what to do next. It was a fitting setting to give up her virginity to someone she trusted and loved with all her heart. It was romantic, too.

But how had he known to do all this? "How long were you here before I arrived?"

"Long enough to make a bed for us," he murmured behind her, before sliding his hands onto her waist and wrapped his arms around her tightly. "I won't hold it against you if you'd rather wait."

"When have I ever changed my mind?"

"Now. Being here with me. I couldn't be more surprised."

She turned to face him. "I never once told you I would not consider you."

A shy grin crossed his face. "So you did think me one of your suitors?"

"Yes, but I want to be honest. I wanted to please my parents more than anything, but it was only lately, Julian, that I thought of you as more than just a friend."

"Since when?"

"The moment you told me that you had never been my friend, I knew we were both wrong. You were always more than that." She kissed his cheek and turned to face the room again. He'd gone to such a lot of effort on her behalf. It was surprisingly endearing to have him make plans to seduce her, especially here in her favorite place. "I think the wine is a nice touch, but only if you drink with me."

"I'd planned to," Julian assured her as he bumped the door shut with his hip. He locked the door for good measure. "I doubt we'd be caught by surprise up here, given the way the house creaks and groans, but let's not take any chances."

"No one would imagine us together. They were all too busy congratulating themselves on marrying me off, and now plotting how best to show off Lavinia so she captures a husband. They are going to be so disappointed."

"Everything will work out the way your mother wants, I'm sure. Perhaps even better than she dreamed," he murmured with a masculine rumble, giving Portia chills. This was a side of Julian she wanted much more of.

"What bargains have you made now, my lord?"

"Nothing yet, and when I do, you'll be the first to know."

"I would appreciate that."

Portia lifted her hands to her hair. She was done wasting time and quickly removed the pins. The long strands spilled down her back. Julian moved back, and she started to blush. However, she reveled in the forbidden thrill of his scrutiny now. Perhaps she'd always enjoyed the way he watched her all the time.

He moved around her, and she shivered when he lifted her hair and his hot breath fluttered against the back of her neck. He began to nibble on her throat as she unfastened a few buttons at the top of her gown.

"You are so beautiful," he promised. "And I know I don't deserve you."

Portia smiled. "You're just saying that so I'll keep undressing."

"Absolutely." He chuckled quietly. "I don't want to risk waking up from this dream."

"I'm not a dream. I may be spoiled, occasionally foolish, and I've nearly made the worst mistake of my life, but this is honestly the most right thing I've ever done. It's me whose been dreaming I could be happy as a duchess. I don't deserve *you*," she promised.

When her gown was undone as much as was strictly needed, Portia wiggled out of it and allowed it to pool around her feet. Instead of leaving it there, Julian swept it up and laid it over the back of a chair as neatly as any maid might.

When he turned back, he was grinning. He put his arms around her again. He was very gentle but skimmed his hands up and down her sides in a bewitching caress. "Stunning."

Portia glanced down at herself. She was still wearing stays and a chemise yet. "Wait till you see the rest of me. It might be a little vain, but I've seen myself naked. I'm as good as or better than Lady Windermere's portrait."

"I don't know. That portrait was very well done." Julian's arms tightened about her, pulling her into him. "Would you allow me the honor of disrobing the rest of you later so I can confirm your claim?"

"Only if you undress, too."

"If I must," he said with a small laugh. He removed his coat and waistcoat, showing his garments the same care as he'd done with Portia's clothes. She blushed and looked away for a moment but turned back, just in time to see him lower his breeches.

Julian's legs were long, pale, and very lean as he moved about. She lifted her gaze up, to find he was still wearing an almost sheer linen shirt that had seen better days. She lifted her gaze higher still and noticed him studying her.

Portia backed up a few steps and grinned. "I want you to undress fully."

"I can do that." He grinned, pulling his shirt up over his head.

Portia's breath caught, and then she swooned a little. His male form was simply beautiful. Julian was nicely muscled but oh so thin. But as she drew closer to him, her heart skipped a beat as she noticed his ribs were visible. She could probably count them.

Julian reached out and slid a finger under her chin, lifting her gaze. "I'm up here, sweetheart."

Portia ignored his rebuke and ran her hands over his body, learning his skin. He was much too thin, but for now there was nothing she could do about it. She moved until they were standing close together and slid her hand slowly down his back. She covered the round globes of his bottom with both hands and squeezed, as he did the same to her. They laughed.

"Lovely," she whispered, and then stretched up.

Julian kissed her for several minutes, slipping his talented tongue in and out of her mouth until she was panting. He drew her down to the bed he'd made for them. "You look tired."

Portia made herself comfortable but pulled the sheet up to cover them both. She rolled onto her side, facing Julian. "I have been having the strangest dreams of late. I am locked away, with Montrose banging on the walls, demanding to be let in."

He brushed her hair back from her face gently. "Dreams are often a reflection of the truth we won't listen to."

"You were with me, and I felt so safe because of you."

He kissed her fingers softly. "Of course, I'd never let any harm come to you."

"I believe that," she promised. Then Portia yawned suddenly, unable to stop. Julian pulled her tight into his arms. They lay nestled like that for a while, and Portia never wanted it to end.

Chapter Twenty

Julian's heart was beating so fast, he feared he'd crack his own ribs. When he'd come here early this morning, he never imagined this sort of reception, but it certainly removed any doubts.

Portia would not marry Montrose.

Her freedom was all that mattered to him. He lightly brushed a hand down her back, seeking to wake her from the deep sleep she'd suddenly fallen into when her head had touched his shoulder. He liked that she felt so safe with him, but they had quite a bit to talk about and to do yet.

Portia stirred in his arms finally and stretched. "Is it still raining?"

"It is," Julian murmured as he found her hand and clasped her slender fingers in his. "It hasn't stopped all morning. You've been asleep for several hours."

His stomach growled, and he wished his hunger far away. Portia had heard, though, and quickly sat up to pull her picnic basket across the floor.

A sandwich landed in his lap and a glass of wine was poured for him, too. Portia found something for herself and nibbled on a chicken leg while she peeked at him. "Have you been awake all this time?"

He'd been too keyed up for sleep. What they had started

that morning could have a devastating effect on other people. Portia's parents would be angry with them both, and her sister's chances of making a match would suffer unless they did things the right way. Most of all, he still did not know how—or how soon—Portia intended to break her engagement with the Duke of Montrose.

"I've been awake most of the morning. I didn't want to miss a moment of having you all to myself."

She chuckled softly as she peeked under the sheet at her state of undress, and then at his nakedness too. "You've had more of me than anyone else ever will."

That sounded promising, but he didn't want to assume anything where Portia was concerned. He ate quickly, even taking a second helping at Portia's urging. Sleeping with him was one thing. Marrying him quickly, quite another. "I must admit I am very surprised you were the one to suggest this."

Portia flung herself onto her back and glared. "Don't you want to be with me?"

She might be glaring at him, but Julian was much more interested in enjoying the view of her lovely breasts.

He traced the point of one finger over each swell and the valley, and then did it again. "You've kissed a great many gentlemen during the two seasons that I've known you."

She sat up, scowling fiercely. "I hope you're not suggesting I've done this before with one of them?"

Since her pitch was rising in fury, he shook his head quickly. "I know you have not, but I haven't watched over you every minute of your life. I've noticed you are quite adept at slipping away on your own, and I understand your need for liberty very well. You have openly admired the most attractive gentlemen of the *ton* quite often."

"You are one of those."

"Oh no, I'm not," he corrected her. He did not need or want false flattery. He knew his looks lacked that certain flair to make women swoon when he passed them by. "I do not resent that, either. The pretty ones are often foolish."

She resumed her former position, half lying atop him.

"True," she admitted. "Sometimes it was hard not to laugh at the way they'd catch their reflections in any mirror and admire their own faces."

"They should have been admiring yours instead."

She reached out and her fingers slipped under his hair to toy with the shell of his ear. They were a bit too large, and he'd suffered enough jokes for them in the past that he'd long since learned to hide them beneath an overdue haircut. It might be unfashionable but it served a purpose. "For the record, I would not have cared if you had slept with an army of gentlemen. I'm hardly virginal."

Portia's eyes fixed on his, and they narrowed dangerously. "And who have you slept with, my lord?"

He shrugged, trying not to laugh at her flash of temper and the intrusive question. "Only a handful of women perhaps have shared my bed, when I was a young man. Nothing like the number Montrose had memorialized upon his disgusting little stick of wood. Mine were light skirts, every one. Paid well for their trouble. I can barely remember their faces, they were so long ago."

Portia lifted one shoulder, and he could touch her breast more easily. "Were you ever in love?"

He moved his hand up until his fingers rested over her nipple. A pity they were still encased in chemise and stays. Portia's breath hitched as he began to unlace her, and she did not try to stop him. He gently removed her stays and also took her chemise away.

A crimson blush stained her cheeks, and she looked down as he swirled his fingertip around her breasts, teasing her in a way he'd always hoped to do.

"I thought so once, but now, I suspect it was merely an infatuation," he assured her. It was better that Portia have no doubts about the state of his heart. She was about to cast herself into the eye of a storm, and the scandal might be hard to bear if she had doubts about his sincerity. She owned him body and soul. Had for years, too, not that she'd realized it fully yet. He did not believe that would ever change.

Her breath rushed out as he pinched her nipple. He swept one hand down her warm body, lingering over the soft, supple curve of her hip. He moved her slightly so more of her body rested on top of him.

Portia was slowly moving her body against him, too, and he considered whether they should stop this. Although Portia was with him now, obviously, her family could try to keep them apart in the end. It would all come down to the money, and whether he could convince her father that his affection for Portia had nothing to do with the size of her dowry.

Portia suddenly straddled his hips and looked around with a laugh. "I finally understand what you meant now. About gentlemen always wanting to go riding with a lady."

"Do you?" Julian grasped her hips and moved her back. His cock was already thick enough, and with a little maneuvering, he rested beneath her folds. She had a lovely body, and Wade was well embraced by her.

He brought his hands forward to her flat stomach and very slowly moved his fingertips lower, into her curls. "I could show you the stars."

She suddenly moaned as he delved between her folds. "I know about this kind already."

He liked that she had a little experience in pleasuring herself. One day he'd like to watch her do it, too. However, Julian needed to bring her to that point himself. He'd waited a long time to have Portia, after all. But there was no need to rush.

"Wade," she complained as he drew his fingers away.

He returned his fingers to her folds and found her clitoris easily. She began to writhe as he played with her with more intensity.

He grinned. "I should probably stop."

"Don't you dare," she warned, as she lifted her hands up under her hair. She stretched and twisted and rocked against his fingers. The moisture from her body coated his cock, and he groaned.

Portia looked down at him and smiled. "What are you

waiting for?"

"I can't look away from you."

She widened her legs a bit more and began to move against his fingers and cock. She nearly drove him out of his mind.

He grabbed her hips tightly, lifted her up, and held the tip of his cock against her entrance. "I'll be gentle with you," he promised, before he thrust up.

Portia yelped a little, freezing above him. Julian quickly returned his attention to her clit and resumed teasing her. After a moment, Portia made a few tentative movements that drove him deeper into her body. However, it seemed her experience only went so far, and she moved uncertainly.

Julian grasped her hips again and showed her the way.

He held her gaze as her face slowly flushed. Her nipples hardened to points as they bounced free and unbound above him. It was glorious to make love slowly, each using their body to excite the other.

He found her clitoris hardened, and Portia gasped as he teased her there. "Oh, that's the spot," she whispered.

She began to move a bit more purposefully. The friction of her fine cunny gripping his cock was without equal. Julian's desire flared higher. He could fuck anyone if he wanted to, but making love was an art he only needed Portia for.

He captured her breast with one hand and teased her sex with the other. A little pinch of her nipple made Portia moan. "Julian, help me," she cried.

"I'm here, love. I'm deep inside you, where I've always wanted to be."

He abandoned her breast and got a firm grip on her bottom. Carefully, he rocked her hips against his. Portia moaned again, and she continued to work her body against him, too. Her erotic movements nearly unseated him. He'd imagined her passionate for the right man, just not this way for *him*.

Portia's gaze lowered, and as soon as their eyes met, she cried out his name. She jerked, coming hard and long on top of him. Julian gritted his teeth but her gyrations were more than he could hope to resist. He climaxed inside her tight little body, driving into her over and over, unable to stop himself.

Portia collapsed, her sweat-covered limbs sticking to his.

He licked his lips nervously, waiting for complaints. He'd been very much carried away in the heat of the moment, but then so had she, too. However, it was clear that pleasure and Portia were very well acquainted.

She slowly raised her head. Her cheeks were flushed, her lips slightly parted. She looked to have been truly ravished. A slow smile spread over her face, and then she stretched to kiss him full on the lips. "You're wonderful."

Relieved beyond measure that their lovemaking had lived up to her expectations, Julian pulled her into his arms and held her tight. "No, *you're* wonderful," he whispered, pressing a kiss to her brow.

Eventually their bodies cooled and he softened enough to slip from her.

"Julian," she whispered, her face still pressed to his chest. "How do you feel about me?"

Julian smoothed his hand over her head and hair, his heart beating fast at the obvious answer. It burned his tongue, and he waited only a moment to explain. "I've always loved you," he said simply.

"I thought you must." She pressed a kiss to his chest. "What time is it?"

"Almost three, I should imagine." He reached for his pocket watch and squinted. "Actually, almost four."

"We have to get dressed. Hurry. My maid might return at any moment."

Portia sat up, and then bounded to her feet. Julian struggled into a sitting position and leaned against the wall to watch her move about. She seemed unusually energetic to his eye.

Portia poured herself some wine and drank thirstily. "I have to get home. Mother has organized another dinner with Lord Montrose."

Julian scowled. "With Montrose?"

"Oh, don't say his name in that tone."

Julian would use any tone he liked to describe that undeserving bastard. "Are you looking forward to seeing him?"

"Indeed I am, now." She laughed as she attempted to tighten her stays. "Can you help me with this?"

Julian slowly climbed to his feet and crossed to her. He held his tongue, unsure about her current mood. He did not like that she sounded happy to see Montrose straight after they had made love.

He tightened the bindings that would hide her lovely bosom from his gaze as requested. But was it to be forever?

When he was done, she turned and drew his head down for a quick kiss. "Thank you."

She dashed about the room and kept talking while she dressed. "I have so much to do to prepare for this evening. Can you see one of my garters out there? I seem to only have one here."

Julian looked around and found it on top of his shoe. He snatched it up but held it. He wasn't sure what was going through her mind right now, but obviously Portia was not thinking about him anymore.

Her hands rose to slip her gown over her head, wriggling around wildly to get back into her dress. When she emerged again, she was practically perfect. Only her hair looked like she'd just jumped out of bed. Which was true.

She smiled at him, "Did you find it?"

Julian held it up. "I did."

Portia raised her foot and rested it on the edge of the chair. "Will you help dress me?"

Julian moved toward her, and then knelt at her feet. He tugged up her stocking until it was neat and slowly tied the garter just above her knee. "Is that tight enough?"

He looked up and found Portia staring down at him with a smoldering expression on her face. He moved his hand along her inner thigh toward her curls.

Portia made a little sound—half encouragement, half frustration—and her hips retreated from his touch. "Julian, there's no time for that now. If I'm too late, Mother will send someone to get me, and I don't want anyone to find you here with me."

"I suppose you don't, at that."

"No indeed. No one can know about us." She cupped his cheek and pulled him up to stand on his own two feet. "Today will be our secret forever."

He took a step back, utterly crushed. "As you like."

Working without a mirror, Portia smoothed her hair and pinned it into a neat arrangement.

Julian jerked on his own clothes then, tugging them up without caring if it was done right or not. If she had changed her mind about him, it hardly mattered how he looked, did it?

"Did I really leave my slippers downstairs?"

"I think so."

"Hmm," she huffed. "Getting a bit ahead of myself. Dinner will be at eight Wednesday night, make sure to bring Auntie. I don't want her to miss anything."

Julian turned slowly. "Dinner?"

Portia turned around quickly. "Yes, you're both coming to dinner."

When she stepped toward him, Julian took a pace back. "What about us?"

"There is no *us*. There cannot be right now," she explained.

She pulled his head down and planted a hard kiss on his lips. When she drew back, she was frowning. "I made a mistake letting this go so far with you."

Did she mean to pretend they'd never made love? "You cannot unmake what we did today, Portia!"

She squirmed. "I know, but I have to make sure no one suffers for what I've done. Come to dinner tomorrow night, and you'll see what I mean."

Portia gave him one last kiss goodbye, and then fled, leaving Julian even more confused than before.

Chapter Twenty-One

— ◆ —

The dinner at which Portia had expected to end her betrothal had to be postponed at the last minute. Lord Montrose had sent word while she'd been lying in Julian's arms that he would not be able to attend after all. Mother had not taken the snub very well and gone to bed, pleading that she had a migraine. Father had gone out to his club on hearing about Mother, and likely wouldn't return until dawn.

Portia would have no chance to broach the subject of Montrose with him until later tomorrow, most likely.

She pressed a cooling cloth to Mother's forehead. "Does that help?"

"Not yet," she whispered. "Oh, it is all falling apart."

How right her mother was. Portia dreaded telling her the truth. She wet the cloth again and returned it to her brow, trying to decide if she should give some warning of her lack of feeling for the duke. Her only concern was how strenuously her mother might try to talk her out of breaking the engagement with Montrose.

Portia would not change her mind.

Now that she had decided not to be engaged to Montrose, Portia wanted to end the association with him as quickly and directly as possible. That could not be done without looking Lord Montrose in the eye. She owed him that respect at least.

It was absolutely imperative that he never realize she had decided to throw him over because she loved Lord Wade instead. She wanted it to seem unplanned, and therefore less dangerous for Julian. "Did Lord Montrose indicate when he'd be back in London?"

"Not really. I do find that very inconvenient."

Portia wholeheartedly agreed, but likely not for the same reason as her mother. She had prepared a speech, consulting books on etiquette that afternoon, too, but she could not be free to make a better choice until she saw the duke. Of course, she could write out her change of heart in a letter, but that seemed cowardly.

She toyed with the idea again and dismissed it. Julian had once warned her against writing any of her feelings down. He said they could be used against her if they fell into the wrong hands. He was probably right about that.

She would like to write to Julian, though, and tell him how she felt right now. She felt badly that she had slept so long and had needed to leave him behind. She wanted to shout to the world that her heart had finally found a home. She was in love with a man she'd never once expected to fall for…until she had nearly lost him.

She didn't even know why she loved him so well as to throw away her one chance to be a duchess. The only thing she knew deep down in her bones was that she couldn't lose the chance to be Lord Wade's lady.

The things they had done that afternoon in her late uncle's home were her secret, her hidden pleasure. And she wanted to do it all again with him, and soon. When he'd finally told her that he loved her…Portia's heart had almost burst with joy.

He did not care about her fortune, or how horrid she might have been to him in the past. They had moved beyond that, apologized, and she had discovered a man worthy of her unbridled admiration. Quite frankly, she was smitten, and she had a hard time keeping the smile off her face.

Realizing she'd been rudely staring off into space and ignoring her mother's discomfort, she reclaimed the cloth and wet it thoroughly.

Mother touched her arm suddenly. "Are you in love with him?"

Portia started, shocked by the blunt question. She looked at her mother quickly. Was she speaking of Montrose or of Julian?

Mother smiled gently. "I only ask so I might know for certain that you will be happy with Lord Montrose."

Portia let out a sigh of relief. It was too soon to reveal her feelings toward Lord Wade had been irreversibly changed that day. Where Lord Montrose was concerned, she feared disappointing her mother, though. Mother had dreamed that her daughter would marry well and had made her feelings very clear.

However, conscience warred with the truth. The truth won in the end. She did not wish to lie to her mother any more than was necessary. It would be best to prepare her for what Portia would eventually admit. "No. I don't love him, and I don't believe I ever will."

Mother's face clouded with confusion. "I had hoped there was a good reason why he keeps pressing to marry by special license."

"What?"

"He came earlier today to ask again for an expedient wedding. Your father was quite upset about the way the duke will not take no for an answer on that subject."

Portia bit her lip. It was not love that compelled the duke to press for an early wedding. It wasn't even desire, because she'd seen little evidence that he wanted her. Not the way Lord Wade did.

Her heart sank a little more to realize she had badly misjudged the duke. He didn't want *her*, really. He wanted to possess her—like a painting or a fine horse. The sooner the better as far as he was concerned. "Wade said he was used to getting his way. Since school he's been something of a bully."

Mother worried her lip. "We will stand firm and make him understand our decision is final. If he does not respect us now, he never will."

"I do appreciate your support, Mother. I know it cannot be easy to deny so powerful a man."

"We Hayes women must stick together. And don't imagine your father could buckle under the pressure. Your father will do as I wish unless he wants to live alone."

"Surely you would not leave Father," she teased.

Mother's face darkened, and she draped a hand across her forehead. "Why not? He leaves me alone all the time."

Portia wet her lips. "Where would you go?"

"I always thought I would like to live in Oliver's house, but your father would not consider it before. I suppose now you are to marry it remains impossible, since the duke will have the care of it until your son is old enough to inherit."

Portia smiled at the thought of having a child. A son for Lord Wade. Motherhood would increase her happiness, but only if she was to marry Julian.

She imagined living with him in Hanover Square but yearned for Soho instead. He seemed to like Uncle Oliver's house, and it was very large. Julian had once assured her there was room enough to house two families inside. Of course, she'd not considered the possibility of combining their families under the same roof until now, but perhaps there was a way to accommodate everyone. Soho Square was not that far away from Mayfair.

"Perhaps there might be a way. When I am married, I will speak to my husband about it."

Mother smiled sadly. "I don't believe the duke offers too many boons to his acquaintances."

"I imagine he doesn't," Portia agreed. Julian, however, was a very different man, and he did seem to like her mother. He might be persuaded to share. "Let's talk about this another time, after we see Lord Montrose again.

"That could not be too soon as far as I'm concerned. People are beginning to talk about his lack of attention to you." Mother closed her eyes. "I'd like to sleep now."

"Of course," Portia murmured and pulled a light blanket

over her shoulders. "Rest and we'll talk later."

"Could you send a note to Mrs. Lenthall on my behalf?"

"Why?"

"There was something she wanted to talk to me about the other day, and I was so worried about the duke coming to dinner that it completely slipped my mind."

Forgetting so good a friend was not done and absolutely must be apologized for. In person might have been better than a note. "Perhaps I could go in your place."

"Oh, could you?" Mother sighed and rolled over onto her side, tucking her hands under her cheek. "I'd be forever in your debt. Do remember to take your maid. The little carriage, too."

Portia smiled and smoothed her hand over her mother's shoulder. It was Portia who should be grateful. She'd never had reason to call at the Wade residence before.

Portia left the room quietly, rushed to her own to change, and ordered up the small town carriage. With her maid at her side, they undertook the short trip to Hanover Square very quickly. Her heart was beating fast as she looked up at the façade. There was no hint that the family were in dire straights from the outside. The townhouse looked much like all the rest around the square.

An aged butler welcomed her and led her toward a sparsely furnished sitting room, while Portia motioned for her maid to settle on a chair in the hall to wait for her.

Portia froze a few steps into the room. Mrs. Lenthall appeared to be dozing. She glanced quickly for the butler, but he was already backing out again.

Uncertain what to do, Portia affected a sneeze.

Mrs. Lenthall startled awake and, upon recognizing Portia, smiled. "I suppose you've come to see if the rumors are true."

"I'm here on my mother's behalf," Portia promised. "She sends her warmest wishes and apologizes profusely for not being able to come today."

"Her head again?"

"Yes, I'm afraid. She feels simply too dreadful to leave her bed."

Mrs. Lenthall nodded. "The worry of marrying off a daughter causes a remarkable number of ladies to take to their beds at some point," Mrs. Lenthall confided. "I suppose Montrose is not helping."

"I'm not sure what brought it on," Portia said quickly, realizing that she really did not want to talk about the duke even a little bit. "A few hours of rest and a good supper should improve her health."

"We could all do with a good meal now and then."

On a sudden impulse, Portia switched seats to sit beside the older woman. "I've wanted to come and see you many times before today."

"Oh?" Mrs. Lenthall squinted at her.

"I might have been a little dim-witted. I've come to understand that you and Julian have helped pave my way in society without me knowing it. Introductions, parties, and knowledge I'd never have come across on my own. I should have thanked you both long before now for your assistance." She placed her hand on the old lady's, feeling the cold of her skin, and frailty, too. "Thank you so very much for all your help over the years since I've known you."

Mrs. Lenthall sniffed and patted her hand a few times. "It was for a good cause. You're a bright gel. There are not that many Originals left, really."

Portia heaved a sigh and grasped Mrs. Lenthall's hand more tightly. "I do miss the ladies who were taken from us, too. Did you help them the way you helped me?"

A little smile tugged up her lips. "In some ways, perhaps, but they were never in your league."

"I was raised almost the same as the others. A gentlewoman by birth and well dowered."

"If you think your dowry had the slightest influence on my mind, then you are indeed still as dim-witted as you were before."

The lady turned to the side table and poured a small measure of wine into an empty glass. There was but one glass on the table and Portia was offered nothing. She took a sip, and then sighed. "Be a good gel and pull that bell over there. I should at least be able to offer you tea."

"You are very kind," Portia murmured and rushed to do her bidding.

An elderly maid appeared some time later and brought with her a tray of tea and a few biscuits. The tea was very weak, she noticed. Portia said nothing about it, and she declined to take a biscuit but held the plate out to the older lady.

Mrs. Lenthall took one and bit into it with a grimace. "We used to have friends come for tea every Tuesday afternoon when I was married."

"Could you not do that still?"

Mrs. Lenthall raised a glass. "All my friends are dead. What is there to talk to anyone about anymore?"

"Your family."

"Those nephews of mine cause me nothing but heartache."

Portia did not know Nigel, Lord Wade's younger brother, all that well, only that he had gone to the army recently, and that was something to worry over and talk about. "The oldest is very worried about you."

Mrs. Lenthall suddenly raised her lorgnette and studied Portia in more detail, until she began to squirm. "When are you going to tell him the truth?"

"Who?"

"Montrose, of course. You really should put him out of his misery."

Portia fidgeted. "It is complicated. My father—"

"Is a fool, and much too afraid of losing Montrose's favor, little good it will ever do him. But then you know about Montrose's failings, now, don't you?"

Portia nodded quickly.

"Arrogance, impatience, ghastly temper like his father." The older lady smiled sadly. "Old Montrose married three times in his life. Wore out each woman one way or another. Personally, I think they were happy for the peace of the great beyond in the end."

Portia shivered.

"At least my nephew has never tried to tie you down. He always respected your opinion and let you run your own race since the moment he first saw you at your court presentation."

Portia blushed. "He never told me he saw me there."

"Well, of course he would not admit to falling in love at first sight. Men, in my experience, never do."

Portia could feel herself grinning widely, even though she tried not to react. How much she appreciated Julian's restraint now. She hadn't liked him following her, but at least he'd never truly stood in her way. How it must have hurt him when she'd accepted Montrose.

"I take it the news pleases you, dearie," Mrs. Lenthall said as she reached for her wine glass again.

Portia took it from her and set it aside. "You need to stop drinking."

The old lady frowned severely. "I occasionally find you entirely too opinionated. You are not a duchess yet, young lady."

"And I never will be," Portia promised. She leaned forward and kissed Mrs. Lenthall's cheek before whispering in her ear, "Dear Auntie, don't argue with me. I refuse to be less than I am. But remember, you cannot hold a baby and a wine glass at the same time. I will forbid that. So will Julian, too, I suspect."

She sat back and watched the impact of her words on the older woman's face. It took a very long time, but the lady grinned widely until there were tears standing in her eyes. "You didn't come all this way to lie to an old woman, did you?"

"No," she admitted. "Actually, I came to ask you to help me one more time. I will soon end my engagement to Montrose, and I should not like my sister to suffer for my decision."

The old woman blinked furiously, and then wiped her eyes dry. "You have no idea what good it does to this old heart to hear that you will prove me right. I was afraid you had lost your chance to be happily married."

Portia clasped the older woman's hands. "So you'll help me with Lavinia?"

"There is nothing I won't do for you, my dear. We're

almost family. What a remarkable gel you're turning out to be. We need—" The old lady shot to her feet, and then tumbled back to the chaise in an untidy heap.

Portia straightened her up and wedged pillows around her. "You need to sleep first, I think. Lie back and close your eyes. I'll be here when you wake up."

"No, I've been feeling sorry for myself for much too long." She cast a scathing glance at the wine bottle, and her expression firmed. "Fetch me my writing table from over there, and my copy of my Debrett's Peerage, too. It's time to call in a few favors owed to me, and I know which families hide the best scandals. They'll help you and your sister if it silences me."

"I don't want to blackmail anyone," Portia protested.

"We are going to need a plan if we are going into battle with the high sticklers of the *ton*." She squinted at the writing table when Portia set it on her lap, and then at her hand. She moved it back and forth, squinting as if she couldn't see clearly. "On second thought, you had better summon the butler, first. We're going to be at this for a while. This is a job for coffee. A vat of it should be brewed poste haste."

Chapter Twenty-Two

—◆—

Julian assisted Auntie out of the carriage, noting her pallor was somewhat green. "I say, are you unwell?"

Auntie scowled severely. "I don't want to talk about it."

"Why not?" he questioned, preventing her from taking another step. "You usually tell me more than I ever wanted to know. Don't start keeping secrets now."

She looked around quickly and drew herself up straighter. The rented carriage was drawing away, and the Hayes family butler stood waiting on the stair. No one should hear a word they said if she kept her voice low enough. If she were not fit to sit down to dinner, he would try to hail a hack and take her back home again. Portia would understand that his family came first.

Julian drew closer. "Tell me what's wrong with you?"

Auntie sniffed and adopted a haughty expression. "If you must know, I gave up drink yesterday. My head already pains me."

Julian almost cheered. He currently couldn't afford to buy her more wine, and he hated to disappoint her. "I'm so pleased to hear that. Not about the sore head but the other."

"Do keep your voice down, boy," she complained, lifting her fingers to her brow and massaging her temple. "No need to shout it out for all to hear.

Julian struggled not to laugh. He'd been in her condition a few times, not lately of course, but when he was younger. He understood how every noise was amplified. He captured her hand and slid it onto his arm. "You'll feel better after you eat something substantial."

"The gel promised me roast pork for dinner. I haven't had that in such a long time."

"Hmm, and it is your favorite, which makes tonight your lucky night," Julian murmured—and then looked at Auntie sharply. "When did Portia promise roast pork for dinner?"

"Yesterday."

"Why didn't you tell me you saw her?" Julian would have liked to talk to her about Montrose, find out if she was still engaged or not. There hadn't been a whisper about the break so far, and he was getting worried that she'd changed her mind. If she wasn't engaged, he'd be delighted to kiss her witless as soon as they were alone. If she was, Julian wasn't sure what to do, or if they should even be dining with her family tonight.

Auntie took a step forward, dragging him along. "She called to see *me*. It is hardly my fault that you were busy elsewhere all day."

Julian swallowed and winced. He'd been with the Duke of Exeter, discussing how he might be of service. Their talks had been exhaustive but his thoughts had never been far from Portia.

He glanced up at the house and saw Portia in profile, standing at a window. She was not looking outside but his heart thudded a little faster. "I trust she only saw the drawing room."

Auntie smiled quickly. "The gel is not the least bit interested in your wealth, my boy."

"That's good because there is none. She's marrying a duke and will want for nothing," he warned. He wasn't about to tell Auntie that he'd made love to Portia Hayes until…well, never. He was disappointed in himself. He had taken something from Portia that he could never give back. He sighed deeply. "I imagine this might be our very last dinner with her and her family, too. Montrose has not changed, so I doubt we will have the dubious honor of an invitation to dine with her after she marries."

"I think you might be surprised how often you see the gel for dinner."

Julian shook his head and they mounted the stairs slowly.

They were taken into the drawing room, a pretty chamber filled with rich furnishings and flowers. A room fit for a lady and her family. The Hayes family was there to greet them— the mother looked tired, the father cross, the little sister oblivious to all as she entertained them on the pianoforte from afar. It also appeared that Lord Sullivan was to be dining with the family again that night, as well.

But Julian's eyes were drawn to Portia and her wide smile of welcome. He ached to rush over to kiss her.

He bowed, she curtsied. There was nothing he could do openly to prove that he had missed her like the very devil without drawing attention to them.

"We are so pleased you could join us tonight," Mrs. Hayes announced.

"It is our pleasure, as always."

"I have good news," Mrs. Hayes whispered for his ears alone. "We have received an invitation to the event of the year. I am beside myself with happiness!"

He had no time to ask what she meant because the butler suddenly announced Montrose had arrived.

Julian schooled his features to hide his dismay and stepped back to allow Montrose room to greet Portia.

If Montrose were here, she was still engaged to the duke.

However, the duke's greetings toward Portia's parents were perfunctory at best, almost rudely done. Mrs. Hayes was a good woman, albeit a little shortsighted where her daughter was concerned. The father, exceedingly ambitious.

Julian glanced at his aunt and found her grinning at Montrose. "Your grace, what a pleasant surprise to find you here."

"Mrs. Lenthall," he said, looking down his nose at the woman. "How interesting to find you again ready to sup at another family's table instead of your own."

Julian stepped forward, but his aunt placed a restraining hand on his arm. "We were invited to dine with the family, your grace. Unlike some, I would never invite myself anywhere," she noted.

Julian glanced at her sharply and saw her slowly smile at the duke.

"The Hayes family are the most generous and kind of any family I've ever known," Julian added.

Mrs. Hayes beamed a smile at him. "You are too kind, my lord."

"He is kind," Portia agreed, coming up on Julian's other side. "Why, I've never known anyone so generous to help others as the Wade family. They were the first family of the *ton* to welcome us with open arms and have done so for many families."

Wade couldn't help but be confused by what was going on. Auntie and Portia seemed to be in perfect step. "Are we to spend the night complimenting each other?"

"Indeed, no. We have so much more important matters to discuss, and we have promised a feast and mean to make good on that score, too." Portia slid her arm through Julian's. "You are with me tonight, my lord."

Montrose spluttered.

The dream dearest to Julian's heart was to have Portia all to himself at dinner, but not with Montrose looking daggers at him.

Mrs. Hayes held out her arm to the duke, and Julian and Portia walked in to dinner together.

Portia held him back a little so they were not following so close to the others. "He was supposed to come the day I saw you last," she told him, scowling at the dark figure up ahead. "He promised to call today, too, and then amended his acceptance to say that he would be here for dinner. Mother is very cross about it all."

"He knows she won't refuse the honor of having a duke eat at her table." He shook his head. "The man is incapable of being agreeable. What are you and Auntie up to?"

"Nothing you need know about," she promised with a sweet smile he instantly distrusted.

Her fingers toyed with her neckline, drawing his attention down to her breasts. Those had filled his hands, and her body had met with his in perfect symmetry. "I like your gown," he whispered.

Portia gently shoved him sideways into the library and pressed him against the wall. He grasped her hips while she pressed her lips against his and stole a kiss. Her tongue flickered out to meet his, and they stood kissing like that a moment or two. However, they could not stay in this room. They were expected to join everyone else soon.

He glanced down at her bust and wet his lips as he skimmed his fingers across the hard peaks of her nipples through her gown.

"I like your buttons," she said, eying his waistcoat.

He frowned and looked down. "Just the buttons?"

"There are only four on your waistcoat. Four less than I had to contend with the other afternoon," she murmured.

Julian considered that and grinned. "Less is better?"

"More efficient," she whispered, and the hot look she threw him almost knocked him off his feet. She laughed wickedly and pecked another kiss on his lips. "I think I shall make that the first requirement of my husband, that he economize on buttons."

"I'll consider that a priority."

"Please do so," she murmured.

Julian pulled her back into the hall and along to the dining room. Everyone noticed their late arrival.

"There you are," Montrose exclaimed, eyes narrowing.

Portia glanced at the duke but it was a dangerous smile that flitted across her lips. "A pressing matter of business detained me."

Julian helped her sit, trying not to laugh at the look of shock on the duke's face, and he took the chair at her side. He placed his own napkin in his lap and sat back, looking at everyone at the table again. Auntie sipped water. Mrs. Hayes, wine. Mr. Hayes seemed at a loss for words, while Portia's younger sister fiddled with her napkin, glancing shyly at Sullivan.

Conversation resumed slowly, and Julian turned to Portia. "Did you hear that Lord and Lady Windermere left London this morning?"

"I had not." Portia smiled. "Do you know what brought it on?"

"Lord Windermere sent a note to say he has decided to take his wife to the seacoast for the rest of the summer. A honeymoon trip."

"How romantic. I do like to hear of husbands and wives traveling together after so many years of marriage."

Julian nodded. "It seems…economic."

"Ah," Portia said, just as Montrose sniggered.

Portia's hand settled on Julian's suddenly. "Did Mother tell you our news?"

"She mentioned something but did not elaborate. What makes her smile so happily?"

"Exeter has sent an invitation to join him for a month this winter."

"Oh, what a boon for Lavinia!" Julian exclaimed, and then cast a glance along the table to where Montrose sat. The dukes did not get along, and Exeter had been only too happy to repay Julian's future help with a promise to invite the Hayes family to the country. Julian glanced at Portia quickly. "For everyone?"

"For Mother, Papa and Lavinia." She smiled and took a small sip of the soup that had been placed before her as they spoke. "I expect my inclusion will sort itself out eventually. Once I marry."

Julian leaned toward Portia slightly. "I would say so."

"How do you like your lobster soup, my lord?"

Julian glanced down at his bowl and dug in. The first mouthful melted his senses. "This is truly excellent."

"I though you might enjoy that one. I hear it is your favorite."

Julian and Portia spoke in pieces all through the meal. He was very sorry when the last dishes were cleared away. He didn't want to part with Portia, and nearly said so. However, he soon noted Lord Montrose was glowering at them.

As soon as Mrs. Hayes suggested the ladies repair to the drawing room, Montrose was on his feet and rounding the table to capture Portia's arm. "I'll take you in."

Julian goggled at the breach of etiquette. The duke had no manners for delicate company and was only getting worse the older he got. Julian got to his feet, too, and Sullivan joined them all.

Portia freed herself. "Actually, Lord Montrose, might I trouble you for a word in private, now that you finally have time to see me."

His jaw clenched tight. "I think that's a good idea, too."

Julian swallowed at the hard edge to Montrose's words. He was furious. Julian didn't want Portia to be alone with this man, not when he was in a temper, and he was about to say so when, to his complete surprise, Auntie came up to Portia, linked their arms like sisters, and drew Portia out of the room.

"This way, your grace," Auntie called.

Mr. and Mrs. Hayes drew together to whisper, appearing very concerned. They did not, however, follow after their daughter and Montrose.

Julian sat back down slowly but stared after the retreating figures until he heard a door close down the hall.

Sullivan slid into a chair beside Julian. "I thought he would explode! Bravely done."

"We were only talking."

Sullivan chuckled. "That was always enough for him to become jealous of anyone when they got too close to his lovers."

"She is not that to him."

"You know what I mean," Sullivan chided.

Unfortunately, he did. If Montrose found out he and Portia had made love, he might hurt her. Julian got to his feet and slipped from the room to follow Portia for his own piece of mind.

Chapter Twenty-Three

Portia swept ahead into the library with Mrs. Lenthall at her side without waiting to see if the glowering Duke of Montrose followed. It was all his fault it had to be this way. He was a tardy suitor and expected everyone to bend over backward to please him at all times. No matter how rude he was or how inconvenient his arrival, Portia and her family had been expected to feel *honored* to be inconvenienced.

She turned around and faced him. The duke was a handsome man but he was arrogant, inflexible, and rude to her friends and family. She gritted her teeth. She had intended to be gentle about ending their engagement, but after listening to him needle Julian and his aunt about their reduced circumstances yet again, well…she was much too angry to be bothered with the niceties anymore.

Auntie sat herself down on a nearby chair to act as protector and chaperone with a wide smile on her lips.

Her presence gave Portia all the courage she needed. "Your grace," she began. "I am glad you came tonight."

He drew close and nodded. "I have neglected my responsibilities, so here I am."

She winced. "Is that what you think I am already? A chore that must be completed out of duty?"

"That is not what I meant."

"But that is what I heard and what I feel." She drew herself up. "I have something to say to you that is most unexpected. Over the past weeks, I have striven to know you, and I must say you have proven impossible. You promised I would have time to get to know you, but you've done nothing but neglect me."

"You will not be neglected after our marriage," he promised.

"After marriage doesn't interest me. After marriage you will most likely do whatever you like with anyone you like too. But before marriage, I expected better—I expected to be courted. I imagined you to be a man who would at least try to make me fall in love with you before we wed. Two shoddy kisses and you have failed most thoroughly."

The duke's face darkened. "What do you know of kisses?"

"Enough to know you are terrible at it," she insisted. "You don't enjoy kissing me, or seem to want to, and I'd prefer you didn't now. Did you give any thought to what I might have wanted from my future husband? Was I just expected to put up with long silences and the scowls you directed at my dance partners?"

The duke's jaw clenched and she sensed he was on the edge of an outburst. Now seemed like a good time to stop. She'd said enough. "Lord Montrose, it is my duty to inform you that we do not suit."

He stared without saying a word.

"Do you understand me? I no longer wish to become your duchess."

He took a pace toward her, standing over her so tall and forbidding now. Any trace of polite engagement faded away, to be replaced by a look of complete shock. "No."

"Yes."

He took another menacing step toward her, and she had little choice but to take a step back. She did not want his body touching hers.

"You are mistaken," he announced.

"I am not. I have ended our engagement, and as a

gentleman, you must accept it."

His gaze grew cold. "I could crush you. I could ruin your family!"

"I'm sure you will do your best," she murmured. Threats would change nothing and she could not relent. The last thing she wanted was to be his duchess. Not when there was a chance she could be the wife of a good man instead. "But that statement just proves how very odd a man you are. The rules of polite society demand you accept the situation and withdraw. Threats do not work on matters of the heart. You care not for me or for the good of my family."

He glared at her for a full minute, and Portia held her tongue while he mulled over her words in silence.

He narrowed his eyes even more. "You asked too many damn questions anyway."

Montrose spun about on his heel, strode away, and slammed the door shut behind him.

Portia waited, trembling with relief while he demanded his hat and gloves, and then he was finally gone from her life.

"That was very well done, dearie," Mrs. Lenthall murmured. "You would have made a formidable duchess."

Portia grinned. "I thought so, too, once. Shall we join the others?"

"Indeed we should. Julian was looking a little worried for a while there."

Portia turned and saw Julian retreating back to the drawing room, where everyone else must be by now.

The easy part was over. Telling her parents that she would no longer be a duchess was bound to be the most difficult discussion of her life. It was also bound to sour the night and make them very angry with her.

The only bright spark was that Julian was here, and he must know she was free to hear his proposal now. About time. She pressed her hands to her cheeks and laughed softly as she followed Mrs. Lenthall to the hall. She paused outside to listen, realizing that Lord Wade, and even Lord Sullivan to an extent, fitted into the family already—far better than Lord

Montrose had ever tried to.

She stepped into the room with Auntie and smiled at everyone. "What have we missed?"

"Nothing of importance." Julian promised. "Sullivan was just inviting us all to join him for a few weeks of country air."

She moved to sit beside Julian. "A trip to the country is just what we all need."

"As I was saying, how about you all visit my estate for a few weeks next month," Lord Sullivan continued. "We could take long walks, picnic by the river, and perhaps even fish if you are inclined."

Auntie sighed. "Northport's gardens are lovely in the summer. I visited long ago, when I was a girl. I doubt much has changed, but I don't know if Wade would be willing join us."

"Oh, that is a shame," Mother murmured. "Are you sure you cannot?"

Portia glanced at Julian, catching him watching her with a smile playing on his lips. "I think I might actually have my hands full next month. Perhaps the month after I could, though."

Summer in the country was not her wish, either. She wanted to be married to Julian as soon as possible. She still had to ask him about Soho Square, and whether they might live there instead of his own townhouse. There was so much to do in that house and none in the other but decorate it. In four weeks, or perhaps less if he were able to obtain a special license, she hoped they would be newlyweds.

Lavinia cleared her throat. "Do you fish, my lord?"

"Indeed I do," Lord Sullivan promised her. "Do you?"

"Oh yes. I am a very keen angler. I caught more than my papa once, but I was only a little girl at the time."

Lord Sullivan's smiled indulgently. "Truly?"

The pair then discussed fishing as if no one else was in the room.

Julian leaned a little closer to Portia, his fingers resting on the edge of her skirts. "Do you fish as well, Portia?"

"I could learn to," she said, taking note of his hand's movement. Fishing was not a favorite pastime but she would learn to like if Julian wanted her to.

"You will not ever have to sully your hands with worm guts because of me," Julian promised with a laugh as he quickly caressed her thigh. "I find it as dull as watching paint dry."

"What will you do then if you are not fishing?"

His brows lifted suddenly. "What we did the other day would suit me very well."

A thrill flowed through Portia's body at his gravelly tone. "Me too."

Her mother glanced toward the door. "Will Lord Montrose be joining us soon, Portia darling?"

She sighed, knowing her peace was at an end. She had to tell them now. "No, he's gone."

"Without saying goodbye?"

"I for one am glad to see the back of him," Sullivan promised.

Julian nodded. "You were magnificent, by the way."

"Thank you." She looked to her parents, buoyed by his praise. "Mother, Father. I have an important announcement to make. Tonight, I ended my engagement to Lord Montrose."

Portia's father turned red, and then he paled. "What?"

Mother gasped. "Portia, what have you done? You were to be married. I have everything arranged! And what about your sister?"

"I did what I believed was necessary. Accepting his proposal was a mistake. He was not what he first appeared to be." She took a deep breath. "You should know, too, that Lord Montrose threatened to make trouble for us if I didn't marry him, but that only made me more determined not to. He is no gentleman."

Mother swooned.

Portia rushed over to help her.

"Are you really not going to get married now?" Lavinia asked suddenly.

She smiled at her sister. "I would have been very unhappy if

I had married Montrose."

Lavinia's brow furrowed. "What does happiness matter? You would have been a duchess."

"Trust me, happiness is the *only* thing that matters when you marry," Lord Sullivan explained gently, and then he winked. "I think she did a very brave, very right thing."

Father stormed from the room. Portia sighed heavily and wondered if she should follow and explain, or at least be there to be scolded. "He wouldn't even look at me."

"He'll come around eventually. I got the impression he wasn't so keen on Lord Montrose anymore, anyway. It happens once people get to know Montrose's true nature. He's a hard man, impatient and very demanding. He's the worst fellow to ever inherit that exalted title. What you have done tonight *was* very brave, Portia. Never doubt that," Julian murmured. "The *ton* will probably hold you at fault at first but not for very long, I imagine. Your popularity and easygoing character will bring true friends back to your side and ensure your place in society remains unchanged."

She looked at Julian fondly. "It is only because of you and your aunt that I became popular."

"Nonsense," he argued. "It would have happened eventually. You have a great heart, and you have never been afraid to befriend anyone and everyone. Most women in your position don't. Not if they dream to catch themselves a title."

"I have dreams aplenty."

"I'll do all I can to assist," he murmured with a twinkle in his eye.

Mother moaned suddenly and covered her face with both hands. "Oh, dear. Oh my! We will suffer for this."

"I can assure you they will care little by the end, dearie," Aunt Hesper soothed. "The *ton* has a short memory, especially when reminded of their own misdeeds. They will forgive by the time she marries another and move on to the next scandal almost immediately."

Mother glared at Aunt Hesper in obvious exasperation. "Have you understood *nothing*? Who will marry my daughters now that one has shown herself to be so particular? If a duke is not good enough for Portia, who would even ask her to marry?"

Auntie stood slowly. "You've nothing to worry about on that score. Let's you and I have a little talk before you borrow trouble where there is none. Do you happen to have a powder? My head is aching like the very devil."

Mother instantly helped Aunt Hesper to her feet and they whispered to each other all the way out the door.

Portia leaned closer to Julian. "What is wrong with Auntie?"

"She gave up the drink yesterday."

"Oh, I was hoping she would take my advice."

"She did it for you?"

"I warned her that no mother would allow a tipsy woman to hold their children. She aches to see the next generation of Wade in the nursery."

Wade's eyes drifted across the room to where they had an audience still.

Lord Sullivan and Lavinia were still sitting with them, watching them avidly, but Julian took up her hand anyway. It was high time for him to do what he should have done a long time ago. He brought Portia's fingers to his lips and kissed them softly. "We're on the right path now."

"Yes, we are," she agreed, clutching his hand tightly. Portia raised her free hand to touch his face. "Together."

He nodded. "Together."

"What are you doing holding my sister's hand like that?" Lavinia asked, interrupting the tender moment with an ill-timed question.

"Quiet now, Miss Lavinia," Sullivan warned. "Your sister is in the middle of something vitally important."

"Indeed," Julian promised with another twinkle in his eye for Portia.

"I'll explain later," Portia promised her sister without looking away from Julian's face.

"He should not be holding her hand, and she should not be

messing up his hair," Lavinia declared loudly. "Mother would not like it. It isn't proper."

"He's about to propose," Sullivan remarked. "Something that does not require witnesses. Why don't you and I find a book to look at in your library? I understand you are a great reader."

"Do you like to read?"

"When I have time," he answered, and surprisingly, Lavinia left the room with him.

Portia, already lost to Julian and the spell of anticipation they were weaving together, did not worry about any possible impropriety. Desire, attraction, love, and honesty compelled her to stay right where she sat now. She wet her lips, impatient for what came next.

"I have waited so long for this day," Julian murmured.

"I was dreadfully slow in understanding. Forgive me."

"Already done. Besides, some alterations cannot be rushed. I prefer to do things right when I can."

Portia arched her brow. "Like long courtships and extravagant wedding feasts."

"I have no objection to either one." He leaned in and kissed her cheek. "Whatever you require is yours. Just tell me what would please you."

Portia flexed her fingers in his hair, loving the feel of it slipping through her fingers. "I have already been courted by you, when you consider our history. Long walks, dancing, conversation and confidences shared. Even my favorite flowers."

"It's been a very long courtship indeed, if that's how you see our history. Three years nearly since I first laid eyes on you. I have something that I must say first, though." Lord Wade cupped her face lightly and drew closer. "I'm entirely without funds, pockets to let, a fortune hunter. My house on Hanover Square will be gone soon, too, I hope. I've sold everything of value just so I could stay in London to see you. I have no ties to anything but you and my small family. My future is in your delicate hands."

"Good." She smiled despite the pain his confession caused her. "I happen to have a good dowry, and that includes a house meant for my son. I would like us to live there when we marry. Your aunt, and your brother whenever he visits, could stay, too, if they want, and my mother and sister will visit often, I hope. We could be very happy there."

"I'm always happiest when I'm with you," he promised. He slid off the settee and knelt at her feet. "What color is your garter tonight," he whispered as his fingers grazed her ankles.

Portia grinned and slowly raised her gown up one leg to show him. His hand settled on her knee firmly—but then footsteps rushed toward the room.

Father had terrible timing.

"What the devil are you doing on your knees?"

Julian discreetly flicked her gown down over her leg as he rose. "Perhaps we might talk in private, Mr. Hayes."

Although her father frowned, and she worried that it was too soon for this conversation, Father did agree to leave again with Julian.

Portia wished Julian good luck in a whisper and then sat back, breathing a sigh of contentment. Father might say no to Julian today; he was broke, and Father abhorred fortune hunters. But eventually he would come around, because Portia would say yes to no one else.

Mother and Mrs. Lenthall returned, followed by Lavinia and Lord Sullivan. The earl seemed uncharacteristically quiet, and Lavinia seemed to be blushing furiously.

It took two cups of tea before Julian and her father returned. Father headed for the whiskey, but Julian once again settled at her side with a firm nod. "I forgot to tell you that when I was speaking to the Marchioness of Ettington the other day, she vowed to host a ball when I married."

The whisky decanter landed heavily on the silver tray. Father turned, eyes wide.

"A ball at Ettington House?" Mother exclaimed in astonishment. "What an honor!"

"Indeed. Actually, it was more of a threat, now I think

about it closely." Julian shook his head. "I think the Marchioness of Ettington may not be finished making me pay for that thing I said to her before she married."

"Poor Julian. You must learn to hold your tongue around proper women more often." Portia laughed softly. "Thankfully, you needn't worry about offending me anymore."

"I never once did," he admitted with a laugh. "I grossly underestimated the marchioness' nature then, though. Her penchant for revenge is quite unexpected."

"I definitely need to further my acquaintance with Lady Ettington," Portia declared. "She seems like someone I could be friends with."

"Winter at Exeter's estate should be interesting. You, Anna, Lady Windermere, and Lady Ettington together for a month under the same roof? I should probably be afraid," he whispered. "The trouble you ladies could get into boggles the mind."

"You'll be there to watch over me." Portia sighed and caught his hand in hers. "We are going to be all right, my lord."

He stared back at her. "Will you marry me, Portia Hayes?"

Portia's eyes prickled with the threat of tears. She was so happy, she couldn't speak for several very long seconds. "Yes!"

"Oh, my word!" Mother exclaimed as she collapsed again.

This time she really did swoon, although they tried to rouse her.

Mrs. Lenthall winked. "She's had one too many shocks for today. Give her time, and I think this calls for a celebration as soon as she wakes up. Do carry on with what needs doing."

Portia held Julian's hand to her cheek. "I love you, Julian, with all my heart."

Mother roused then. "David, where are you," Mother called, stretching out her hand blindly to her husband.

Father sighed and moved to stand over his wife. They exchanged a long look, and then he caught up her hand. He patted it soothingly. "It's all right, my dear. Everything will be all right now," he promised. "Lord Wade will look after her well enough.”

“But he's a fortune hunter,” Mother cried in a scandalized whisper.

“He is not!” Portia declared in his defense. “He's never cared about my fortune. He loves me!”

“I don't believe he is after her money, either,” Father announced, eyeing Julian through narrowed eyes. A half smile turned up his lips suddenly. “But she's your problem now, my lord. Don't let her change her mind a second time.”

“Never. I've a fair idea how to keep her happy.”

Portia blushed as Julian smiled down upon her.

He winked, and then grasped her about the waist and brought her to her feet. He spun her around in a tight circle.

Portia leaned into him and looped her arms over his shoulders. She stared into his eyes. “I do love you.”

“That's all I ever wanted.” Julian's smile widened, and then his lips were at her ear. “But I'll need a peek at those garters of yours again before I leave tonight.”

How delicious was it to whisper scandalous intimacies to each other in a crowded room with someone you loved? “I'd planned to show you more than just my garters.”

Lord Wade sighed deeply. “As long as I'm the only one you tempt.”

She winked. “I can guarantee you that, my lord.”

Julian framed her face suddenly and pressed his lips to hers in a hard kiss that never seemed to end.

Epilogue

———◆———

Portia gasped as the new carriage rounded a corner, throwing her into the well-padded side. "Julian, please," she begged.

He chuckled. As a husband of three weeks, Julian was well pleased with the desperation of his wife's plea for mercy. He slid his fingers into her sex again and returned his lips to torment her dripping folds with hungry kisses. Portia was so close, he could almost feel her body vibrating with lust.

The carriage was cloaked in darkness, interior lights snuffed as they moved along the dark streets, barely an arm's reach away from other people.

Portia enjoyed the danger of discovery, almost as much as his touch. Although he could not see her body, he knew her very well. Most likely she was a little embarrassed by her pose, but not enough to stop him pleasuring her. He adored being a husband, and he never hesitated to drive Portia wild when he saw a chance to be wicked.

He had brought little to the marriage but his hunger for her.

This was not even the first carriage encounter they'd enjoyed, but it was the most adventurous. Julian had an insatiable appetite for her body but time was short. He loved nothing more than to shock her by whispering sweet seductions in her ear at every opportunity. The way she seemed to melt at the mere suggestion of intimacy kept them both well satisfied in the bedroom, and the hallway, and the storage cupboards on occasion.

However, tonight there was little time to dally. They were going to their first *tonnish* engagement since their marriage. They should be arriving at Lady Fox's soiree at any moment.

Portia suddenly pressed her hands down on Julian's head, urging him to satisfy her quickly. He doubled his attentions, lapping at the little bud at the junction of her thighs and twisting his fingers into her body again and again, until Portia finally cried out softly.

He stayed with her until she settled then withdrew to his own side of the carriage, willing his erection to subside. It wouldn't do to present himself to tonight's host with his sword at full attention.

Portia sat up slowly, scowling. "You don't play fair, husband."

"You needed the distraction, wife." He grinned. "I imagine your cheeks have a delightful glow about them now. You were looking a little pale when we left home."

"Of course I am anxious about tonight." She straightened herself, and then pressed her palms to her cheeks. "It is our first social engagement as husband and wife."

"No one cares about anything Montrose has said about you. He doesn't even know the truth about *us*, either."

Montrose had made an attempt to disparage Portia, and the *ton* had risen to her defense in a way they rarely did for anyone. He'd had plenty to say about them marrying, too. However, with the Duke of Exeter's congratulations, the *ton* suddenly saw nothing wrong at all.

Largely ignored—and angry about it—Montrose had returned to the country to lick his wounds.

The carriage rolled to a sudden stop and, thankfully, when Julian alighted, he was in full control of his body. He held out his hand to assist Portia's exit but she staggered onto the pavement as if her legs were weak still from her climax.

"Goodness," she exclaimed as the carriage drew away. She stood at his side, fluffed out her costume and breathed deeply, lifting up her breasts quite by accident.

Julian was very tempted to call the carriage back. Surely he could find the time to feast on the bounty inside that scrap of bodice. She was about to fall out of it anyway. "You take my breath away."

"As did you, my lord. Quite thoroughly."

She wound her arm through his and he led her up the stairs to enter the townhouse.

Their hosts, friends of his for years, greeted them with exuberance and warmth. No one but Montrose had yet to declare Julian had married better than he deserved, although there were times he wondered if he really hadn't. He had no concerns about money any longer. The great weight of apprehension about the future had lifted from his shoulders the moment he'd moved into Portia's late uncle's home and declared it his own.

That was not to say they had finished moving things in and out of rooms. Old Uncle Oliver had hoarded everything that seemed to have come his way. A week after their marriage ceremony, they'd placed the knocker on the door. A trickle of visitors had became a deluge as word spread that Julian and Portia were happy to return any lost items they might unwittingly have inherited.

Julian drew Portia to his side as they met the waiting hosts. "We are delighted to be with you tonight, Lady Fox. Have you met my wife yet?"

The couple laughed because they were well acquainted with Portia already, had attended their wedding, too, but still congratulated them on their marriage. Julian could not quite get enough of telling people that Portia was his lady.

Lady Fox drew close. "It was high time someone good took you off the market."

"You're not the first to say so," he whispered back. "I never knew my bachelorhood was of such concern to others."

"To those you helped find happiness, it is."

Julian smiled.

"You might not believe it, but Exeter has graced us with his presence tonight," she whispered.

"Excellent." Julian was not done helping the duke, and he did have a question.

Julian and Portia's arrival was announced and the assembly cheered. He led Portia into the ball, bursting with pride to have her on his arm at last. He might never get used to the feeling of satisfaction he experienced as other men looked upon her grinning countenance. He was finally the luckiest man in any room now.

They had gone no more than a few feet into the ballroom before they were swamped with well-wishers and congratulations. Portia was asked to dance time and again, and it wasn't too long before she announced her card was full. Those who had missed out tried to claim a dance at a future ball there and then. Julian laughed along with everyone else and took great delight in sending them on their way.

He peeked at her dance card. "So who is the lucky swain to dance with Lady Wade first tonight?"

"That would be Lord Grindlewood," she murmured with a slight frown. "I always thought I would be less in demand as a married woman."

"No doubt one of them will try to steal you away from me before the night is over." He pressed a kiss to her brow. "Who is your partner for the supper dance?"

She turned to him, a shy smile on her lips. "That would be you, my lord."

"You saved me a dance?"

"Of course. Didn't you want to take me into supper?"

He pulled Portia close. "I suppose I could do that, or I could do what I've always longed to do with you at supper, instead."

"What was that?"

"Lure you to a dark corner and kiss you witless," he promised.

Portia laughed and leaned into him a little more. "I think I'd like that. How do we do it?"

"Meet me on the terrace as soon as your dance with," he took her card and peered at her list of partners, "Sullivan is over. I'll be watching for you, as always."

She took her lip between her teeth and her eyes glowed with lust. He'd planned to only steal a kiss and hold her tonight, but perhaps his wife would rather he be more thorough in his seduction.

She exhaled slowly, and her eyes fell to his chest. Her fingers toyed with the buttons on his new waistcoat. As instructed, he'd happily economized on buttons when he'd visited his tailor. There were just three on this one, easily undone, too. He brought her hand to his lips and kissed it. "You shouldn't look at me like I'm a meal, darling. What will people say?"

"I want them to say we're a love match."

"They will soon enough," he promised.

Her first partner was coming their way, but Portia suddenly lifted up to whisper in his ear, "I can't wait to be alone with you again later."

He held her close a moment longer. "I might be desperate to put my hands on you again by then, too, so don't keep me waiting."

She grinned. "My lord, you say the most exciting things to me."

"As long as I'm the only scoundrel you listen to."

She nodded. "The one and only."

Portia was swept away by Lord Grindlewood to dance under the bright chandeliers, smiling merrily. Julian watched as she was passed from man to man, but they always brought her back to him at the end of every set. Portia basked in their attention, and couldn't help but flirt with her partners and other men. But just when he feared he'd been forgotten, her eyes would lock on his, and she'd smile in a way that filled his heart with love.

He was very lucky indeed.

If you enjoyed Lord of Sin don't miss
The Winter Wishes Anthology
and a brand new distinguished Rogue

One Enchanted Christmas

An Excerpt

Lady Meg Stockwick covered her cold nose and mouth again and blew out a breath, hoping to warm her face a little bit. Meg was not used to traveling in the winter months. She was not used to traveling at all really. She was doing her best not to become an icicle.

Her brother was to blame for her discomfort, not that he seemed to care.

Until recently, she'd never had reason to venture from the family home on the coast of Dorset. But it was Hector's home now; her brother had assumed control of their father's estate and title upon his death, and she was supposed to obey the new viscount—even if she couldn't seem to stop questioning his decisions.

"It's not too late to turn back," Meg told him urgently as Hector's new traveling chariot began the slow descent into yet another blindingly white valley. "We could be home by Christmas morning."

"It certainly is too late. We're almost there," her brother assured her as he scrubbed the damp from the window with his fist. "You will enjoy yourself."

Meg doubted that as she huddled more deeply into her coverings. The sun had come out to shine at last and brought with it Hector's enthusiasm for new surroundings. He had been saying she'd enjoy herself repeatedly for the last day, and she was still quite sure he was wrong. Spending the anniversary of the worst month of her life in Derbyshire, at the home of a terrible rogue, was not her idea of fun.

"We should still celebrate Christmas the way we always have," Meg insisted, determined to win her brother over. "In our home. I had everything in hand before you arrived."

"Next year you can do as you wish," he promised. "But this year I have other plans than sitting in Dorset all alone."

Meg shivered, wishing her brother had stayed in London. His return had heralded an upset of all her plans for the holidays. And now she was here, far from home and all she'd ever known. Meg had heard nothing good about her brother's closest friend in the past few years and now she would be forced into close proximity with him for weeks.

She had known Lord Clement as a boy, but it had been a decade since she'd lain eyes on him. She had heard enough to form a clear picture of his character though. Lord Clement was often gallivanting about London with her brother, too important to visit their little coastal village. Meg believed him to be a terrible influence on her older brother.

She heaved a heavy sigh. There was only one thing to look forward to this holiday. Lady Vyne, the rogue's mother, was certain to be better company. Lady Vyne had written Meg many comforting letters in recent years following the death of her mother and then her father so soon after.

Hector suddenly began gathering his possessions—book, handkerchief, and a pouch of sweet meats he'd procured along the way—and stuffed them into a leather satchel he'd kept at his side for the entire trip.

Meg hugged her book close to her chest. "Mother and Father are still with us in spirit," she argued.

Hector shifted forward to stare at her, his expression grave. "If Mother and Father are spirits as you continue to claim, and watching over us as well, then surely they've heard our itinerary many times from your own lips and will have hitched a ride."

Meg wished that might be so. Did ghosts ever take a holiday? "That is how they met. Father climbed into the wrong carriage, and they fell in love."

"By the time they reached the fourth turnpike," Hector said softly.

"Love at first sight." Meg wanted so much to believe in the

impossible right now. Even though she had Hector still, she felt very alone without her parents. There was no one to tell her secrets to and no one who gave her theirs to keep. Two years of death, first her mother and then her father, and the constant period of mourning had been hard to bear for everyone. Her closest friends had married and moved away to start new lives with their husbands already. She had lost touch with all but a few.

Hector had been away in London when their father had died, but he had rushed home to be with her for the burial. He had not stayed long, traveling back to London to meet with Lord Clement while she had mourned alone.

And now Hector insisted she must travel with him. In the winter!

"Cheer up, old thing," Hector said. "Who knows what might happen during the holidays."

Nothing good, she suspected. Not if Lord Clement was anywhere in the vicinity of her brother. She might not see much of Hector either. That was not how she wanted to see out the year.

Meg huddled farther beneath the warm furs, trying to resign herself to the fate her brother had forced upon her. "I'm still in mourning," she reminded him. "Even if you forbid me to be."

He shoved his satchel aside roughly. "It was past time!"

Meg glared at him. "Papa deserved to be mourned for a full year as we did with Mother. Six months is hardly long enough."

"Enough is enough," he cried, smacking his fist on his thigh. "You will do as I say, and be grateful I care enough to take you to visit my friends at all. I am the head of our family and you will enjoy yourself." Her brother scowled. "I insist you make merry."

Meg glared at him. "You cannot make me pretend."

Hector pinched the bridge of his nose, a sure sign she was trying his patience. "You will not embarrass me by spoiling Christmas for Lord Clement and I."

Meg pressed her lips together tightly, affronted that Hector thought more of Lord Clement's happiness than hers. "You don't seem to care what I want anymore," she grumbled even though knowing she was being difficult. This trip had been a tax on her nerves. She'd barely slept last night in yet another strange bed.

She slumped in her seat as her eyes pricked with the threat

of tears. There were days she did not like her brother. He gambled away his fortune and spent far too many nights out in society. His improved situation had gone to his head. She'd also heard gossip he had a woman in London too—the sort Mama had whispered must never be acknowledged.

"I do care. Very much, and it is high time I did right by you and brought you out in society." Hector nodded. "Gentleman have to see you in order to ask to marry you."

Meg blushed at the idea of marrying a stranger. Hector was all for that. "You speak such nonsense. No one will notice me here."

"On the contrary, Lady Vyne is sure to host at least one dinner during our stay. There's a village not far from the manor house, too, and we will be here until after Twelfth Night don't forget. Anything can happen in that amount of time."

Meg turned up her nose. "That village has an alehouse, I assume?"

Hector grinned widely. "Every village tends to have at least one. Gentlemen come for miles around and some of them call on Lady Vyne, and Clement, too. They will assist with any introductions if they deem the connection suitable."

He had an answer for everything. "As if Lord Clement would stir himself on my behalf."

Hector chuckled. "He's a good friend."

"I thought I was that to you once," Meg grumbled.

"You're worse. You're my unmarried little sister. It is required that I adore you," Hector teased, grinning as he tapped her nose. "Even when you are out of sorts. If the signs of merriment bother you so much, just try not to scowl at everyone for the duration of our stay. Don't spoil Christmas for the rest of us. Mother and Father would hate to know you were so miserable."

She heaved a heavy sigh. Hector was probably right, but Mother and Father had made this time of year special. She had hoped to do the same but for Hector instead. "I will do my best. To honor their memory."

Hector turned his attention back to the view. "Excellent."

Meg glanced out the foggy windowpane, too. It wasn't Hector's way to let grief smother his good spirits. He had lived away from home for a long time. He'd not borne the worry of caring for either of their parents as they had declined.

He meant this trip as a way to end their mourning.

Meg might never end hers, no matter what happened. Her life had not been the same since her mother and then her father had passed, and it could never improve.

Frustrated that her breath had fogged the window again, she rubbed a circle on the pane with her fist and glared at the rolling fields of white powder until she realized she was looking down at their destination.

The manor on The Vynes estate, a widespread yellow stone structure, sat at the end of a long, winding road. Snowy mounds hiding what might be garden shrubbery dotted the landscape, bordered by low stone walls around the dwelling. But everything that could be pretty or green was hidden beneath inches of snow. There was no warmth here.

Meg desperately missed the rolling blue of the sea and the sound of crashing waves upon the shore near her home. It had been three days since she'd been bundled into this carriage, and two uncomfortable nights sleeping at posting houses along the way.

She focused her gaze back on the nearing house with a sense of foreboding. The family they were visiting were a good bit wealthier than they were, and it was a larger family, too. Lord Clement had a mother and father, Lord and Lady Vyne, a younger pair of unmarried sisters, and an infant brother as well. It was going to be a noisy few weeks in the country, and awkward to be with another family.

But Hector grinned as the carriage began to travel around the circular drive that would bring them to a stop before an impressive pair of oak doors. "Ready to dash inside and begin to make merry?"

"If my legs haven't gone numb yet." She smiled with false brightness. "As ready as I'll ever be."

But there was little chance this was going to be a happy Christmas. Meg was sure it might just be the worst ever.

About Heather Boyd

Determined to escape the Aussie sun on a scorching camping holiday, Heather picked up a pen and notebook from a corner store and started writing her very first novel—Chills. Years later, she is the author of over thirty sexy regency historical romances. Addicted to all things tech (never again will Heather write a novel longhand) and fascinated by English society of the early 1800's, Heather spends her days getting her characters in and out of trouble and into bed together (if they make it that far). She lives on the edge of beautiful Lake Macquarie, Australia with her trio of mischievous rogues (husband and two sons) along with one rescued cat and a new puppy who is proving a big distraction.

You can find details of her work and writing at
www.Heather-Boyd.com